DEADLOCK

Saki Aida

6'
5'9"
5'6"
5'3"
5'
4'9"
4'6"
4'3"
4'
3'9"
3'6"
3'3"
3'

6'
5'9"
5'6"
5'3"
5'
4'9"
ID No.
DATE
40375
07:04:27
ID No.
DATE
39806
POLICE

NO SMOKING

DEADLOCK

Written by

Saki Aida

Illustrations by

Yuu Takashina

Translated by

Bitter Sweetheart

Deadlock is rated MATURE for Intense Violence, Graphic Sexual Content, Strong Language, Horror, Death, Murder, Mature Themes, Blood, Nudity, Sensuality, Rape, Racism, and Adult Activities. Reader discretion is advised.

Originally published in Japan in 2006 by TOKUMA SHOTEN PUBLISHING CO, LTD., Tokyo.
English translation rights arranged with TOKUMA SHOTEN PUBLISHING CO, LTD. through Rightol Media.

TRANSLATION: BITTER SWEETHEART
ILLUSTRATIONS: YUU TAKASHINA
COVER and INTERIOR DESIGN: ADDIS
INTERIOR CHAIN ART: RARA
EDITOR: SOFIA
EDITOR-IN-CHIEF: ADDIS

Printed In Canada
First Printing: September 2025

10 9 8 7 6 5 4 3 2 1

In Loving Memory of
Saki Aida

A brilliant storyteller, a master of suspense, and a voice that captivated hearts. Through your words, you brought complex characters to life, weaving tales of justice, love, and redemption that will endure for generations. Your stories live on, inspiring and moving those who turn their pages.

May you rest in peace,
as free as a swallow,
knowing your legacy will
never be forgotten.

TABLE OF CONTENTS

CONTENT WARNING:

Please be advised that this volume contains extreme content that may not be suitable for all readers. This content contains several **RAPE** scenes.

Your well-being matters.
If you or someone you know needs support, help is available:

National Domestic Violence Hotline (USA)
1-800-799-7233
Text "START" to 88788
thehotline.org
Available 24/7, confidential, and free.

PROLOGUE

Lying in the darkness, Yuuto listened intently as the sound of footsteps drew closer. Amid the footsteps, the jangling clicks of metal striking against metal reached his ears. Hope surged swiftly and fiercely within him, but he forced it down with brutal resolve.

Cut it out! he told himself.

How many times over the past two weeks had he heard footsteps only to be disappointed each time?

"Yuuto Lennix," said a voice as sharp as a blade. "Get up."

The order echoed mercilessly in the narrow jail cell; Yuuto opened his eyes and stared unblinkingly at the blank wall before him.

"I *said*," the deputy chief's voice grew distinctly irritated by his insolence. "Get up!"

With casual slowness, Yuuto sat upright on the bed and turned his gaze toward the iron bars of his cell.

"Get over here and hold out your hands."

Obediently, Yuuto approached the metal bars and extended both hands through the gap between them.

The deputy chief handcuffed him before opening the cell door. "You're getting on a bus in an hour," he said. "But first, you're getting a pat-down and changing clothes."

"Where is the bus taking me?" Yuuto asked calmly, voice soft.

"Schelger Prison," he replied, his voice all business.

A sigh of relief escaped Yuuto's lips. He had been haunted by the fear that a mistake would send him to the wrong place.

"Yeah, you've got some real shitty luck," the deputy chief commented, misreading his reaction. "You'll just have to get over it."

It was natural for him to reach this conclusion; most criminals would be horrified to learn they were being transferred to an infamous prison known for its many layers of security.

For Yuuto, Schelger Prison was the one place on Earth where he might find a way to escape the abyss that had swallowed him.

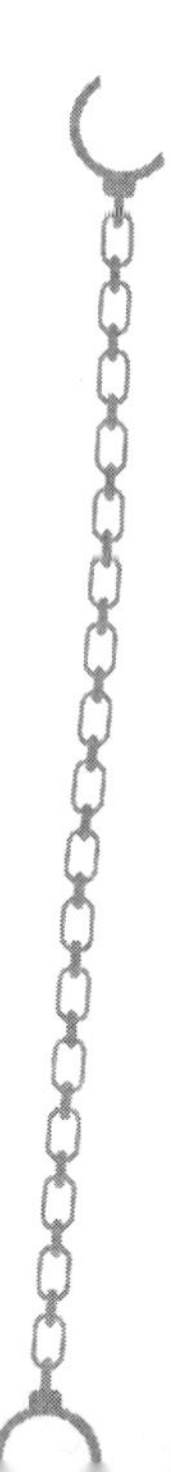

CHAPTER 1

"Hey," a young, White, blond man seated next to Yuuto whispered, "is this your first time in prison?"

The man had boarded back in San Jose, California, and couldn't be older than twenty. His boyish face radiated innocence, but was now pale with anxiety, like a carsick high schooler.

"Yes," Yuuto said shortly, shooting the kid a quick glance.

Metal partitions separated the front and back of the prisoner transport vehicle. Several prison guards stood behind them, shotguns at the ready, their eyes trained on the prisoners.

"This is my first time, too," the young man replied. "Man, talk about unlucky. I mean, we're getting locked up in *Schelger Prison* of all places! I heard that—"

"Hey!" Barked a voice behind them. "No talking on the bus."

The kid's runaway mouth snapped shut.

Heavy tension hung in the air as the vehicle rumbled northward, carrying over twenty prisoners clad in red jumpsuits. Bright summer sunlight streamed through the barred windows, a harsh contrast to the somber mood inside.

A rare wave of sentimentality washed over Yuuto as he squinted against the glare, watching the passing landscape. When could they have the chance to stand in sunlight again, unshackled beneath the sky?

The bus reached Schelger Prison much sooner than Yuuto had

anticipated. The facility loomed, vast and imposing—so far beyond anything he'd imagined that its true scale seemed unfathomable. A towering fence stretched into the horizon, wrapped in thick coils of barbed wire. He wouldn't have been surprised if it were electrified, too.

Their bus came to a halt before the prison gate. Surveillance towers flanked both sides, armed guards perched above with fingers poised on rifle triggers. The sight of them, ready to fire at a moment's notice, confirmed that Schelger Prison's reputation as the most secure maximum-security facility in the country was well-deserved. Within its century-old walls, over two thousand inmates served out their sentences.

The gate whirred open, and the vehicle lurched into motion once more. It moved past a large, fenced-in area, where Yuuto noticed a basketball and outdoor tennis courts. A crowd of inmates in denim jumpsuits clustered throughout the space, chatting among themselves.

When the bus stopped for the second time, it was in front of a large building. Guards were already stationed outside and stepped forward to open one of the partitions, instructing the prisoners to exit in a single file.

A White, male guard with a hooked nose and sharp, dangerous eyes was waiting outside.

"Welcome to Schelger Prison!" he shouted, like a drill sergeant straight out of hell, once the prisoners were lined up. "Before we get started, let's clear a few things up. First—while you're here, the guards' word is the law. Second—no matter what kind of job you had on the outside, or how badass of a gangster you were, it means nothing inside these walls. Third—we won't tolerate any shit. If we catch you disobeying orders or acting shady, you'll get shot. Just look at the surveillance tower over there!"

The man pointed a finger at a tower that overlooked the recreation area. More heavily armed guards with rifles stood inside, watching the inmates below.

"For example, if a riot breaks out in the recreation area, the first thing the guards will do is fire a warning shot into the air. The moment you hear that, you hit the dirt—face-first, no questions asked. If any more shots are fired, they're going straight into one of you. Oh, and here's something you better engrave into your thick skulls," he informed them, pausing as his eyes swept over the crowd. "Every guard in those towers is a sniper, and they keep their aim sharp by practicing for three hours every day."

After finishing his speech, the man motioned for everyone to enter the building before him. Like cattle being led to slaughter, Yuuto and the other prisoners shuffled forward in a straight line, their hands and feet bound in manacles. From behind them, inmates in the recreation area peered through the chain-link fence, jeering and shouting insults.

"Hey, blondie," someone shouted. "I'm gonna make you my bitch. I'll be seeing you later."

"Aww, man," another voice groaned. "I can't stand it! I wanna fuck one of those cuties so bad!"

Among the sea of vulgarities that were thrown at them one after another, one was addressed solely to Yuuto.

"Hey, you yellow bitch over there! You, yeah, *you.*"

Yuuto looked toward the speaker, where a bulky, twenty-something-year-old Black man smirked, drumming his fists against the fence. He had a silver piercing in his right ear, a beanie pulled low over his eyes, and the build of a pro football player.

"I've never had a slut like you before," the guy breathed. "C'mon, give me a taste. I'll pound that ass of yours real good with my massive cock."

Swallowing a wave of humiliation, Yuuto looked away, though not before he saw the man flip him off. The harassment, the racism—it would only get worse from here on out. If he let himself get angry every time, he knew he wouldn't make it out alive.

With no women in the prison, the young men with pretty faces became prime targets. At twenty-eight, Yuuto was somewhat older for such attention, yet his Asian heritage made him appear much younger. He hadn't shaved since being thrown in jail, partly for that reason. He wasn't sure how much his unkempt beard would deter anyone, but if it kept him out of even a little unnecessary trouble, it would be worth it.

The first thing the guards did after getting the prisoners inside was conduct a strip search. Then came a full-body examination, and it was thorough—the guards didn't let anyone through until they had searched every inch and crevice, top to bottom.

Literally.

Before his arrest, Yuuto would have found having his asshole inspected an unbearable humiliation. His lengthy incarceration had built up his tolerance for that kind of shit, dulling his emotions until the process stirred only mild annoyance.

From the moment the court had judged Yuuto guilty, he became their bitch. Like a good little dog, he'd learned to open his mouth, stick out his tongue, and even spread his ass cheeks on command. As an inmate, there was no such thing as dignity.

After changing into the prison clothes he was given, Yuuto was led to a separate room to undergo the administrative procedures for his admission to Schelger. As he waited, the door swung open abruptly, revealing a middle-aged man dressed in a three-piece suit.

The officer in charge quickly stood up. "Warden Corning, sir," he saluted hurriedly. "Is there something I can help you with?"

"Just doing a routine inspection," the warden answered, shooting a quick glance at Yuuto. "It's an important part of my job to know what's going on in this place." He then picked up Yuuto's file from the officer's desk. "Yuuto Lennix, twenty-eight years old, from Los Angeles." He paused, glancing up from the file to glare at Yuuto. "I see here you worked for the DEA before your arrest. Is that right?"

"This man is the warden of Schelger Prison," the officer growled,

his voice sharpening when Yuuto didn't respond. "Speak when spoken to and answer him!"

"Yes, that's right," Yuuto replied.

"What kind of work did you do there?" the warden asked, pressing further.

"I was a special agent."

The warden raised his eyebrows, surprised at Yuuto's flat reply, and shook his head. "It's disheartening to see someone sworn to fight crime become a criminal. To take the life of your own partner? You really have no shame."

Yuuto fought to keep his face blank, but inside, his rage boiled red-hot. The warden didn't know shit.

Killing his own partner.

That accusation was an unbearable insult. Yuuto hadn't harmed a single hair on Paul McClane's head. Paul hadn't just been Yuuto's partner; he was also a dear friend. The loss felt as tragic as losing a family member. Yuuto had cherished Paul more than words could convey.

Before Paul's death, the two of them had infiltrated a drug trafficking ring in New York as part of their work for the DEA. About a year after they first made contact, they got deep enough into the ring to arrest the person at the top. Only two weeks passed before everything fell apart—Paul was found stabbed to death in his room.

Yuuto was four years younger than Paul and had a deep respect for his more experienced partner, both as a person and as an DEA special agent. While Yuuto often recklessly dove headfirst into danger, Paul always had a clear head. His steady nature, along with his ability to devise complex strategies on the spot, had proven invaluable time and time again. Paul had been someone Yuuto could trust with his life.

Now, he was gone.

When Yuuto first heard the news, he was stunned, left in a daze.

The nightmare deepened when his fingerprints were discovered on the kitchen knife used to kill Paul, leading to his arrest on suspicion of murder.

During the interrogation, one of the detectives had shoved the murder weapon right in front of Yuuto's face, forcing him to admit that the knife had come from his own kitchen.

In a frantic effort to prove his innocence, Yuuto desperately tried to explain that someone had taken it without his knowledge. Still, the police, having received testimony that he had argued with Paul at a bar the night before the crime, weren't buying it.

In their minds, he had already been guilty.

While it was true that Yuuto and Paul had fought that night, it hadn't been anything serious. It wasn't unusual for them to get into heated discussions over how to proceed with an investigation—and that was all it had been at the bar. To outsiders, their drunken quarrel might've seemed worse, but neither of them would have held a grudge over something so minor.

Yuuto had attempted to explain this to the police, yet they refused to believe him, given that he was living alone and lacked an alibi.

Despite everything, Yuuto remained convinced that the truth would come to light through their investigation and had steadfastly chosen to believe this—until he learned the findings from the search they performed at his house.

Police went through the property, found cocaine, and seized it. The second the cocaine turned up, everything changed. It didn't matter who it belonged to. He was already guilty in their eyes. They hounded Yuuto without mercy, demanding he admit to their version of the "truth"—that he murdered Paul to keep his drug habit hidden.

Yuuto was convinced that whoever had broken into his home to take the kitchen knife had also planted the cocaine. It was evident that Paul's death and arrest stemmed from a meticulously planned scheme.

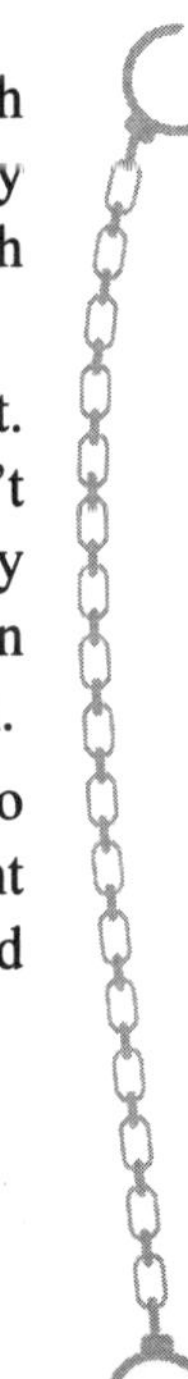

Whenever questioned, Yuuto consistently claimed that Paul's death and the framing that followed were orchestrated by members of the drug-trafficking ring they had dismantled.

During the arraignment, he pleaded not guilty.

A trial ensued, and ultimately, the twelve jurors—eight White, two Black, and two Hispanic—convicted Yuuto of Paul's murder. That was the first time he truly hated his own skin. He couldn't help but wonder: if he'd been White, would things have turned out differently?

It was an undeniable fact that race influenced decisions in the courtroom; if a Black man was tried for killing a White man, his chances of receiving the death penalty were exponentially higher. This wouldn't be the case if a White man had killed a Black man, or if one Black man had killed another. In the American judicial system, White lives are prioritized over others.

"You were arrested in New York," the warden went on, snapping Yuuto out of his thoughts. "So, why did you get transferred all the way to Schelger?"

Since transferring prisoners across state lines was illegal in California, the decision appeared particularly strange.

Yuuto, faced with the question he had been dreading, feigned calmness. "I asked to be somewhere closer to L.A." He started, "My family's out there. But all those places were packed, so they shipped me out here instead."

The warden let out a small hum of agreement, nodding his head. "They've got a real overcrowding issue there."

Shortly after, the officer in charge concluded the legal proceedings. Yuuto rose to leave, but the warden called his name before he could exit the room.

"Lennix. Remember—the DEA's on the inmates' hit lists too, not just the police. So keep your past buried," he warned, his tone becoming derisive with every word. "I don't tolerate unrest in my prison. Remember, as long as you're here, you're just another inmate, penned up and fed slop like cattle. Actually, cattle have more value—at least you can slaughter them and make a nice meal. Something to think about at night."

It was a vile comment for someone in his position, and it pissed Yuuto off. With a man like him in charge, it was no surprise that the other prison staff followed his lead.

CHAPTER 2

With his legal paperwork completed, Yuuto underwent a medical checkup, followed by an overview of the prison rules. Afterward, he received a blanket, a selection of toiletries, and a photo identification with his inmate number, 40375. He would need to recite that number and his name at least five times a day for headcount and lockup.

"Yuuto Lennix and Matthew Kane, follow me," ordered a young correctional officer. "You will be assigned to Block A, in the West Wing."

The second name belonged to the kid Yuuto had spoken with on the bus earlier that day. As he gathered his things, he shot Yuuto a look of relief—grateful, it seemed, that they'd been assigned to the same block.

Matthew had a distinctly childlike appearance, which was accentuated by his slim build; he likely weighed no more than one hundred pounds. Moreover, he was short; the top of his head barely reached Yuuto's eyes. Yuuto, who stood at five foot eight, estimated that the kid was probably two inches shorter.

As the correctional officer led Yuuto and Matthew to their cells, he informed them that he was in charge of Block A. "You're an unlucky man, Kane," he added, casting a cryptic smile over his shoulder at Matthew. "They usually only send the more troublesome inmates to Block A, or those facing long sentences. Guys like you, with just two years, should be in the low-security East Wing. Unfortunately for you, that section's packed."

"I'll be transferred if there's a vacancy, right?" Matthew demanded, his face twisting with the anxiety of a high schooler who had just been assigned detention.

The guard paused briefly, then murmured that it would depend on the timing.

"I-I'm fucked, aren't I?" Matthew mumbled weakly, his voice squeaking with tension.

Yuuto felt a pang of sympathy for the kid. With a newcomer like him, there was no way the other inmates would keep their hands to themselves. Not that Yuuto was in a much better position—his only advantage was the experience he'd gained from five years of successful drug busts. His specialty had been high-risk infiltration and undercover work. While working his way into gangs and cartels, he had encountered more than a few rowdy, violent drug dealers. As a result, he became an expert at remaining calm in any situation, even when facing fear or despair.

Still, Yuuto knew that although his former job had provided him the tools to survive, the inmates here would pursue him with relentless fury if they ever discovered what he had once done for a living.

Block A was located in the innermost part of Schelger's West Wing. As Yuuto walked through the large gates, he was greeted by a remarkable view. The expansive, warehouse-like area inside was enormous, so extensive that it seemed to go on indefinitely.

The left side of the building was lined with four floors of cold, lifeless iron jail cells, from ceiling to floor. Waist-high steel mesh barriers partially obscured the walkways leading to the cells. Now and then, prisoners leaned against the rails, arms resting on top, peering down at Yuuto and Matthew with curious eyes.

On the opposite side of the room was a gun rail—an overhanging observation deck. Narrow walkways, about a meter wide, ran along the second and fourth floors, giving any guard stationed there a clear view into the cells across from them.

"Kane, your cell's on the first floor." The correctional officer who'd brought them to the ward pointed to one of the cells. "Right over there."

Matthew hesitantly walked over.

"Hawes," the correctional officer called. "You've got a newbie. Keep an eye on him for me, will ya?"

The elderly Black man sitting on one of the beds inside the cell glanced at Matthew, then threw his hands up dramatically. "Guthrie, you gotta be kiddin' me. A White boy?"

Guthrie laughed as he shoved Matthew inside the cell. "You two get along now. Cause any trouble and it's solitary for both."

"Come on, Lennix." Guthrie turned his back on Yuuto and started heading up the stairs without checking to see if he was following. "Your cell's on the third floor."

"So, cellmates are paired together regardless of race?" Yuuto asked, keeping his tone mild.

Segregation was, of course, unconstitutional across the country; the Supreme Court had ruled that race should not influence housing assignments, regardless of a penitentiary's location. Despite this ruling, that didn't mean it was always followed.

Inside prison walls, racial differences often sparked serious tension. Just a year earlier, a riot had erupted in a Los Angeles facility due to growing conflict between Black and Latino inmates. By the time it was over, nearly two thousand prisoners had been drawn into the chaos.

"There are no restrictions within the common facilities," Officer Guthrie answered as he led Yuuto up the stairs. "When it comes to the cell blocks, White inmates are generally placed in Block B, Latinos in Block C, and Blacks in Block D. Prisoners of other races get slotted into a cell here in A Block—along with anyone we can't fit into their corresponding ward at the time."

Yuuto felt a bit reassured by the words. Given that A Block was home to a variety of races, it was unlikely he would come across any extreme racists among the inmates.

"Where are you from?" Guthrie asked. "China?"

"No, I'm Japanese-American."

"Oh, interesting. We don't get many Japanese here," he remarked, glancing back at Yuuto. "You've been paired up with a White guy named Dick Burnford. He's a crafty bastard, not someone you should trust. If he goes after you, it won't be because of race."

Guthrie continued moving, reaching about halfway across the third-floor walkway before stopping. "Looks like the asshole's not even here," he muttered, peering into a dimly lit cell. "You've got the top bunk. Anything you've got with you can go in that cabinet over there. If you've got any more questions, just ask Burnford."

With those parting words, the correctional officer was gone.

Yuuto stepped into the cell and tossed the few items he had onto his bunk, then gave the space a quick glance. The bunk bed was against the wall to the right, but beyond that, the cell was bare. The only other notable features were a toilet and a sink with a wooden cabinet above it, tucked behind an opaque vinyl curtain.

A closer look revealed that the mattresses were thin, rock-hard, and stained. Not that Yuuto could see them clearly—with only a sliver of sunlight filtering through a tiny, iron-grilled window, the cell remained dim even in the middle of the day. The walls, meanwhile, seemed to have collected grime for years. Yuuto couldn't even begin to guess what color lay beneath the ugly, ashen gray.

Still, none of that bothered Yuuto more than one other aspect of the cell: it was incredibly small.

The space was so narrow and claustrophobic that he wouldn't have been surprised if it had originally been intended for solitary confinement. The thought of living there, day after day, squeezed in with some unknown man, made Yuuto feel like he was suffocating. He let out a long, defeated sigh into the dim, stifling darkness of his new home.

"Hey, do you mind if I come in?" Turning around, Yuuto found Matthew standing just outside the cell door, offering an awkward smile. "Why don't we chat for a bit? I'm Matthew Kane. Your name's Yuuto, right?"

Yuuto let out an even longer sigh. He knew Matthew was probably feeling lonely and scared, but Yuuto didn't want to get too emotionally attached. He'd have his hands full just keeping *himself* in one piece, let alone anyone else.

Oblivious to the irritation on Yuuto's face, Matthew entered the cell and sat on the lower bunk.

"Hey!" Yuuto snapped. "Matthew, get up."

The kid gave him a puzzled look. "Why?"

"'Cause that's not my bed."

It was clear from Matthew's expression that he still didn't get it, but he obediently stood up.

"I have another cellmate who could return at any minute," Yuuto said, his tone firm. "What would you think if you found some random-ass dude on your bed? There's no guarantee the guy's chill enough to laugh it off and give you a free pass just because you are new."

"Okay, fine," Matthew said, shrugging. "I still think you worry too much. If the guy gets pissed, all I have to do is apologize, right?"

This kid's problems are none of my business, Yuuto reminded himself firmly, but he couldn't shake the feeling of deep worry. It was bad enough that Matthew was timid and somewhat cowardly, but his flippant attitude would soon earn him a place on people's shit lists. Moreover, there was no shortage of angry, confrontational dudes in a place like this.

"Anyway, have you taken a look at the guidebook yet?" Matthew picked up the pamphlet Yuuto had left on top of his bunk and let out a snort. "They listed murder among the things we're not supposed to do. Like, come on, did they really have to write that out? Made me laugh."

The guidebook, which outlined the rules of prison life and the penalties for prohibited behavior, had been distributed earlier.

"It means," Yuuto pointed out, "a lot of violent shit happens here."

"What do you mean?" Matthew exclaimed, shock written all over his face. "There are guards everywhere!"

Just as Yuuto sent the kid a pitying look, a voice filtered in from outside the cell, "Twenty-three."

Yuuto whipped around, his eyes landing on a young White man standing in the doorway of his cell.

"Sup, guys," the newcomer said. "Welcome to Block A. I'm Michele Ronini, but you can call me Mickey. Nice to meet ya."

Mickey extended a hand, and Yuuto gave it a quick shake after introducing himself.

Seemingly pleased by Mickey's friendly attitude, Matthew gave an unguarded smile and shook his hand firmly. "Likewise."

Mickey, cheerful and with a pointed nose and sharp features, had an Italian appearance that matched his name. The tips of his naturally curly, dark brown hair stuck out in all directions, and he looked to be about the same age as Yuuto.

"I'm Matthew Kane. You can just call me Matthew," the kid introduced himself. "Oh, but what did you mean by twenty-three, Mickey?"

Mickey leaned against the cell wall. "That's the number of guys who got killed last year," he said nonchalantly. "So, that's what? About two a month? Someone gets their ass beat at least once a day."

A spasm passed over Matthew's smiling face. His shoulders twitched as though someone had smacked him hard across the back.

"Oh, don't worry," Mickey added cheerfully. "Statistically speaking, you're more likely to die in a car crash than get merc'd in here."

CHAPTER 3

When five o'clock rolled around, Mickey asked if Yuuto and Matthew wanted to head to the dining hall with him. With all the inmates eating together, getting there early was crucial to avoid the frustratingly long wait in line.

As they stepped off the stairs and onto the ground floor, Mickey called out to a guy standing nearby, "Yo, Nathan! Just the man I wanted to see. Let me introduce you to my new friends. This guy is Yuuto Lennix, and this guy's Matthew Kane. They just got set up here in Block A. Guys, this is my roomie, Nathan."

"Nathan Clark," Mickey's cellmate smiled and reached out his free hand to shake theirs, the gesture a bit awkward with a stack of books tucked under one arm. "Nice to meet you."

Nathan looked to be around thirty, with smooth chestnut hair that was especially striking. Tall and slender, he might've seemed frail if not for the surprising breadth of his shoulders. His fine nose and thin lips gave him an intellectual air, though a hint of nervousness lingered in his features. Even so, his gentle smile and relaxed demeanor lent him a calm, easygoing aura.

"Come to the dining hall with us," Mickey said.

"Sure," Nathan replied easily. "Just hang on one moment while I drop off these books."

Yuuto watched as he made his way up the stairs to the third floor, moving at an unhurried pace. There was something serene about him—like a Buddhist monk, detached from the world and free of its burdens.

While they waited for Nathan to return, Mickey started talking about himself, even though no one asked. They quickly learned that he had landed in Schelger after a failed bank robbery attempt and had already served five years of his sentence.

Apparently, he also had a secret route for smuggling in contraband. The guards hadn't figured it out yet, and he was running a thriving business supplying a wide range of items to other inmates. From how he talked about it, it was clear he was proud of what he'd built.

"If there's ever anything you wanna get your hands on, just let me know," he said. "Porn mags, drugs, knives—doesn't matter what it is, I can get it. Oh, unless it's a woman. That's beyond even me."

Internally, Yuuto smiled wryly. No wonder Mickey was being so friendly—he'd just found himself two brand-new customers.

When Nathan finally returned, the four of them headed off for the dining hall. Mickey strode ahead, whistling, while Yuuto and Matthew walked alongside Nathan.

As they went, Nathan gave the two newcomers a quick overview of the place: the prison was built around a central yard, with a Central Building and three wings. The West and East Wings housed the cell blocks, while the North Wing contained the gym and workshops. The Central Building—shaped like a T—held administrative facilities at the front, including the warden's office, control center, and guard rooms. Toward the back were the dining area, recreation room, infirmary, library, and educational areas.

Security checkpoints were positioned at key gates, with metal detectors installed in certain zones.

"Plenty of ways around those, of course," Nathan said, a mischievous smile playing on his lips. Though they'd only been speaking with him for a short time, Yuuto could already tell Nathan was smart; his explanations were detailed yet concise.

At the entrance to the dining area, the guards gave them a quick pat-down. Yuuto quickly noticed how careless the inspections were—it wouldn't be hard to smuggle in a small blade. In a shoe, tucked into a collar fold, slipped behind a belt. If someone wanted to hide something, there were plenty of options.

Inside the dining area, the kitchen bustled with inmates in white aprons; guards stood around the room, eyes restless, monitoring every movement. Following Mickey and Nathan's lead, Yuuto and Matthew grabbed plastic trays and joined the back of an already long line.

The menu consisted of fried fish or chicken, cheese grits in paper cups, salad, and a few other items. Additionally, inmates could take as much bread, coffee, and orange juice as they desired. The room was packed and loud, with overlapping conversations, and beneath the endless chatter, the air was thick with the sour scent of sweaty men, nauseatingly mixing with the aromas wafting from the food.

Yuuto tried to take his mind off the smell by studying the layout of the dining hall. White inmates had taken over the tables on the right side, while the back and left sides were occupied by groups of Black and Latino men, respectively.

He was still trying to figure out where he fit in, given his Asian heritage, when Mickey and Nathan walked by and headed to a table near the center of the room. He followed them, with Matthew close behind. Looking around, Yuuto noticed that the surrounding tables had a mix of people sitting together.

The very center of the dining hall, it seemed, was quietly understood to be a mixed-race zone.

As for the food, his expectations had been low, and sadly, it didn't even manage to surpass them. Nothing tasted remotely appetizing. Still, it was edible, and that was good enough. He needed the energy to keep moving.

Silently, Yuuto shoveled bite after bite into his mouth. He didn't speak. In his mind, he imagined fueling a machine: his body was the engine, and food its fuel.

Matthew was attracting more attention than he realized. Inmates passing by leered at him and let out wolf-whistles, like he was some hot girl strutting down the street.

Mickey theatrically snapped his fingers and pointed at Matthew. "Yo, Marshmallow Kane."

"It's Matthew," he corrected flatly.

"When you're done eating, Marshmallow Boy," Mickey drawled, ignoring Matthew, "you better head straight to the commissary and buy yourself a chastity belt. I hear NASA makes 'em just for us. You can even take a shit with one on!"

Matthew just stared at him, dumbfounded.

Mickey laughed at his joke, slapping the table before adding. "Well, even with one of those, your ass won't last three days. I'll bet three full packs of cigarettes on it."

Matthew's expression darkened into a frown, but he didn't say a word.

"You really should be careful," Nathan said, his tone suddenly serious. "The guards might step in if someone's about to get killed, but they tend to turn a blind eye to rape. Don't go anywhere alone unless absolutely necessary, and avoid trouble spots whenever possible. Oh—and avoid gang members at all costs. If a group corners you, don't fight. Just give them your ass, let them do as they please, and hope they let you walk away alive."

Matthew scoffed.

"I don't get it—what exactly are they escaping from?" a voice said from behind him. "Please, enlighten me, Mr. Lawyer."

Nathan furrowed his brow, and at the exact moment, Yuuto tensed as a hand clamped down on his shoulder.

"You guys look like you're havin' fun," the voice continued. "Mind if I join the welcome party?"

Yuuto glanced over his shoulder, and recognition hit instantly—it was the same man who'd called out to him through the fence earlier that day. Black, solidly built, with a beanie pulled low over his forehead and a silver earring glinting in his ear. He wasn't alone. A small group of rough-looking men loomed behind him, clearly part of the same crew.

"Someone gonna introduce me to this pretty little thing?" the man asked. "Been dyin' to meet him ever since I saw him step off that prison bus. C'mon, baby, what's your name? Mine's Bob Trenkler, but everyone calls me BB."

BB leaned in, his face creeping closer until Yuuto turned away, offering him nothing but the back of his head. One of BB's buddies leaned around him, trying to get a better look.

"Hey, BB," he said. "The White boy over there is way cuter."

"Shut the hell up, dumbass," BB snapped. "Who the fuck wants some baby-faced kid whose balls haven't even dropped? You don't know how to pick your women."

BB pressed his nose against the back of Yuuto's neck and inhaled deeply. His eyes fluttered shut, his face going slack, like he'd just tasted the first bite of something decadent.

"God*damn*! That's the shit right here," BB breathed into Yuuto's ear. "I've got me a real first-class bitch."

"Get your filthy hands off me!" Yuuto snapped, slapping BB's hand away.

BB's crew immediately lost their shit and the room erupted with noise.

"You little punk! You talking to BB like that!"

"Yeah, you got a death wish or somethin'?"

Their faces flushed with rage as they closed in, surrounding Yuuto from every angle. A chorus of shouts erupted around them—onlookers egging it on, yelling things like "Get him! Kick his ass!" and "Fight, fight, fight!"

Suddenly, a deep, menacing voice cut through the turmoil, "Move."

The noise died instantly. Heads turned, the tension in the room thickening.

"Let me through," the voice continued in a quiet but deadly tone. "I just want to eat my goddamn lunch and be done with it."

The crowd slowly parted, revealing a White man holding a tray. The man had a well-proportioned, muscular build and a face so strikingly handsome that it wouldn't be an exaggeration to call it beautiful.

Yuuto couldn't help but stare.

The tall man, with slightly long blond hair casually tied back, seemed completely unfazed by the tense atmosphere. He walked right past the Black men with combative eyes and sat down next to Yuuto

"Trenkler, what the hell are you doing over there?" a nearby guard barked, finally catching on to the disturbance. "If you're done eating, get out of the dining hall!"

"Relax," BB called back, grinning as he stared at Yuuto. "I was just sayin' hello to the newbies." Leaning in just enough for Yuuto to hear, he murmured, "I like 'em feisty. Next time we meet, how 'bout a little date? I'll take *real* good care of you, pretty boy."

Then he turned to the man sitting beside Yuuto, his expression darkening. "Oh, and Burnford? Don't get too cozy. Even Choker can't keep you in his sights all the time."

With that, BB and his crew backed off and disappeared into the crowd. Around them, the dining hall seemed to collectively exhale, though whether it was in relief or disappointment was hard to tell.

"Jeez, Yuuto," Mickey groaned, finally breaking the silence. "You caught the eye of the worst motherfucker. That guy's Bad Bob—the leader of the Black Soldiers. He's in here on a hundred-fifty-year sentence for turning four people into Swiss cheese with a machine gun. A total psycho."

"Black Soldiers?" Yuuto snorted, forcing a smile. "That's the name they went with? Sounds kinda lame."

"This isn't a joke, dude," Mickey warned, frowning as he shook his head. "The gangs run Schelger. And the Black Soldiers? They're one of the top three. The other two are the Chicano gang, Locos Hermanos, and the ABL—a bunch of White supremacists. Look, Yuuto, I'm telling you, if you wanna make it out of here in one piece, don't screw with any of them."

"Got it, Mickey," Yuuto said dryly. "Straight to the commissary it is. I'll pick up one of those NASA-grade chastity belts."

"Yeah, yeah," Mickey rolled his eyes at hearing his own dumb joke thrown back at him. "You do that."

"Hey, Dick," Nathan called out, "this guy is your new cellmate."

The man who'd been quietly eating looked up at Nathan, then shifted his blank gaze to Yuuto. When Yuuto introduced himself, the man replied briskly, "Dick Burnford," and returned to his meal.

Yuuto quietly observed his unfriendly cellmate. If he had to sum him up in one word, it'd be: good-looking.

His features were masculine and sharply defined, the kind of good looks that drew universal notice. He was tall, well-built, and impressively toned. The only blemish was an old scar running from his forehead to the corner of his eyebrow. In prison, though, a scar like that only added to your appeal.

It wasn't the body or the scar that gripped Yuuto most—it was his eyes, calm and piercing, blue like a still lake. Not bluish-gray, not greenish-blue, just pure blue.

Blond hair and blue eyes weren't exactly uncommon, but most White people's features tended to darken with age. Someone who kept both so perfectly was rare.

"How old are you, Dick?" Yuuto was curious about the man he would be living with, so he used the question to start a conversation.

"Twenty-nine," Dick said without looking up from his tray.

"Oh. You're one year older than me—I'm twenty-eight. How long have you been here at Schelger?" Yuuto kept his tone light and casual, but Dick offered no reply. Not a grunt, not even a glance.

Just silence.

"Matthew, how about you?" Mickey cut in brightly, either to save Yuuto from more awkward silence or just eager to keep the energy going.

"Almost twenty-one."

"You look like you still cry for mommy, baby face," Mickey teased with a grin. "What'd you do to land yourself here?"

Matthew pushed his grits around with his fork. "It's no big deal," he mumbled. "My buddy and I stole some whiskey from this old guy's liquor store. My friend swore the man was senile and said we'd be in and out, no problem. The old man caught us, and we got into a scuffle. Then, my friend ended up stabbing him with the knife he had. He only stabbed him in the arm, but the old man got so startled he fell and hit his head. He suffered a severe brain contusion. I got two years."

"Damn," Mickey said, giving Matthew's shoulder a sympathetic pat. "Started as shoplifting, ended in armed assault. I bet even the guards felt bad when you landed in the West Wing. You're one unlucky bastard."

"What about you, Yuuto? How long you in for?"

"Fifteen years."

Mickey let out a low whistle and leaned in, eyes gleaming with curiosity. "What'd you do?"

"Nothing."

Mickey and Nathan exchanged a look—one of those silent conversations that clearly said, *Yeah, right*. But Yuuto didn't care. Let them think whatever they want. He'd told the truth, plain and simple.

"I'm innocent," he declared firmly.

"Ah, well," Mickey scratched awkwardly at his cheek. "It happens. You must have shitty luck too."

Maybe they thought he was crazy. Yuuto didn't care. The interrogation, the trial—no one had believed him. He'd been falsely accused of killing a fellow agent and sentenced to fifteen years. Compared to that, being seen as a weirdo by other inmates was nothing.

"Hey!" Matthew suddenly piped up, cutting through the silence. He pointed at Nathan. "That Black guy earlier called you 'Mr. Lawyer,' right? Were you one before you got sent here?"

"Nathan volunteers at the law library," Mickey said, cutting in before Nathan could speak.

Mickey struck Yuuto as the kind of guy who always had to get a word in.

"This guy knows the law inside and out. He files complaints to the Department of Corrections for inmates whose rights have been violated or who are being mistreated. He helps long-term prisoners research laws and case precedents to build petitions for sentence reductions. He's incredible. Just recently, one guy got ten years shaved off thanks to a loophole he found, and another got parole. Honestly, he's more dependable than any outside lawyer. Nathan can even meet with Warden Corning directly."

The admiration in Mickey's voice was unmistakable. And there was no doubt that several other men in the prison looked at Nathan as their savior.

"The warden only sends for me to give me lectures," Nathan corrected dryly. "Apparently, all the trouble I cause gives him migraines."

Yuuto smiled. "When did you get into studying law?"

"College, but only a bit," Nathan replied with a shrug. "My major was in criminal law, which is, let's just say, pretty *relevant* these days. Now I get to see how theory holds up against reality."

The joke was lighthearted, with no hint of self-pity, and Yuuto found himself really liking the guy for it.

Then there was Dick.

Still unfathomable. Still a man of few words. But those subtle moments didn't escape Yuuto: the quiet amusement at Mickey's joke, the unexpected answer he gave Nathan. He wasn't warm, and he wasn't cold either. Just...*polite.*

Yuuto could work with that. Honestly, he preferred such a roommate over a troublemaker like Mickey.

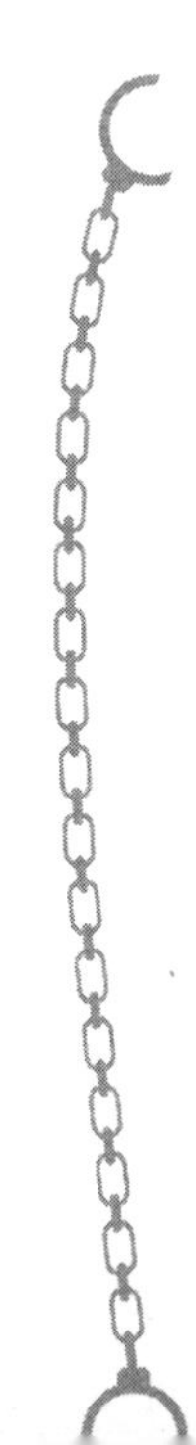

CHAPTER 4

With the six o'clock lockdown headcount approaching, Yuuto and the others returned to Block A after finishing their meal. It was like a mass migration—waves of inmates moving toward their respective cells.

Suddenly, an angry voice rose from the moving crowd—a fight had broken out. In an instant, onlookers swarmed around, and furious shouts echoed down the corridor.

Matthew tried to make his way toward the commotion, but Nathan held him back. "Don't," he warned. "Getting involved in stuff like this will only get you in trouble. If you're late for headcount, you won't like the punishment that comes with it."

Mickey gave Matthew a nudge on the shoulders to get him moving forward. "Fights happen all the time," he said. "Soon, you won't think they're interesting at all."

Matthew let out a gloomy sigh but obediently started walking.

"Low calcium can make you irritable, you know," Nathan said mildly, as if that explained everything.

The five of them started pushing through the crowd, but Yuuto only made it a few steps before getting yanked back by the arm. By the time he realized the danger he was in, it was already too late—a group of BB's cronies had dragged him into a nearby washroom.

They were the same ones who'd threatened him in the dining hall.

The man holding Yuuto's arms yelled, "Do it!" and the other three men lunged at once. One punched him hard in the stomach; another struck the back of his head. Yuuto collapsed to the floor from the pain and shock, and a flurry of ruthless kicks followed.

Yuuto could have put up a decent fight if he'd wanted to, but he knew he couldn't beat the four men all by himself. Instead, he opted to curl up into a ball to try to stop them from damaging anything internal, then raised his arms to protect his head. The storm would pass—he just needed to wait it out.

"Next time you decide to mouth off to BB," one of the men said as they landed another kick, "we won't be so gentle, you little bitch. Remember that."

"Guys." Yuuto wasn't sure who spoke. "Let's go."

After beating him down with brutal efficiency, the men scattered. Moments later, Nathan and Mickey appeared, hurrying to where Yuuto lay crumpled on the floor.

"Yuuto, hang in there. Are you okay?"

"Damn," Mickey muttered, voice dripping with hatred. "Black Soldier bastards—"

Whatever he was about to say next died on his lips when Nathan barked at him to find Dick.

Yuuto's new roommate came rushing into the bathroom just as Nathan managed to get him into a sitting position. Dick stared into Yuuto's eyes, "Can you see my face?"

"Yeah," he groaned. "Two eyes, one nose, one mouth, one handsome guy."

"Seeing as he's cracking jokes," Dick said, rolling his eyes. "I think he's fine. Come on, help me take him back to our cell."

With Nathan and Mickey's help, Yuuto managed to stand, though every breath felt like fire. Pain throbbed through his chest with each inhale.

"Get moving," Dick said curtly. "The guards find out you've been fighting, and you're going straight to solitary." His voice lowered, turning into a grumble, "Lucky me, getting a troublemaker from day one."

The snide tone struck a nerve. Yuuto snapped, scowling, "I

haven't done shit."

"Oh? If you ask me, you brought this on yourself," Dick said coldly. "Mickey warned you, but you just laughed him off." Yuuto felt his face stiffen as Dick continued, "Don't think being the victim gets you a free pass. The guards don't care who started it, only that there was a fight."

"So, what?" Yuuto asked, disbelief clear. "You're saying if they come across someone getting jumped, they'll just hoist everybody up? That's fucked up."

"You can think it's fucked up all you want, but this place's your life now," Dick said, peering outside the bathroom without even glancing at Yuuto. "Let's go."

At Dick's signal, Nathan and Mickey started walking, Yuuto limping along with them. Every step sent a jolt of pain through his body. He couldn't bring himself to say that he couldn't walk—getting beaten so easily was humiliating enough.

"Where's Matthew?" Yuuto asked Mickey, noticing that the boy was nowhere to be found.

"We made him head back to Block A on his own," Mickey answered. "After noticing you'd vanished and seeing the Black Soldiers run out of the bathroom, we had a pretty good idea what happened. No point dragging a short-term prisoner into a mess, right?"

"Good call." Yuuto smiled through the pain, feeling relieved at Mickey's kindness.

"What's going on here, Nathan?" asked the guard at the entrance to Block A, his voice edged with suspicion. "What happened to the new guy?"

It was Guthrie, the guard who'd escorted Yuuto and Matthew to their cells.

"He got pushed and fell. It was crowded, so he got kicked around by some others," Nathan replied smoothly, his voice calm and steady.

This seemed convincing enough for Guthrie—he jerked his chin toward the inside of Block A, as if to tell them to hurry along.

Yuuto could hear Mickey let out a sigh of relief.

When they reached the stairs, it took all of Yuuto's willpower to haul his aching body up the three flights to the third floor. After Nathan and Mickey deposited Yuuto on Dick's bed, the pair hurried off to their cell. An ear-splitting buzzer sounded just a few minutes later, echoing across the entire block.

A guard's roar echoed throughout the building: "Step back!"

"The doors close automatically after the buzzer goes off," Dick explained. True to his word, the doors suddenly slid shut, trapping them inside. It hit Yuuto with a sudden, visceral force that he was now truly a prisoner, confined within a small cage.

Once the guards finished headcount, the doors reopened. Meanwhile, Dick had ordered Yuuto to lie down on his bed. As he gingerly stretched out, Dick peered into his eyes again, then ran his cold hands over Yuuto's body to check the severity of his injuries. He asked questions as he went, like whether Yuuto had a headache or was feeling any nausea.

"Dick. How's Yuuto doing?"

Nathan and Mickey had come back to visit.

"Well, I was in the middle of finding out," Dick said wryly. He turned back to Yuuto. "Does it hurt to breathe?"

Yuuto nodded.

Dick turned to Nathan and Mickey. "He might have a cracked rib."

"What should we do?" asked Nathan.

Dick shrugged like it wasn't his problem, then got to his feet. "There's nothing we *can* do other than wait till it heals. I'm heading to the infirmary—I still have work left to do. Choker's not doing very well."

Yuuto waited until Dick had left the cell, then turned to Nathan.

"Is he a doctor?"

Nathan shook his head as he applied a wet towel to Yuuto's swollen face. "No, but he knows a lot. He works as an assistant in the infirmary, so he's used to treating injuries," Nathan answered, hesitating briefly before continuing. "Yuuto, if it's really painful, you should tell the guard. Your request won't be processed until tomorrow, so you'll have to get through the night without the infirmary."

Yuuto thanked Nathan for his help, but told him he was fine without a visit to the infirmary. Even if he went to see a doctor, the best they could do for a cracked rib was give him a chest wrap.

Out of nowhere, Matthew burst into the cell with a shout, his eyes going wide at the sight of Yuuto's swollen, battered face. "Yuuto, what happened? You look horrible," he said, his eyebrows knitted. "Was it those Black guys who were bothering you at the dining hall?"

"Yeah," Mickey answered in Yuuto's stead. "Honestly, he was lucky. There wasn't much time before lockdown, so they didn't have the time to rough him up too bad."

Matthew bit his lip, staring angrily at Yuuto's face. "They went this far over that little comment? They're insane."

"Guys, can I have some time alone?" Yuuto cut in. "I want to rest for a bit."

Obediently, Nathan, Matthew, and Mickey left. Yuuto was now alone with the pain. His chest throbbed, and every inch of his body ached. Even lying still, he had to fight to keep groans from escaping.

Gritting his teeth, Yuuto endured.

He wasn't a stranger to violence. He'd been discovered while undercover, fought armed suspects, and even taken a knife during a drug sting. Working for the DEA had always been a dangerous job.

Nothing about this was the same—ambushed, helpless, and denied even the bare minimum of medical treatment. Alone in the dark, Yuuto lay in silence, misery settling into his bones. He had to hold himself together.

You're a former DEA special agent, Yuuto chided himself. *This shit shouldn't get to you. You've survived worse. You've overcome so much.*

Pride was the only thing Yuuto had left. He'd lost everything, but his dignity, his belief in himself? No one could rob him of those unless he allowed them to.

He wasn't about to let self-doubt take root now.

What he feared most wasn't failure—it was losing faith in his own abilities altogether.

The last thing he ever wanted to become was a coward, someone who only thought about squirming out of every problem. He cursed himself silently, furious at his weakness. No one had forced this on him.

He had chosen it.

Yuuto had volunteered to come to Schelger Prison. Yes, he had family in L.A., but that wasn't the reason. There was something else—something critical that brought him all the way from the East Coast to this prison on the West Coast.

Truthfully, it wasn't that he was standing at the edge. He had already fallen. The incident had stripped him of everything: his job, his status, the trust he'd once earned. Nothing he did could bring any of it back.

But at rock bottom, he'd been given a single sliver of hope.

That hope lived here, in Schelger Prison.

Yuuto had been sentenced to fifteen years in prison for the murder of Paul McClane, and it had plunged him into the depths of despair. Yet it was in that darkest moment that the FBI quietly approached him.

"Lennix. How are you holding up?" The man, Mark Heiden,

appeared before him with the familiarity of an old friend. He had flashed his identification to Yuuto in the meeting room of the detention facility and introduced himself as an investigator of the FBI's Counterterrorism Division, Domestic Terror Unit. He was just a pretty face in an expensive suit.

Yuuto found it difficult to like him, given his elitist, haughty, and condescending attitude, which was so typical of the FBI. Yuuto had been confused at first, wondering what the FBI could want from him. He didn't have long to linger in confusion; Heiden's next words left him reeling.

"We want you to find someone inside the prison. If you find him, we'll promise you immediate release on parole."

The story was all too suspicious, and Yuuto was hesitant to believe the FBI's claims at first.

Heiden flashed a cocky grin at his apprehensive expression before launching into an explanation. "Are you aware that over the past year, there have been a series of small-scale acts of terrorism in various places throughout the United States? They're believed to be the work of a single group."

"I've heard it on the news," Yuuto answered.

The incidents had made headlines as the "Silent Terrorism" attacks. No group ever claimed responsibility, and the bombing targets seemed random. Experts were divided—some believed it was the work of a fundamentalist cell, others suspected far-right extremists, and a few dismissed them as the actions of thrill-seekers.

"Two months ago, while investigating these incidents, the FBI arrested a White male in possession of explosives at a supermarket in Connecticut," Mark recounted. "His testimony revealed he belonged to a radical cult. However, he refused a plea bargain and remained silent on everything else, so we couldn't uncover the full scope of the organization."

Once Heiden realized that the man was terrified of the group's retaliation, he offered witness protection to ensure his safety; the man, moved by Heiden's earnestness, finally agreed to talk.

"To summarize, this is what he told us: the organization wields enormous power. Those who betray the organization are killed. All acts of terrorism are decided by a single person, the leader. The past terrorist attacks were only child's play—in the future, something will occur on a larger scale." Heiden listed everything in a quick succession. "Vague things like that. We couldn't get much from him on the leader in question either. The Bureau made the decision to transfer him to our headquarters in Washington for a more comprehensive interrogation. That transfer, however, never took place."

"Why not?" Yuuto asked.

"He was killed," Heiden shrugged helplessly. "Shot just outside the detention facility. A rifle was recovered from the roof of a nearby building, but the suspect escaped, even with the police locking down the area almost immediately."

Yuuto was unsettled by the cult's bold and cold-blooded tactics. A mysterious terrorist group, already dangerous enough with their repeated attacks, but assassinating one of their own for speaking out? That wasn't normal.

"Is this really just a crazy cult?" Yuuto pondered out loud. "Could there be a larger criminal organization backing them?"

"We considered that, too, but there's not enough information about the organization itself; at this stage, there's nothing we can say for sure," Heiden said, pausing before adding as an afterthought, "The subject remained conscious for a short time after arriving at the hospital and provided us with a particularly interesting statement."

Yuuto leaned forward, feeling on edge.

"The leader's name is *Corvus*. Likely just a nickname. Supposedly, he is secretly operating from inside a prison." Heiden tapped the table with a finger. "Corvus is apparently a White male in his early thirties; a convicted murderer with military training, and a large burn scar on his back."

"I see," Yuuto murmured, absently looking at the man's neatly trimmed nails. "You want me to find this guy."

"Exactly. We believe Corvus is imprisoned at Schelger Prison in California."

Only then did Yuuto realize the FBI was serious about this offer. If this Corvus guy was a dangerous figure connected to multiple terror attacks—and possibly planning more—it made sense that the FBI would do whatever it took to catch him, even using backdoor methods.

"There's going to be a major international summit in New York this fall, with several world leaders attending," Heiden said, almost as if speaking to himself. "If a terrorist attack happened around then, it'd be catastrophic. That's why the FBI sent agents to Schelger and checked the personal data of every inmate."

Yuuto understood. "You still couldn't find him."

"No," Heiden confirmed, before continuing his explanation in a flat tone. "There were dozens of White male murderers in their thirties. Some had military training but no burn scars. Others had scars but no military experience. None of them fit all the criteria.

"There was division within the Bureau. Some thought the dead man's information was false. Others said parts of it were likely true, and we should broaden our criteria, or that we should thoroughly investigate every possible match. With no suspicious history on record, it was clear no inmate would yield under pressure. That's when the suggestion was made to infiltrate and search for Corvus from the inside."

Yuuto figured it was a win-win for the FBI. Sending an actual agent into a high-risk prison was too dangerous. But Yuuto, already a prisoner, posed no such risk. If he failed or died, the Bureau wouldn't be held responsible. With his future hanging by a thread, they knew he'd do whatever it took.

Yuuto knew he was just a disposable pawn to them. Though the stakes were unclear, it was a proposition he had little choice but to accept. While failing to find Corvus wouldn't lengthen his sentence, the promised reward could easily be a bluff. He had to keep that in mind. Otherwise, this sliver of hope could easily turn into crushing despair.

He made up his mind and told Heiden that he would do it. There was no reason to hesitate.

The deal came with strict conditions: Yuuto would not get any help from the FBI and was only allowed to contact them if he uncovered solid information. Under those terms, with no special privileges, he was sent into Schelger Prison as just another inmate.

The FBI had given him a list—twelve suspects, all confined to the West Wing—and Yuuto committed each name and face to memory.

Just before they parted ways, Heiden leaned in and said, "Corvus means 'crow' in Latin."

A jet-black shadow among the inmates, Corvus was somewhere in that flock, unseen, waiting. Yuuto wouldn't walk free until he found him. The irony wasn't lost on him: once a man of the law, Yuuto now pinned all his hopes on a terrorist.

Sometime during the night, Yuuto had fallen asleep without realizing it, but was woken up by the unpleasant ringing of the buzzer. Opening his eyes, he saw Dick sitting at the edge of the bed, reading a book. Remembering he was still in Dick's bed, he was about to apologize, but Dick spoke first.

"Final headcount," he said without looking up from his book. "After this, the doors will be locked until morning. Lights go out at eleven o'clock."

Yuuto nodded and sat up, stifling a groan from the pain. A guard appeared, so he stood as best he could and gave his name and ID number.

Now he could sleep undisturbed until morning. Yuuto let out a breath of relief and reached for the ladder to climb up to the top bunk—but Dick stopped him.

"Don't," he said. "Use the bottom bunk. No way you're climbing up and down in the shape you're in."

Dick switched out the blanket and pillow, giving up his bed without fuss. Grateful for the gesture, Yuuto accepted without protest. As he sat back down, Dick handed him a plastic cup of water and what appeared to be a pill.

"Painkillers. I swiped some from the infirmary."

Surprised by this unexpected kindness, Yuuto thanked him and swallowed the pill.

"If you're thinking of telling the guard BB's guys attacked you," Dick said bluntly, arms crossed as he watched him, "don't."

"Because they'll retaliate?"

"That, and in here, the guards are the enemy of all inmates. Even if you get stabbed, you don't say who did it. In prison, we follow our own rules," Dick explained in a condescending tone. "There's a Chinese guy named Fei in Block A. He's the leader of the Asian group. Introduce yourself and join up with them tomorrow."

"Why?"

"Why?" Dick repeated, raising his brows in mockery. His good looks, paired with an ironic grin, gave him a disturbingly cold air. "After everything you went through on your first day in prison, you're still asking why. Your head really is empty, isn't it?"

"BB made it clear in front of everyone—you're his prey. He might seriously come after you. You wanna be his woman?"

Yuuto's face tensed, reacting more to Dick's scornful tone than to what he was saying. "Of course not. I'd rather die than become his—*Ugh!*"

Dick suddenly grabbed Yuuto's shoulders and shoved him back onto the bed. The jolt sent a sharp pain through his ribs, knocking the air out of him.

"Lennix, you talk tough, but how are you going to protect yourself in this state, hm?" Dick taunted in a low voice. "Want me to rape you right now so you can learn firsthand how powerless you are?"

Dick grabbed Yuuto's crotch. The pain was so intense, Yuuto forgot to be afraid. "Dick, what the—"

"If you don't want BB, how about becoming mine? Be exclusive to me, and no one else will lay a finger on you. You give me your body, and I'll protect it. Think of it as a transaction. What do you say?"

The weight of Dick's body was suffocating, and his grip on Yuuto's crotch was unbearable. Drenched in cold sweat, Yuuto shoved at Dick's chest with all his strength. "Get off!"

How humiliating. If he weren't injured, he'd have punched this guy already.

"Even if I get raped, I'll never be anyone's possession. I don't need anyone protecting me—so stop insulting me!" Yuuto glared at Dick, fury clear in his eyes.

Dick met his gaze unflinchingly, then suddenly smirked and let go. "You've got guts, I'll give you that. Let's see how long that spirit lasts."

Yuuto felt both anger and relief. The thought of constantly guarding his chastity from a cellmate was unbearable.

"Listen," Dick continued flippantly, "even if you say no, if a group of guys gang up on you, there's nothing you can do. In here, you're clearly prey. I think you already know the answer. That's why you're hiding behind that pathetic stubble, trying to throw people off, right?"

Dick's cold sarcasm cut deep. It was one thing to know your own weakness, but hearing it thrown in your face was another.

"You still haven't understood the true nature of this place." Dick

went on, "If you stay naive, you'll get hurt. Nathan and Mickey might be kind, but they won't risk their necks for you. Until you can defend yourself like they can, join a group. If you get attacked again, I won't lift a finger. I'm not like Nathan or Mickey. I've got no interest in cleaning up after some dumb newbie."

With that rapid-fire monologue, Dick abruptly ended the conversation and climbed up to the top bunk. Yuuto's resentment flared at Dick's overbearing attitude. Maybe what he said wasn't wrong, but did he have to be such a jerk about it? *Who the hell did he think he was?*

Whatever goodwill Yuuto had felt toward him earlier, he quickly took it back. Dick Burnford was undeniably handsome, but his charm was entirely ruined by how unbearably rude he was.

CHAPTER 5

"There's one good thing about coming to prison," Matthew said with a puffy, sleepy face as they returned to their cell after breakfast.

Yuuto asked him what it was.

"It forces you to go to bed early and wake up early," he answered, pouting before adding in a whisper. "Not that we can do anything else."

Yuuto had to agree. First headcount was at 6:30 a.m., breakfast started at 7:00 a.m., and lights were out at 11:00 p.m. It was a more disciplined schedule than most teenagers today maintain.

During the day, most inmates were assigned to work or participate in an activity. Whether it was a paying job within the prison, a rehabilitation program, or an educational program, their daily good behavior was directly tied to opportunities for parole or sentence reductions, known as "good time." There didn't seem to be many prisoners just idling around.

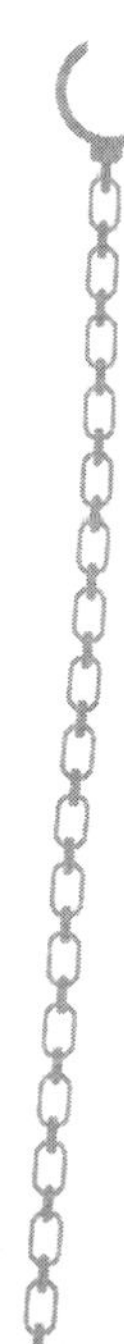

"Are you getting used to your job?" Yuuto asked.

"More or less," Matthew nodded.

Thanks to Mickey's connections, he had gotten a job sorting and delivering mail. As for Yuuto, he was temporarily helping Nathan out in the library. Typically, new inmates who wanted to work were assigned strenuous jobs, such as kitchen duty or cleaning. Yuuto and Matthew were considered lucky newcomers for meeting helpful seniors so early.

After the second headcount back in the cell block, Yuuto headed to the central building with Nathan to the library. A few prisoners were already gathered outside, waiting for consultations with Nathan.

"It's always busy, isn't it?" Yuuto remarked, eyeing the crowd. "There's never a shortage of visitors."

"Everyone's desperate to shorten their sentences, even if just a little," Nathan replied.

Yuuto was assigned the task of classifying legal documents and typing reports, and Nathan praised him for quickly picking things up. It reminded Yuuto of his days assisting one of his professors during his college years.

"How's your body holding up? If it's too much, you don't have to push yourself," Nathan asked kindly, always concerned about Yuuto's condition.

"I'm all right," Yuuto answered. "No problem."

Three days had passed since he got beaten up. His body still ached, but the pain in his ribs was subsiding, and he was relieved he hadn't suffered any fractures. Despite the bruises all over his face and body, since the work wasn't too physically demanding, Yuuto could manage it.

Although he wanted to start chasing Corvus immediately, he knew he had to heal and secure his footing in the prison first. He repeatedly reminded himself to be patient.

"I know it's frustrating, but you must endure," Nathan told him. "Losing your temper won't do you any favors."

"Yeah. I know."

"If someone picks a fight with you in public and you run away, you'll be labeled a coward," Nathan said, sighing. "That's why prisoners who care about their pride or masculinity often fight back, even if it means getting thrown into solitary confinement. I understand the impulse, but it only leads to trouble." His voice was gentle, yet it carried a hint of warning: "Don't let your emotions get the better of you."

Yuuto was still seething with anger toward BB and his underlings, but spending time with Nathan, a true pacifist, made him realize he couldn't afford to get dragged into the prison's foolish atmosphere.

The more he got to know Nathan, the more Yuuto liked him. In a world where nonsense and injustice reigned, maintaining rationality and common sense was extraordinary. Though Nathan appeared calm and laid-back, he was far more strong-willed than he seemed.

Inside the prison, apathy and hostility coexisted in a strange, uneasy balance. Most of the time, inmates drifted through their days with indifference, but the slightest spark could ignite sudden bursts of violence. Hot-tempered prisoners started fights over the most ridiculous things—a glance, a bumped arm, a rumor—the list was endless.

"It's sad that fighting is their only outlet for all their bottled-up energy," Nathan said. "Especially now, racial tensions are the biggest problem. It's been dangerous for about a year."

After their last morning consultation, Nathan began explaining, his expression gloomy, "Just last month, a fight broke out between Black and Chicano inmates. A Black gang member was stabbed, and in retaliation, the Black Soldiers attacked the Chicano boss, Rivera. They were defeated, and three of them were seriously injured. Rivera was sent to solitary, partly for his own protection against further retaliation."

"What do you mean?" Yuuto asked as he shelved some law books.

"Rivera is a charismatic man who once led the largest Chicano street gang on the outside. If the Blacks killed him, a full-scale race war would break out—no doubt about it," Nathan explained. "You know how, in baseball, when a fight starts, everyone storms the field?"

Yuuto nodded.

"It's the same here. If a big fight breaks out, everyone joins in. If the fire spreads, it could even reach outside the prison. That's why Warden Corning is trying to convince the Black Soldiers' boss to avoid conflict."

"You mean BB?"

"No. BB's only the second-in-command," Nathan shook his head. "The real boss is a man named Choker."

Nathan explained that Choker, though still under forty, was bedridden with terminal cancer in the infirmary. Despite being close to death, he continued to command the respect of the Black inmates, and even BB couldn't openly defy him.

"Choker is cooperating with the warden to maintain peace. Should he die, and BB take over? The consequences could be catastrophic. BB is aggressive and combative. Also, Dick takes good care of Choker—he's the only White inmate Choker trusts."

Yuuto recalled BB's words in the dining area and finally understood them.

"No one here would try to pick a fight with Dick, anyway, even without his connection to Choker," Nathan said.

Indeed, the other prisoners seemed to keep their distance from Dick.

"Because he's terrifying?"

"Yeah. He isn't a violent man, but he is unbelievably strong and a skilled fighter. When Dick arrived about a year ago, there was a massive inmate nicknamed Fat Thompson—he was built like a wrestler, and even the gangs hated him. Thompson targeted Dick as soon as he arrived. Dick ignored him at first, but one day, Thompson attacked him in the showers. They fought fiercely, and Dick ended up breaking Thompson's neck."

"What happened to Thompson?"

"He died. Dick took down a man the size of a grizzly with his bare hands. Incredible," Nathan said with a wry smile, and Yuuto stared at him in astonishment.

"Did Dick's sentence get extended, even though it was self-defense?"

"No. Thompson's killer was never officially identified. Nobody snitched because everyone hated Thompson. Since then, no one's dared to mess with Dick. The gangs resent him for not kissing up to them, but he doesn't swagger around or act arrogant, so the regular inmates generally like him."

Yuuto was shocked by the story, especially after having seen Dick's morose yet nonviolent demeanor.

"Dick told me to join a group for safety. What do you think?" Yuuto asked.

"It's safer that way. If you belong to a strong group, others would think twice before messing with you. That doesn't mean you're in the clear. No matter how careful, trouble could still find you—like a traffic accident. Even if you drive safely, someone could always rear-end you."

"That's true."

After finishing their morning work, Nathan stopped by the prison commissary and bought a pack of cigarettes, the cost deducted from his pre-registered bank account. Wages from prison jobs were deposited into that account, so inmates without savings had to work hard if they wanted to afford cigarettes and other essentials.

"It's a bit late, but here's a welcome gift," Nathan said, offering the sealed packet to him.

Yuuto, who didn't smoke, hesitated. He didn't resist after Nathan pointed out that cigarettes were the currency here.

"I'll give you a few examples," Nathan said. "If you want to use the tennis court, you give one pack to Alonso, one of the upper members of Locos Hermanos. If you want banned porno magazines, you give two packs to my brother Mickey. Want a late-night snack? A pack to the kitchen crew. There are many ways to use these. Of course, cash would be helpful, but if you don't have a nice girlfriend, it's not that easy to bring it in."

Apparently, a significant amount of money circulated inside the prison, much of it brought in by daily visitors, along with drugs such as marijuana.

Yuuto, who had been a DEA special agent, could easily imagine how visitors smuggled drugs in: wrapped in folded bills, concealed inside condoms hidden in the anus or vagina, or sometimes baked into heartwarming homemade cookies.

"Alcohol is harder to sneak in, so most inmates go for easier-to-get drugs instead. There's also a lot of gambling during sports games. Even in this cage, huge amounts of money move—and the gangs control it all. Some guards even help the gangs for extra cash. It's a really hopeless place."

Nathan suggested getting some fresh air, so they went to the yard, where inmates were grouped by race. They found a quiet spot and sat down.

"Yuuto. About what you said in the dining area. Is it true you were framed?" Nathan asked hesitantly. His hazel eyes reflected his reluctance to touch on such a delicate issue.

Yuuto just nodded without averting his gaze.

"I'm innocent," he said with conviction. "The coworker who was murdered, Paul, was my best friend. I didn't kill him. Someone set me up. With all the evidence pointing in my direction, there's nothing left for me to do."

"I see," Nathan replied and lowered his gaze to his feet. He stayed silent for a while, deep in thought, before looking back at Yuuto and muttering softly, "Actually, I was wronged, too."

"What?"

"I was framed, too. I don't talk about it, though—bringing it up would just isolate me here," Nathan said with a sad, resigned smile. "I was imprisoned two years ago for a murder I didn't commit."

Yuuto was left speechless by the sudden and unexpected confession.

"They said I killed my mother. She wasn't a good woman; she

was careless, had many boyfriends, and a tendency to sleep around. She was my only family, though; I still loved her. Someone broke into our house and shot her. My debts and failed business ventures made it easy for the police to jump to the conclusion that I killed her for the insurance money. They only focused on the evidence that made me look guilty and ignored everything I had to say. It's incredibly frustrating."

Nathan lifted his gaze and watched as the inmates fought over a basketball. "Most men here are criminals, sure. They're the misfits of society, the bottom of the bunch. Among them, there are those whose sentences are ridiculously harsh, or who couldn't afford a proper defense. That's why I do what I do now. Still, I know some would mock it. What can a guy do for others when he can't even help himself, right?"

Yuuto was deeply impressed by Nathan's aspirations. Despite being trapped in the same unfortunate situation, Nathan wanted to help others—something that couldn't be accomplished through kindness alone. Yuuto felt ashamed of himself for merely lamenting his misfortune and thinking only of being saved.

"Yuuto, if you serve your sentence diligently and do your best, your time will be shortened. You're serving a fifteen-year sentence, right? If you're lucky, you might be released on parole in about half that time. To make that happen, you need to stay away from the bad influences here, be a model prisoner, and work hard to get out as soon as possible." Nathan said before he stood up. "Come on, let's head to the dining hall."

Yuuto watched Nathan's back, quietly savoring his words. At best, he might get seven or eight years. It would be half his sentence, but it still felt far too long for someone innocent like himself. He knew he could never become a person like Nathan. No matter how hard he tried, he could not quietly accept his misfortune.

There was no other way out of here.

His only option was to find Corvus.

CHAPTER 6

Two weeks had passed since Yuuto arrived at Schelger Prison, and he had started checking the FBI's list of inmates as much as he could. That said, he couldn't simply approach them and start asking questions or blatantly snoop around. For now, he limited himself to casually observing them when he happened to spot them in places like the dining hall or the recreation room, or checking out who they associated with.

Yuuto deliberately thought of his mission as an "investigation." If he acted based on personal feelings or motives, it would only cloud his judgment and cause him to lose his composure.

Former DEA special agent Yuuto Lennix had been assigned a special mission: to go undercover inside a prison and track down a dangerous terrorist. The narrator's voice in his head made it sound like something out of a third-rate action movie, and he nearly laughed at himself. As long as treating it as "just work" improved his odds, he'd gladly play the awkward Superman or even the laughable Spiderman, no matter how ridiculous it seemed.

Mickey had taken a real liking to Matthew and was constantly by his side, looking out for him. Mickey was a bit of a clown but well-connected. Thanks to being recognized as Mickey's protégé, Matthew's chastity had been preserved so far. That said, he still got his ass groped in passing and received blatant invitations on a regular basis. Some inmates persistently hit on him whenever they found an opening. Still, perhaps because of Yuuto's earlier incident, even the carefree Matthew had grown excessively cautious—and for now, he had managed to avoid the risk of rape.

Meanwhile, Yuuto's days were so uneventful that it was almost anticlimactic. He hadn't yet been approached by BB, the inmate he remained most wary of, and none of the inmates subjected him to the routine newcomer bullying. Was it because BB had picked on him on his first day? It seemed that most inmates treated Yuuto with a certain caution, as if they were afraid to get involved with someone marked by BB.

"Yuuto, let's go to the rec room," said Mickey one day after dinner, as Yuuto was reading a book in his cell. Matthew, of course, was with him. The rec room was the prisoners' main social hub, a place where they could interact freely with people from other blocks. Thinking it would be a good opportunity to observe some of the targets, Yuuto decided to go along.

As the three of them headed out, they spotted Dick and Nathan through a hallway window. The two were sitting on a bench beside the empty basketball court, deep in conversation as dusk settled in.

"Hey, Mickey," Matthew said. "Dick and Nathan are over there. Let's invite them."

"Don't bother," Mickey said, shaking his head. "When they go out of their way to find a spot with no one around, it means they don't want to be interrupted."

"Why? Are they talking about something important?"

Mickey raised an eyebrow. "No, you idiot, they're whispering sweet nothings to each other."

"What?" Matthew was shocked. "They're like *that*?"

Mickey burst out laughing, and Matthew, realizing he'd been tricked, pouted. "That's mean! Don't trick me like that."

"Nah, I wasn't really lying. They're not lovers, but they're definitely close. They get along really well, like best friends. Nathan trusts Dick a lot, and Dick only lets his guard down around him. Having a real friend in a place like this, you've got to envy that."

Now that Mickey had said it, Yuuto realized it was true—Dick and Nathan *did* sometimes talk alone like that. Whether they were walking along the edge of the yard or sitting together in a quiet corner, there was something about the way they spoke to each other that gave off a strange, almost impenetrable atmosphere. It felt like no one else could step into their world.

"Oh, looks like they're done talking. They're coming this way."

"Yeah, the grounds are about to be locked up," Mickey said. "All right, let's call them over."

As the two passed through the central gate, Mickey called out to Dick and Nathan, inviting them to the rec room. Nathan smiled and agreed, but Dick brushed it off with a curt, "I'm tired."

Still, Mickey wasn't the type to give up so easily. "Come on, it's Sunday night," he urged. "Let's all have some fun! Come along."

"Mickey, I want to rest in my room."

"Hey, hey, Mr. Cool Guy who loves being alone. Come on, man, there's nothing but scruffy guys in here. You can act all brooding and mysterious if you want, but there's no cute girl around to squeal, 'That's so cool!' So drop the act and lighten up a little, yeah?"

After being pestered nonstop, Dick finally gave in with a wry smile, clamping a hand over Mickey's mouth. "Fine, I'll go, just shut up already." Mickey's easygoing, joke-loving nature could even coax a playful reaction out of Dick every now and then.

Seeing that side of him, Yuuto couldn't help but wonder why Dick was always so cold toward him. Dick's attitude had been consistently curt. Even though they shared a cell, they hardly ever spoke to each other. Dick wasn't the talkative type, sure—but he had no trouble holding long conversations with Nathan, so it wasn't like he disliked talking altogether.

So Yuuto concluded that Dick just didn't like him, and he made an effort not to talk to him more than necessary. Sharing that cramped space, with every breath audible yet no words exchanged, wore on Yuuto more than he'd expected. He hadn't hoped they'd become friends, but he did wish they could at least exchange a few casual words about the weather. Even that small hope was crushed again and again by Dick's complete indifference. Their cold, distant relationship hadn't changed one bit since the day Yuuto arrived.

What was it about him that Dick hated so much? Yuuto hadn't said or done anything to offend him. Sure, he'd caused a bit of trouble on the first day by getting injured, but he'd been the victim. It didn't seem fair to be hated over something so minor. Besides, Dick was rude enough to push Yuuto down when he was injured, even if it was just a joke—so if anything, they were even.

If there was a specific reason Dick did not like him, Yuuto wished the man would come out and say so. The last thing Yuuto wanted was to be the one to ask Dick why he had a problem with him. He felt like he would make himself vulnerable.

Since it was Sunday night, the large, hall-like recreation room was packed with prisoners. Mickey quickly spotted an open table and rushed over to secure seats. Once seated and sipping the warm soda Mickey had bought, Yuuto looked around.

Some groups were playing cards, others chatting animatedly. In the back were pool tables, foosball, and speedball games, though gang members had already claimed those; inmates who couldn't join in simply watched the games to pass the time.

Even in a place cut off from society, Sundays still carried a relaxed atmosphere. Church services were held in the morning for Christian inmates, and there was no factory work. Perhaps because of the influx of visitors, the prison had a strange, restless, almost giddy energy all day. With about two hours left before the nightly headcount, it seemed like everyone was trying to make the most of the remaining evening.

Mickey took out a pack of cards from his pocket and suggested a game of poker. When Yuuto asked if they were betting cigarettes, Mickey grinned and fished a handful of small coins from his other pocket instead.

"These'll be our poker chips. Split 'em up evenly. We'll play five-card stud. No strict rules—just make sure everyone joins every deal. Checking is allowed."

"It's not exciting if nothing is at stake," Matthew complained.

Mickey just grinned mischievously as he shuffled the cards. "Kid, you really think we're playing for nothing?" Mickey asked with a raised brow. "We'll decide the winner by who's got the most coins. The loser has to do a dare, and the winner gets to call the shots."

"I don't wanna do dares," Matthew whined, but everyone ignored him.

And the game began.

Each player studied their hand with sharp focus, tossing in coins or folding as the rounds went on. Poker was a psychological game. Yuuto glanced around the table at the other four. Mickey frowned and cursed at his cards—but he was probably bluffing. Nathan kept his usual easy smile, while Dick wore a perfect, unreadable poker face. The only open book was Matthew, whose every emotion was clearly visible on his face.

At the end of the third round, Yuuto was in second place. Dick was first. Feeling an odd sense of rivalry toward Dick, Yuuto decided to go all in during the final round. He had a full house and was confident he would win. Mickey, who was in third place, also went all in with his coins, possibly to challenge Yuuto.

During the final reveal, as hands were exposed one by one, the unexpected happened: Mickey held a straight flush.

"No way," Yuuto gaped. "Did you cheat when you dealt?" he protested, stunned at losing everything so close to the end.

Mickey, the winner, gave him a mean-spirited grin. "What was that?" he sneered. "For a sore loser like you spouting pathetic excuses, I've got the perfect penalty game. Yuuto, go over to the Sisters' table and say this to the one you find most attractive: 'My lady, may I have the honor of kissing your lovely hand?'"

"You're kidding, right?"

"There's no joking in the world of gambling." Mickey leaned back smugly and declared it with absolute finality. Yuuto turned his gaze toward the table where the Sisters had gathered. About ten flamboyant inmates, who called themselves female, were crowding around two tables, chattering loudly. Their flashy appearance made them stick out like a sore thumb.

The "Sisters" were men who preferred to be women. They always wore heavy makeup, painted their nails, and stood out even among the general prison population. Of course, dressing up as a woman could only go so far in prison, so they got creative—tying their uniforms at the waist to give the illusion of curves, wearing lace camisoles underneath, or wrapping large cloths around their waists as makeshift skirts—doing their best to look feminine within the limits of what was allowed.

"Go on, Yuuto. Or what, are you such a coward you can't even hit on a single girl?" Mickey teased.

Yuuto gave him a withering look. "But they aren't girls."

"Doesn't matter what they've got dangling between their legs—inside, they're all cute girls. And every one of them's crazy about good-looking guys."

No one tried to stop Mickey's mischief. Nathan and Matthew were stifling their laughter, and even Dick was smirking, watching to see what Yuuto would do.

Yuuto cursed under his breath and looked back at the Sisters. Then he noticed something. A dark-skinned Sister sitting at the far end of the table near the wall was being spoken to by a man: Joe Giverny, an inmate from Block B and one of the names on the Corvus suspect list.

Yuuto quickly decided and stood up. He glanced at Mickey. "I'll go, but you will pay for this, Mickey."

Putting on a grumpy act, Yuuto headed toward the Sisters' table. As he approached, the chatter died down, and the Sisters stared at him, eyeing him up like he was on the menu.

"What's the matter, baby? Do you want us to suck your dick?" a plump Black Sister said humorously and the group burst into raucous laughter.

Yuuto glanced around at them, then subtly turned his attention to Giverny. The man ignored him entirely, focused solely on a Latina-looking Sister with a serious expression.

"C'mon, Tonia. I didn't mean anything by it. Cindy just kept running her mouth, and I lost it. It won't happen again, I swear. Please—let me get back together with her," Giverny pleaded, almost desperately.

"You've got some nerve saying that," Tonia replied coolly in a husky voice. "You know how many times you've hurt that poor girl? Cindy's done with you. She says she never wants anything to do with a guy like you ever again."

Tonia, the Sister he was talking to, had a striking appearance. Her age was hard to guess, but her glossy black hair was neatly tied up on top of her head, and even with subtle makeup, her facial features were beautiful enough to stand out.

"Come on—"

"Give it a rest. If you even think about going near that girl again, I won't let it slide. Now get lost. I don't want to see your annoying face anymore." Tonia turned her head away in disgust, and Giverny's attitude shifted instantly.

"You fucking tranny!" Giverny sneered, voice thick with venom. "Acting all high and mighty just because I tried to be nice? Who the hell do you think you are?"

Furious, Giverny pulled something out of his pocket. A small blade peeked out from his clenched fist—a box cutter. Yuuto moved fast, grabbing Giverny's arm.

"Don't even think about it," Yuuto muttered into Giverny's ear, holding him back with as much strength as he could muster. "What the hell are you doing waving something like that around?"

"Who the fuck are you? Let go!"

"Calm down," Yuuto said to him. "What do you think this is gonna get you? Look. The guard's watching."

Giverny snapped his head toward the wall, where a guard was indeed watching them. His face tightened when he realized the guard's eyes were fixed on him. Noticing the tension, the guard began slowly walking over.

Giverny froze.

"Hey, Giverny. What's going on over here?"

"N-Nothing!"

Yuuto discreetly slipped the box cutter from Giverny's hand and tucked it into his own pocket before the guard could notice.

"Show me your hands. Now."

It was a close call. Giverny, visibly shaken, raised his hands. Not convinced, the guard ran his hands over him, checking for anything hidden. Finding nothing, he simply warned, "Don't cause any trouble," and walked away.

"I'll give this back, but don't go waving it around again," Yuuto said, returning the box cutter to Giverny and patting his shoulder. "You cooled off yet?"

Giverny, looking pale and defeated, nodded. "Y-Yeah. I'm good. If the guards get suspicious, I'm screwed. I'm outta here."

Clearly rattled, Giverny hurried off.

Watching him go, Yuuto silently crossed his name off the Corvus list. An impulsive, short-tempered, and weak-willed guy like that couldn't possibly be the leader of a dangerous cult or a terrorist mastermind. After Giverny disappeared, the Sisters all began badmouthing him at once.

"He always blows up over nothing. Such a pain in the ass."

"He only acts tough with people weaker than him."

They hadn't realized that Giverny had almost attacked with a knife. But Tonia had seen through it.

"Thanks for stepping in, sweetie. If he'd cut my face, I'd have been so traumatized I'd have to cry myself to sleep every night," Tonia said, turning her full attention to him. "You're new here, aren't you?"

"I'm Yuuto Lennix, from Block A," he nodded.

The brown-skinned Sister kept her legs crossed, looking up at Yuuto with a wicked little smile at the corner of her lips—the kind of smirk that said she knew exactly how to make herself look irresistible.

"I'm Tonia," she said. "You're that new guy sharing a cell with Mr. Handsome, Dick Burnford, right? I hear BB already claimed you from day one? Poor thing, being chased around by a beast like him. Is that cute little ass of yours still intact?"

Her teasing, husky voice was dripping with sultry energy, like a nightclub hostess who's smoked and drank too much. Yuuto gave a wry smile and answered, "So far, yeah."

"Did you need something? We don't talk business in the rec room."

For a moment, Yuuto didn't understand what she meant—then it clicked. He realized what kind of "business" the Sisters dealt in. Embarrassed, he shook his head. "That's not what I'm here for."

"Then, what do you want?"

CHAPTER 7

Hearing that question brought Yuuto back to why he was there in the first place—the dare kiss. Since he'd already spoken to Tonia once, he chose her as his target.

"I have a favor to ask," Yuuto mumbled awkwardly. "It's kind of rude and inappropriate, but, if you don't mind, could I… kiss your hand?"

The Sisters who had been eavesdropping all squealed at once. His face burned with embarrassment. *Damn Mickey*, Yuuto cursed as he glanced back. Mickey was up and waving his arms like a lunatic, clearly having a blast.

Tonia noticed Mickey's reaction and broke into a knowing smile. "Did you make some dumb bet with that show-off Mickey?"

Yuuto felt genuinely relieved when Tonia, quick on the uptake, offered him an opportunity to explain himself. "The kiss is a dare for losing at poker."

"I see," Tonia said with a sly look. "I don't mind a kiss on the hand, but on one condition—come to my room tomorrow for tea. First floor of Block C, all the way at the end. Okay?"

Yuuto immediately nodded. The Sisters' shrieking was already starting to attract curious glances from nearby inmates, and all he wanted now was to get this over with and leave.

"Monday after lunch, then. I'll be waiting." With the poise of a noblewoman, Tonia gracefully extended her slender hand.

Yuuto took her hand, leaned forward, and gently pressed his lips to the back. Maybe it was her refined beauty, or perhaps it was simply Tonia's aura, but even knowing she was a man, it didn't feel awkward.

When he lifted his head and gave her a shy smile in gratitude, Tonia responded with a warm smile, as if they were already old friends.

"That's not fair, Tonia! I want a kiss too!"

The other Sisters shrieked like schoolgirls and swarmed Yuuto, clinging to him. He barely managed to shake them off and retreat to his table.

Almost immediately, Nathan, his expression tense, asked, "What were you talking about with Giverny?"

"He was all riled up, so I just told him to cool it," Yuuto replied vaguely as Mickey leaned in with a grin, not caring one bit about his encounter with Giverny.

"Not bad, Yuuto. Of all people, you go and kiss Sister Tonia?" Mickey said with a low whistle. "You've got balls. Lucky for you, Rivera's in the hole, or you might be six feet under."

Yuuto shot him a wary glance.

"Rivera? The boss of Locos Hermanos?" he asked, failing to connect the dots. "And what do you mean, *lucky*?"

"Tonia belongs to Rivera. Before that, she was with Henry, the leader of the White gang, ABL. On top of that, she's the Sisters' leader. Prettiest woman in Schelger, no doubt, but lay a finger on her, and you're gambling with your life."

You could've mentioned that before I went over there, Yuuto thought with exasperation, then sighed. If he'd known, he wouldn't have asked to kiss someone that dangerous. Getting dragged into a jealous vendetta over a dumb poker punishment was the last thing he needed.

"Don't worry, Rivera's the magnanimous type," Mickey said, waving a hand around dismissively. "Someone flirts with Tonia, he just shrugs it off—'Course they would, my girl's a knockout.' Never gets mad. If there's anyone you should be watching, it's Henry Galen."

Yuuto's ears perked up at the name. Henry Galen—he was one of the men Yuuto had been investigating, and given his background, he was also a prime Corvus candidate.

"What kind of guy is Galen?"

"Check him out yourself. The big bald one by the pool table," Mickey said, pointing toward the back.

Yuuto looked over and spotted a massive, bald man leaning on a cue stick, one arm wrapped around the waist of a pretty, delicate-looking young guy. He was whispering something in the boy's ear, and the kid responded with a sweet smile, resting his head on the brute's shoulder.

"He's a white supremacist—hardcore neo-Nazi. Word is, he was part of a far-right group on the outside, a real die-hard. Cold-blooded and scary as hell. You'd better watch yourself around him."

"Who's the guy with him?"

"That's Galen's girl. Name's Lindsay. She's only been here about a year, but cozied up to Galen quickly. Now she acts like the queen of the block. Honestly, Tonia's way hotter than that brat, but Galen's got crap taste."

"I dunno, I think she is way cuter," Matthew chimed in. "If it were me, I'd totally go for Lindsay."

Mickey smacked his dopey little buddy on the head. "Idiot. If I weren't looking out for you, you'd be sashaying around like one of the Sisters by now, mincing through the prison halls. Don't go getting all picky about girls, punk."

Scolded, Matthew sulked and went quiet.

"Tonia invited me to her cell for tea. You think it's safe to go?" Yuuto asked, a touch uneasy.

Mickey, clearly pleased, grinned and offered some advice. "That's just the Sisters' tea party. You'll be fine. If you're uncomfortable going to Block C alone, I'll go with you."

"That'd be great." Yuuto smiled at Mickey's helpfulness, though in the back of his mind, he was already wondering if Tonia might know something about Henry Galen.

When it was time for the night headcount, Yuuto and the others returned to their cells.

"You handled Giverny pretty well back in the rec room. He had a knife or something on him, didn't he?" Dick said, standing in front of Yuuto who was now reading the paper.

"You saw that?" Yuuto asked in surprise. "Even from that far away?"

"No," Dick shook his head. "I couldn't make out what he was holding from where I was. I figured it out from the way he moved—and from the way you stopped him. When the guard came, you snatched it and hid it in your pocket, didn't you? Why'd you cover for him?"

"I don't know," Yuuto replied with a shrug. "Just acted on instinct. No special reason."

In truth, Giverny's panic and fear had gotten to him, and he'd moved without thinking. It had nothing to do with Giverny being part of his investigation.

"You were watching him from the start. Were you interested in him?"

Yuuto wasn't sure what kind of interest Dick was implying, but he couldn't help being impressed by the guy's sharp observation skills. "Not really. He kept pestering the Sister I was planning to ask for a kiss, so I was watching, thinking he was just in the way."

Dick looked like he had more to say, but instead, he sat down on the edge of his bed with a shrug that seemed to say, *Whatever.*

"You're talkative today," Yuuto couldn't help but point out. "What's gotten into you?"

Dick gave yet another lazy shrug. “Just felt like talking.”

“Why?”

“Who knows? Maybe because you’re starting to act like a real prisoner.”

“Is that an insult or a compliment?” Yuuto asked, frowning.

“That’s for you to figure out,” Dick said with a slight smile. “Why’d you pick Tonia for the kiss? Because she’s hot?”

Yuuto had actually approached her because of Giverny, but he couldn’t say that. Instead, he tried offering a believable excuse, “She reminded me a bit of my mother. Her name is Leticia, and she is a Chicana, like Tonia.”

Dick gave him a surprised look. “You’ve got Latin American blood?”

“No,” Yuuto shook his head. “She was my stepmom, and married my Japanese-American dad when I was ten. She has a son who is three years older than me, so at home, we speak both English and Spanish. I’m fluent in Spanish—and Spanglish.”

Spanglish was almost a new language in itself, a slang-heavy blend of English and Spanish spoken by Latinos in the United States.

“Where’s your family now?” Dick asked.

“My dad died in a car crash two years ago. After that, Leticia, who had always been in poor health, moved to Arizona to live with her sister. She took Lupita, my twelve-year-old half-sister, with her. My stepbrother Paco works for the LAPD.”

Yuuto had deeply mourned his father’s sudden death. Even now, that grief had not faded. At least his father had been spared from seeing him like this—a small mercy in the midst of everything.

“Your brother’s a cop?”

“Yeah. He’s a good guy—nothing like me.”

A cop with a criminal in the family. Just thinking about Paco made Yuuto feel a heavy guilt pressing on his chest. Not a single accusation came from Paco. He had stood by him, even as the guilty verdict was read, and told him, *"I believe in you, no matter the outcome."*

Yuuto had moved out for college and started working for the DEA in New York right after graduating. He only saw his family once or twice a year, but they meant everything to him. Even though they didn't share the same blood or skin color, their bond was unbreakable.

He'd begged Paco not to visit—said it was too painful to show his face. Instead, a letter had arrived two days ago.

It mentioned Leticia being hospitalized again, Lupita living happily with her cousins, and Paco doing fine at work. In the end, he wrote: *When you're ready, I'll come to see you. Just let me know.*

"How about you?" Yuuto asked. "Where's your family?"

Dick shook his head. "Don't have one. I grew up in the system—an orphan."

"I see," Yuuto muttered. It sounded cold, even to him, but he didn't want to toss out some shallow words of pity. Even after a short time, he could tell Dick wasn't the type who wanted cheap sympathy. "You've been alone since leaving the orphanage?"

"Pretty much. I had friends when I became an adult. A lover, too. All of that is gone now."

If prison had cost him someone important, that was a harsh fate. No matter how close two people were, it didn't mean they'd stay by your side after you became a criminal.

Yuuto suddenly found himself wondering what crime Dick had committed. What had brought him here? How long was his sentence? It was a question he couldn't ask. Among inmates, it was the one subject you didn't bring up.

The buzzer rang, signaling lights out, and Dick climbed up to the top bunk. A few moments later, the lights shut off.

Yuuto told himself to stop prying. In a place like this, some things were better left unknown.

CHAPTER 8

After the post-lunch lockdown headcount ended and the cell doors opened, the block was once again filled with its usual buzz. Countless voices, footsteps, music, and the sound of televisions all intertwined, forming a familiar noise that filled the entire building.

Yuuto glanced at the mirror above the sink while washing his hands and casually ran a hand through his hair. With his untrimmed beard and shaggy hair, he thought he looked pretty damn scruffy.

"You dollin' yourself up, Lennix?" Dick said from behind, reflected in the mirror. "Lemme tell you straight; there's no point. Tonia's not the kind of girl you can land."

"What's not gonna happen?" Yuuto asked flatly.

"You're missing the touch of a woman, right? I get it. Don't waste your time with her. She's way out of your league."

Dick clearly thought Yuuto had gone to Tonia's cell with sleazy intentions. The accusation was so off the mark it pissed Yuuto off. "Don't be stupid. I'm not going to see her for that."

"Don't be shy," he said, ignoring his protests while nodding knowingly. "I mean, she is gorgeous and looks every bit like a real woman. I wouldn't blame you."

"I said that's not it, damn it," Yuuto snapped. "What, are you jealous? Just because she invited me, the new guy—"

"Hate to break it to you, but I've got plans with Tonia, too," Dick said, already walking out of the cell. "C'mon, no need to bother Mickey; I'll escort you to Block C myself."

Yuuto hurried after Dick, who had already disappeared down the corridor. He had no idea what was going on. Once he caught up with Dick, he asked, "You're going, too? Are you friends with her?"

"Well enough to get invited to her tea parties now and then. I usually pass, but she specifically asked me to bring you along this time."

Yuuto could understand why the Sisters would fawn over someone like Dick, but it was still surprising to hear he actually accepted their invitations.

When Yuuto pointed this out, Dick gave a faint smirk. "Didn't want to leave a clueless rookie like you alone with them. The Sisters' tea parties are another world, man. Scary stuff."

Yuuto felt a sudden creeping fear at Dick's threatening remark. What if he were to get attacked by the Sisters and stripped naked the moment he set foot inside Tonia's cell? *No, they wouldn't go that far,* he told himself.

When they reached the ground floor, Matthew came running up. "Yuuto! Dick! You guys headed to Tonia's? Can I come too? Bring me along!"

"Nope," Dick said flatly. "Uninvited guests ain't welcome."

Matthew let out a sullen "Tch," and pouted. Yuuto tried to placate him, promising to ask Tonia to invite him next time, then followed Dick out through the Block A doors.

"That kid's been getting too relaxed lately. I saw him walking with a couple of Chicano inmates the other day."

"What's wrong with that?" Yuuto frowned. "He's not allowed to talk to them now?"

"That's not what I'm saying. With Rivera still locked in solitary, the Chicanos are getting restless. Real agitated."

To Yuuto, everyone in this place seemed irritable, but maybe Dick could pick up on shifts in the prison atmosphere that he couldn't.

"Rivera's Tonia's man, right? Still not out yet?"

"Yeah. The guards are trying to figure out the right time to let him out. He's got a lot of sway with all the Chicanos. If he gets shanked by a Black inmate, we'd have a full-blown riot. And not just here; prisons all over California would go up in flames."

After taking everything in, Yuuto hesitated, then muttered, "You sure this tea party won't make it look like I'm trying to jack his girl?"

Dick smirked and muttered under his breath, "Don't flatter yourself," making Yuuto scowl.

"It's not like that," Yuuto shot back. "I just don't want any trouble."

Since the rec room incident, Dick had eased up around Yuuto. He'd actually respond when spoken to and didn't act like just being near him was some kind of punishment. It made their time alone a lot more bearable.

They underwent a security check at the gate to Block C. Dick wasn't known for causing trouble, and he wasn't the violent type, but the guards still frisked him with an extra dose of caution. Maybe it was his calm, unreadable demeanor; it gave off a sense of unpredictability, like he could snap at any moment.

There was definitely something about Dick. He seemed laid-back, but there were no openings in his guard. Even without glaring, he had a quiet intensity that made people instinctively step aside when passing him. That unsettling vibe wasn't lost on the guards either.

"You never introduced yourself to Fei?" Dick asked over his shoulder after they passed through the gate. Yuuto remembered the advice he'd gotten before, and the name rang a bell; Fei, the old Chinese boss from Block A.

"I did, but I didn't ask to be a part of his gang."

"Why not?"

"Just because we're all Asian doesn't mean we think the same. Different countries, different customs. I was born here in the U.S. I didn't grow up as part of any ethnic community. Just having the same skin color doesn't mean we'll get along."

"I get that," Dick acceded, "but inside prison, race matters."

To Yuuto's surprise, Dick didn't shoot down his reasoning like he might've in the past. Between that and the tea party invitation, maybe he was finally starting to accept him a little… or so Yuuto hoped.

"Then let me ask you—what about Block C?" Yuuto continued, wanting to get his point across. "There's gotta be fights, right? Even if they're all Latino, you've got Mexicans, Puerto Ricans, Cubans… They all speak Spanish, sure, but their cultures are different. There must be some clashes."

Even outside prison, Mexicans tended to cluster in California and Texas, Puerto Ricans in New York, and Cubans in Miami. It was hard to believe they'd suddenly drop those differences just because they were behind bars.

"You're right," Dick agreed. "I guess if the Blacks and Whites disappeared, we'd be seeing conflicts amongst Latinos themselves next. With the Chicanos far outnumbering everyone else right now, there's no immediate threat."

People naturally form groups to protect themselves, and race was the easiest way to draw the lines. Inmates had no choice but to cling to visible identities.

Prison really was a microcosm of society. Latinos had surpassed Black Americans to become the largest minority in the U.S., and among them, Chicanos made up the majority. So it wasn't surprising that they also had a serious influence behind bars.

"Anyway," Dick added, stopping as they reached the last cell at the end of the corridor, "where we are going now? No race wars; White, Black, Brown, Yellow—everyone's thrown into the mix, talking men, food, and fashion like their lives depend on it. Ready for this?"

As Dick said this, he turned to Yuuto like he was about to kick off a battle, a smirk firmly planted on his lips. From behind the curtain-draped doorway came the loud chatter of voices. Yuuto nodded, tense.

Dick stood at the threshold and called inside in a low but theatrical tone, “Ladies, may we intrude on your secret garden?”

The curtain flew up.

“Oooh, look who it is!” A curvy Black Sister wiggled her hips and purred, “Girls, Dick’s here! And so is that polite little cutie who kissed Tonia’s hand!”

A chorus of excited squeals erupted, and in an instant, Dick and Yuuto were seized by a dozen hands and dragged inside. Even though he’d braced himself for the worst, the scene that greeted Yuuto was beyond anything he’d imagined.

The cell was clearly a double, much larger than the ones they lived in, and it was packed tight with at least ten Sisters. The air was thick with perfume and heavy makeup. Yuuto’s head spun.

They were swarmed like movie stars by a mob of die-hard fans, hands groping them, lips landing kisses, bodies swirling around them for a frantic few moments until they were forcibly seated, one on each bed. The Sisters then crowded in close, all trying to sit beside them.

“Welcome, Yuuto,” Tonia said warmly from a chair in the back. “Dick, I’m glad you came too.” She handed him a teacup brimming with hot tea, and finally, Yuuto started to feel human again. “Help yourself to some cookies too,” Tonia offered. “I bake them myself.”

He had no idea where she got the ingredients or how she baked them, but Tonia’s cookies were surprisingly good—chewy, fragrant, and just the right amount of sweet.

“Tonia,” Dick asked, “any idea when Rivera’s getting out?”

“Soon, I think,” she replied and lit a cigarette. “I’ll still worry once he’s back.”

“Choker’s not looking to fight with Locos Hermanos. Things’ll be fine.”

“I hope you’re right. BB’s been ignoring Choker’s words lately, so I’m not completely at ease.”

Even as Tonia and Dick spoke in serious tones, Yuuto found

himself helpless in the clutches of an older Sister seated beside him. She was plump, her face caked with heavy makeup, and she kept patting his head and stroking his cheek. Leaning in close, her eyes sparkled with amusement.

"Everyone," she exclaimed loudly, "don't you think this cutie would look better without the scruff?"

The others chimed in immediately with cheers of agreement. Yuuto gave a weak, defeated smile. He knew facial hair didn't suit him; it was pointless to argue.

"You should shave it, honey. Don't you think so?"

"Wait—uh, no," Yuuto protested. "I'm not so sure—"

"I say we do it! Off with the beard!"

In yet another bout of glee, several Sisters suddenly jumped him and pinned him to the bed. He thought they were joking until one of them came at him with shaving cream and a razor.

Panic rising, Yuuto turned to Dick for help. "Dick! Do something!"

"I'm with them." Dick replied, his only ally betraying him, "That shaggy beard's gotta go,"

"You'll look great without it, Yuuto." Tonia added with a smile, "I always thought it didn't suit you either."

Utterly abandoned, Yuuto gave up. *Fine. Let them do whatever they want.* At his visible defeat, the Sisters cheerfully got to work. With bubbly foam and gossip in the air, they lathered his face and carefully shaved him smooth. One of them wiped his face with a warm towel.

"There! So much better. You've got such a handsome face. It'd be a crime to hide it!"

"Your skin's so smooth! I'm so jealous! The guys won't leave you alone now!"

Yuuto almost muttered that he *grew* the beard to avoid exactly that, but it seemed too pathetic to say out loud. He just lay there silently, scowling slightly as he touched his now bare chin.

"All done, Yuuto. Look, Tonia, doesn't he look handsome now?"

When Yuuto sat up, Tonia's eyes widened in admiration.

"Wow. You really are a stunner," she breathed, genuine shock in her voice. Then she turned to Dick with a sly smile. "Don't you think so, Dick?"

Dick, still holding an unlit cigarette between his lips, nodded with clear surprise.

"Yeah," Dick agreed with a nod. "I figured you had a decent face under all that, but I didn't think losing the beard would change your appearance this much."

Being stared at so intently by Dick was unbearable. Yuuto covered the lower half of his face with one hand and grumbled, "Quit looking."

"What? Embarrassed?" Dick smirked. "You're acting like someone stole your bra."

Yuuto's face flushed hot, not with anger but sheer embarrassment. He had never shown his bare face to anyone in prison and felt like sitting naked in front of a gawking crowd. The discomfort was a touch too overwhelming.

For a while, his new look became the main topic of conversation, and the room buzzed with laughter and teasing. Yuuto wanted to ask Tonia about Henry Galen, but no natural opening came. As he sat there debating how to bring it up, the curtain suddenly lifted, and a young man stepped inside.

It was the pretty boy Yuuto had seen with Galen in the rec room last Sunday. With a confident glint in her eyes, the newcomer scanned the room and lit up the moment she saw Dick. She said with a smile, "So that's what the noise was. You're here."

"Hey, Lindsay," Dick said casually. "How's it going?"

"Not bad."

Unlike the other Sisters, Lindsay wore no makeup and wore her prison uniform normally. It didn't seem like she lacked style—more like she was confident enough to flaunt her natural beauty without embellishment.

"What do you want, Lindsay?" snapped the Black Sister who'd shaved Yuuto's beard, her tone sharp.

Lindsay shot her a frosty glance, then turned to Tonia with a charming expression. "Tonia, you've gotta hear this," she started. "D'you know how Sammy Porter's been all over me lately? I finally gave in just to shut him up, but the bastard didn't even pay me. I'm so pissed. Think you could say something to him for me?"

Tonia's eyes narrowed in exasperation. She said, unable to conceal her surprise, "You're still doing business with Galen around? If he finds out, you're dead, you know that, right?"

"It's fine," Lindsay answered with a dismissive wave. "Just tell him to pay me. If it's you—"

"No." Tonia's voice was ice-cold.

Lindsay's smile vanished in an instant.

"I'd put my body on the line for the poor Sisters who got raped or left high and dry after some bastard skipped out on 'em," Tonia spat out the words like venom, "but I'm not lifting a damn finger for some sneaky tramp hustling behind her man's back. A man who can take care of your every need, no less. Wash your face and start over."

Lindsay's eyes blazed with fury as she glared at her. "Oh, I see. So that's how it is," she said with a bitter nod. Then she leaned in, pointing a sharp finger at Tonia. "You're still sore that I stole Galen from you, huh? What? After all this time, you're still jealous? You are pathetic!"

The Sisters exploded before Tonia could even respond.

"Bitch, who the hell do you think you're talking to?"

"As if Tonia would still be hung up on that piece of shit Galen!"

"Your man got dumped by Tonia—he's a limp-dick loser who can't do a damn thing without a crutch!"

It was like someone had kicked a hornet's nest. The place erupted.

Bombarded by insults, Lindsay stormed off, clearly pissed, but the Sisters were still riled up.

"Seriously, the nerve. Tonia took care of her all that time!"

"She's just a damn brat. If Galen finds out she's been hustling, he might just fucking kill her."

As the Sisters kept trash-talking Lindsay in a loud, furious uproar, Yuuto quietly leaned over to speak to Tonia. "Galen? He's the ABL leader, right? What kind of guy is he?"

Tonia shrugged and ground out her cigarette. "He's in for life, no chance of parole. Supposedly killed three Black men. He's smart, *really smart*, and makes a good boss. I'll give him that. But as a boyfriend?" Tonia shook her head. "Galen is a brutal guy. The kind of guy who can stab someone with a smile. He's sweet on the surface, which is probably why Lindsay underestimates him. She'll regret it. Just give it time."

A cold-blooded, intelligent, and ruthless leader—Yuuto immediately recalled the face he'd seen in the rec room last night. Galen's image overlapped disturbingly with Corvus's. If he could get Tonia alone, he'd ask her then and there if Galen had a burn scar on his back. Even if it wasn't listed in the files, there was a chance he got it after arriving here.

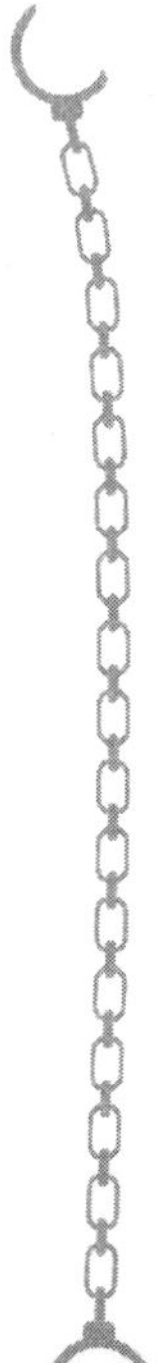

Eventually, the tea party came to an end. The Sisters reluctantly filed out of Tonia's cell, each stopping to shake hands or kiss Dick and Yuuto goodbye. They all looked shy when it came to Dick—like schoolgirls meeting their crush. For his part, Dick wore the role of their gentleman prince to perfection, all smiles and patience, a far cry from his usual surly self.

"You're awfully sweet to them," Yuuto teased with a hint of accusation.

Dick's smile vanished, and he gave Yuuto a cool, unreadable look. "A real man treats ladies with kindness."

"Well said."

"Dick knows what they go through," Tonia said softly. "Even if they play it smart, doing dangerous work like selling your body means getting beaten up sometimes. A lot of them end up in the infirmary."

Her words left Yuuto with a bitter feeling. The Sisters always seemed carefree and cheerful, but beneath that was a mountain of suffering—burdens only those pushed into the shadows ever knew.

"Thanks for coming today, Dick," Tonia said and kissed him on the cheek. Dick returned the gesture and said, "It was fun." She gave Yuuto the same goodbye, then chuckled as she gave him a once-over.

"What? Is there something on my face?" Yuuto asked, puzzled.

"No, quite the opposite," she said, still looking him over. "Without the beard, you've gotten cute. How old are you really? Twenty-five?"

"Give me a break, Tonia. I'm twenty-eight."

"Oh, really? Just a year younger than Dick?" Tonia looked back and forth between them, then gave a dazzling smile. "You're both such handsome men. Different types, sure, but standing next to each other, you make me forget we're in this godforsaken place."

CHAPTER 9

As soon as they stepped out of Tonia's cell, Dick leaned in, whispering teasingly, "You've fallen for Tonia, haven't you, Lennix?"

Not this again, Yuuto thought with a sigh. It was getting old. Still, there was something about Dick loosening up around him that made it a little hard to be annoyed. So instead of showing irritation, he answered with an overly calm expression, "You're the one with a thing for Tonia. Why else would you keep bringing her up?"

"I mean, sure, she's attractive. But unfortunately, I'm not into women."

Yuuto frowned and looked at Dick's face, unsure how to take that. "You mean you're not into women like her?"

"No. I meant it literally. I'm gay."

He came out so smoothly, so casually, that Yuuto didn't even have time to be surprised—he was just flat-out stunned. "You seriously say something like that… *here*?"

They were walking through a hallway packed with inmates, and he was just outing himself like it was nothing. To Yuuto, something like that was as dangerous as handling a live bomb; it required serious caution.

"What's the difference where I say it?" Dick said with a shrug.

"There *is* a difference!" Yuuto nearly shouted, his hand twitching with the urge to backhand him. "What if someone were to overhear?"

Prison was crawling with rape cases. Sure, plenty of guys hooked up with whoever was nearby, but being known as gay was another story entirely. It was fucked up way of thinking, but two guys getting

together was only "acceptable" because there were no women around—it was seen as substitute sex. People could be cool with the Sisters because they were obviously gay, but if a *manly* man admitted he was into men? That shit was taboo. You'd have guys whispering behind your back, calling you faggot, queer, all that crap.

"I didn't think you were the type to run your mouth like that."

"Don't be ridiculous, Lennix," Dick said. "I just spoke honestly about myself."

"I'm saying you need to be more careful." Yuuto snapped, and Dick just shrugged.

"You're a weird one. Most guys would be freaked out finding out their cellmate swings that way. But I get told off for being too open? Didn't see that one coming."

That only pissed Yuuto off more. He glared at him. "Don't fuck with me. I don't discriminate against minorities, and I've got no bias when it comes to someone's sexuality. If you so much as lay a finger on my ass, I will do something about it."

"Oh yeah? Like what?" Dick asked like he was genuinely entertained.

"I'll snap your dick off at the base so it never works again," Yuuto said, jabbing a finger right in front of his nose.

He'd meant to sound threatening, but he was too fired up—and it backfired. Dick burst out laughing.

"What's so funny?" Yuuto snapped.

"It's just… you—" Dick couldn't even get the words out.

It stung. Dick wasn't the type to laugh out loud much, and now here he was, laughing his ass off like Yuuto was the funniest shit he'd seen all year. Humiliated, Yuuto turned and stormed off, only to feel a hand grab his arm from behind.

"Hey, don't be mad, Lennix," Dick said.

"You're always making fun of me. You really piss me off, you know that?" Yuuto said, unable to hold back. "Just 'cause you've got a decent face doesn't mean you can act like you're hot shit."

"I don't think I'm hot shit. I don't recall ever making fun of you."

"Bullshit," Yuuto spat, even more incensed. "On my first day, you said you'd protect me if I became yours. I won't let you say you've forgotten—"

Interrupting Yuuto mid-accusation, Dick shot back, stone-faced, "I was half-serious."

"What?"

"You were a poor newbie getting targeted by BB. I figured, since we were sharing a cell, I might as well throw you a bone. If I claimed you were my bitch, no one would touch you."

"You're a real piece of shit, you know that? Coming onto me out of pity when you don't even mean it—did you really think I'd be happy about that?"

"Oh?" Dick arched a brow at the implication. He asked, not missing a beat, "So you wanted me to come on to you for real?"

Yuuto could only stare, dumbfounded. Say one thing, he'd twist it back. He was usually quiet, but when he felt like it, Dick could talk circles around you.

"I figured you'd turn me down anyway," Dick said with a wave of his hand. "Still, at least now you get just how dangerous this place really is, right?"

"Yeah. No kidding. Lucky me, stuck with such a thoughtful cellmate," Yuuto said sarcastically.

"Don't get so prickly."

"You're the one making me prickly."

Maybe Dick wasn't quite as bad as Yuuto had assumed, but he definitely had a shitty personality. That much was certain.

"I've been a grumpy bastard since the day I was born," Dick said with a shrug, as if he'd heard Yuuto's thoughts out loud.

“Then fix it, if you’re aware of it,” Yuuto muttered. “And Dick—don’t you dare start throwing any flirty looks my way.”

“I won’t. You’re not my type,” Dick said, giving him a pointed look. “I’d rather flirt with baby-faced Matthew.”

Yuuto couldn’t tell whether he felt relieved or insulted by how he said it. Scowling, he shot Dick a sideways glance.

“What’s with that look? Don’t tell me you’re doubting me? Dick said innocently. “Want me to swear to God or something?

“You’re Christian?”

“Nope. Atheist.”

“Bastard.”

Now that they’d opened up a bit, Yuuto had to admit—Dick was kind of a funny guy. Yet, he was hard to pin down. Yuuto still didn’t quite know what kind of person he was. Maybe if they talked more honestly and openly, he’d start to understand him better.

Dick had this vibe, deep down, like he was always keeping people at arm’s length. Maybe most guys in here were like that to some extent, but in Dick’s case, it wasn’t just bitterness or some misanthropic wall. And it wasn’t that weird, antisocial, stubbornness some inmates had, either. Even when he let someone close, he’d subtly step back himself—like the more you tried to get near, the more he’d create distance.

His handsome, cold-eyed cellmate was full of mysteries. In a different way than Corvus, he was shaping up to be another pain in the ass Yuuto couldn’t ignore.

CHAPTER 10

"Congratulations, you did it," Yuuto smiled warmly and gave Bob Wheeler's bony shoulder a light pat. "I'm sure Nathan will be happy, too."

"Thanks, Yuuto. I finally got approved for parole—and it's all thanks to Nathan's advice. Be sure to tell him I said so."

Wheeler beamed as he pulled a photo from his chest pocket and showed it to him; it was the same one Yuuto had seen multiple times before: a chubby wife and two mischievous-looking sons. At this point, Yuuto felt like he might absentmindedly wave and say hi if he saw them in town.

"This one's Jesse, and that one is Steven," Wheeler repeated, pointing at the two kids in the photo.

"I know," Yuuto said patiently. "And your wife's name is Anna, right?"

"Yep, Anna. I'm finally going home to my family," the man's tone was wistful. "I can't wait to have my wife's cooking again."

"Won't be long now," Yuuto said with a firm nod. "All right, I'll leave you to it. I'll make sure Nathan gets your paperwork."

"I'm counting on you, Yuuto. I'll stop by and thank Nathan properly later."

Yuuto gave a faint smile as he stepped out of Wheeler's cell, but the moment he set foot onto the outer walkway, his face naturally hardened, and a heavy sigh slipped out.

Bob Wheeler wasn't Corvus either. He was just an ordinary man. He'd worked himself to the bone for his family, only to be suddenly laid off from the auto parts factory where he'd worked. He'd gone to the manager to beg not to be fired, got brushed off coldly, and in a moment of rage, struck him with a nearby wrench, killing him. He'd undoubtedly committed a crime, but he wasn't a bad person.

Wheeler had approached Nathan asking for advice on how to answer the parole board effectively. Since he was on the list of potential targets, Yuuto, posing as Nathan's assistant, had made repeated efforts to meet with him. From the start, Yuuto hadn't held much hope, but in the end, it seemed like it had been another dead end.

Time kept slipping by without any significant progress in the search for Corvus. Despite his growing sense of urgency, Yuuto continued to steadily investigate each person on the list. He approached them in various ways, trying to draw out their true identity. But it was nearly impossible to judge someone's nature just from a few conversations.

If it were a drug dealer, he might've picked up a scent by now. A terrorist leader was a completely different matter, though. Especially someone as cunning as Corvus, who didn't even reveal his identity to his own followers. They didn't even know what ideology he used to justify his acts.

Still, unless Yuuto started narrowing down the suspects, he'd never make headway. Trusting his gut, he filtered out the targets one by one. Of the twelve originally under investigation, only five remained. One of them was Henry Galen, and Yuuto's hunch that Galen was the prime suspect only grew stronger.

He'd even considered asking Tonia outright if Galen had burn scars on his back, even if it sounded strange. But Tonia was almost always surrounded by the other Sisters, making it hard to catch her alone. On the rare occasion she was alone, there'd always be a tough Chicano guy nearby playing bodyguard.

While pondering what to do, Yuuto was walking toward the central building when he saw Dick and Nathan approaching from the other side. The two didn't notice him as they headed out toward the now-sunset-tinged yard. Yuuto, without thinking, watched them through the window.

Walking side by side near the edge of the yard, Dick and Nathan looked well-matched, both White, tall and handsome. Dick's good looks went without saying, but Nathan also had a refined, well-proportioned face. Surrounded by rough-looking inmates, the two of them seemed like they existed in a different world. And just like Mickey had said, Dick and Nathan seemed genuinely close. Whether it was friendship or respect or something else, one thing was certain: Dick never showed Nathan his usual coldness.

If Yuuto watched closely, he noticed Dick's eyes were almost always on Nathan. It wasn't obvious, but Yuuto got the sense that Dick was constantly aware of him.

It was a bit of a vulgar thought, but Yuuto couldn't help wondering: Did Dick have feelings for Nathan? Dick was gay, so it wasn't out of the question.

If Dick had romantic feelings for Nathan, it would explain why he behaved so out of character around him. It was only natural to be hyper-aware of someone you liked. When they moved, your eyes followed instinctively; when they spoke, you couldn't help but listen.

The two sat on the top bench beside the basketball court, just likc they always did. Dick leaned forward, resting an elbow on his knee, his eyes fixed intently on Nathan as he spoke. Even from a distance, Yuuto could see the seriousness in his eyes.

As he watched them, a strange feeling stirred in Yuuto's chest, something foggy and unpleasant. A mix of unease and irritation he couldn't quite identify. Yuuto was confused by his own reaction. Why should he care who Dick liked? It wasn't his business. It was weird to even think about it.

Just as he tried to look away, thinking there was no point in staring, a different pair of people entered his peripheral vision—and his eyes were immediately locked on them.

It was Galen, the ABL leader, and his lover, Lindsay.

Oddly enough, they weren't accompanied by any of the usual ABL followers. Sensing an opportunity to approach, Yuuto dashed out into the yard and followed them.

Galen and Lindsay slipped into the equipment shed at the edge of the yard. Yuuto slowed his pace, frowning. *What were they doing?* He seriously doubted they were grabbing a ball to play with.

Curious, he pressed himself against the door and listened. A high-pitched, excited voice, clearly Lindsay's, was shouting something. A deeper voice shouted over it. For a moment, Yuuto wondered if something inappropriate was happening between them, but the atmosphere was too charged, too tense, and aggressive for that.

Loud crashing sounds echoed out—clearly a fight, and Yuuto started to worry. It might have been just a lovers' quarrel, but Tonia's words echoed in his mind at that moment, *"Galen is a brutal man."*

That thought pushed him to act. Yuuto threw open the door and stepped inside. Galen turned to look at him from the back of the dim shed. Yuuto's eyes hadn't adjusted to the dark, but one thing was immediately clear—Lindsay wasn't there.

"Where's Lindsay?"

"What are you talking about? You're Lennix from Block A, right? What're you doing here?" Galen grinned menacingly, eyes gleaming with something abnormal.

"I'm looking for Lindsay; I need to talk to her. You came in here with her, didn't you? So, where is she?"

"There's no one here. I've been alone from the start." Galen slowly approached, exuding an overwhelming, oppressive presence that made Yuuto instinctively step back.

"Don't play dumb," he pressed, even as fear began to creep in. "What happened to Lindsay?"

Galen's eyes flared dangerously. *The eyes of a madman,* Yuuto thought as he instinctively took a step back.

"You're a noisy little shit." Galen lifted his thick arm. Just as

Yuuto braced himself for a blow, he caught sight of someone sliding in front of him.

"Galen, don't touch him. He's my cellmate."

It was Dick. The two men stared each other down for a moment before Galen smirked and backed off first.

"Burnford," he said in a low, threatening voice. "You keep that loud mouth of his shut. *Got it?*"

"Got it. Take my word for it."

Still smirking, Galen walked off like nothing had happened. Snapping back to his senses, Yuuto shoved Dick aside and rushed to the back of the shed. Behind a large basket of balls, he saw a flash of blue denim.

"Lindsay?" Yuuto pushed the basket aside and gasped at the sight of Lindsay collapsed on the ground. Frozen in shock, Yuuto watched as Dick knelt beside Lindsay and checked her pulse.

"She's dead." Dick gently closed Lindsay's eyelids, then stood with a grim face, "Looks like he strangled her."

He grabbed Yuuto's arm, pulling him out of the shed. Nathan was waiting at the door.

"Nathan!" Yuuto exclaimed. "Lindsay's dead inside! Galen killed her!"

"What?"

"Both of you, let's go," Dick pushed Yuuto along to get him to walk. "If we stay here, it'll get messy for us."

"Wait, Dick! What about Lindsay?"

"She's dead," Dick said flatly. "Nothing we can do for her now."

"That's not what I mean!" Yuuto shook his head vehemently. "We can't just leave her. This is murder!"

"Someone else will find the body soon enough and raise the alarm. That's why we have to get away before that happens."

Yuuto couldn't believe what he was hearing and unable to hold it in anymore, he shoved Dick in the chest, pushing him away. "Why? We should be honest and tell the guard that Galen murdered her."

"I told you before," Dick said, narrowing his eyes. "If you snitch to the guards, you won't survive here."

"So what?" Yuuto yelled. "I just watched someone get murdered. It wasn't even a fight! She was killed in cold blood! How can I ignore that?"

"Yuuto. Let's just head back to the cell," Nathan said in a calming voice to Yuuto, who was getting agitated by the minute.

"But Nathan—"

"Dick's right," Nathan interrupted. "If you tell the guards, you'll become ABL's next target."

When Nathan said that, effectively taking Dick's side, all the fight drained out of Yuuto. He reluctantly followed them into the building.

On the way back to Block A, Nathan glanced at Yuuto. "Why did you go after Galen?" he asked. "You don't even know him, do you?"

"No, but…" Yuuto hesitated to answer.

Before he could think of an answer, Dick cut in. "Lindsay seemed off, right? That's why you were worried?"

Dick's guess was totally wrong, but Yuuto felt like he needed to go along with it. "Yeah," he nodded. "She looked scared, so I was worried Galen might do something."

Nathan let out a soft sigh and scolded him. "You're more reckless and curious than I thought," he said. "Don't get involved with dangerous men like him or you'll end up dead."

"I'll be more careful," Yuuto relented.

"Please do. Now let's hurry. When someone gets murdered, the prison goes into lockdown."

"Lockdown?"

"Everyone gets locked in their cells. No meals, no visits, no phone calls—nothing. It's part of the investigation and punishment."

Just as they entered Block A, a blaring siren rang out and red emergency lights flashed. As prisoners looked around in confusion, guards began shouting and swinging batons, ordering everyone back into their cells.

Lindsay's body had probably already been found.

A few minutes later, the doors locked shut. Yuuto sat on his bed while Dick stood at the door, peering out.

"Dick. Sorry about earlier." Yuuto tried speaking, but Dick didn't turn around. He continued. "You helped me, but I got worked up. I shouldn't have pushed you."

He'd hoped Dick would just brush it off like always, but when he turned around, his face was icy cold.

"Lennix. I have one favor to ask of you," his tone was flat, and Yuuto tensed. "Don't ever pull bullshit like that again in here. You might think you can do whatever you want, but that's not how it works. Every time you stir things up, it puts my neck on the line. Everything I've built could come crashing down because of you. You're nothing but a burden."

After saying his piece, Dick turned his back again. The rejection was clear, and Yuuto was at a loss for words. Their relationship had improved since the beginning, and they could talk casually now. Just like that, they were back to square one. He didn't understand why, but being hated by Dick hurt more than Yuuto wanted to admit.

It made him feel utterly hopeless.

"Burnford, out." Chief Guard Guthrie came to escort Dick. "Dr. Spencer's asking for you. Says he can't manage without you."

From the neighboring cell, a prisoner named Barry shouted out. "There goes Dick getting special treatment again. Being on medical duty must be real fancy," Barry complained. "Are the infirmary staff really that important?"

Dick slammed his fist against the bars of his cell. Dick snapped, baring his anger."Then you do it! If you're fine wiping the asses of

patients who can't move, I'll gladly trade places!"

"D-Don't get mad, Dick." Barry immediately faltered. "I was just joking. Don't blow up over a joke, that's not like you."

It was rare for Dick to show emotion. After Guthrie and Dick left, Barry called over to Yuuto. "Hey, Yuuto. What's up with Dick?"

"No idea," he mumbled. "Guess he's just in a bad mood."

There was no way Yuuto could admit it was his fault.

CHAPTER 11

The lockdown following the murder of Lindsay Scott lasted twenty-four hours. The inmates, stripped of their freedom, vented their frustration and irritation by banging on the iron bars and shouting, until the entire West Wing rang with noise and fury.

It wasn't until the following day at dinner that the lockdown was finally lifted. Despite the prison and police conducting an intense investigation, the culprit was never found. Still, rumors spread quietly among the inmates; everyone was saying it had to be Galen, that he'd snapped after learning Lindsay had cheated on him. Most people seemed to accept that explanation without question—if anyone would do it, it was him.

Dick stayed in the infirmary the whole time and didn't show up in the cellblock, but when they saw him again after the lockdown was lifted, he was already back to his usual, emotionless self.

The next day, while they were all eating dinner, an elderly Black man approached them. It was Hawes, Matthew's cellmate.

"Hey, Mickey," he said. "You seen that kid of ours anywhere?"

Hawes had been inside for twenty years and was considered a veteran, but he was apparently about to be released soon. Maybe that's why he'd been chattier lately, often stopping by to talk to Yuuto and the others.

"Nope. I had something to take care of this afternoon, so I haven't seen him," Mickey answered. "He should be coming in for dinner around now, though."

"Is that so? That boy promised to rub my back before dinner, but he never came back. Damn kids these days, can't keep a single promise." Hawes grumbled and walked away, unsteady with a tray in his hand.

"He complains a lot, but the old man really likes Matthew," Mickey said with a laugh, and Nathan nodded in agreement.

"Matthew's upbeat and laid-back, so most of the inmates get along with him."

"Yeah," Mickey agreed, his cheerful tone fading. "But that cute face of his keeps attracting all sorts of creeps when I'm not looking. Kid's too good-looking for his own good. What about you, Yuuto?"

Yuuto, absently poking at his salad with a fork, looked up. Caught off guard by the question, he asked, "What about me?"

"I'm asking if you've had more guys after you out since you shaved your beard."

"How the hell should I know?" Yuuto replied coldly.

Seated beside him, Dick let out a smirk that twisted at the corners of his mouth. "He shaved, and now they're treating him like a fresh piece of meat again. No wonder Lennix is sulking."

Despite the obvious jab, Yuuto felt genuinely relieved at Dick's teasing tone. It was safe to assume he wasn't mad anymore.

"I'm not sulking."

Dick's comment had rubbed him the wrong way, but he couldn't deny it. After shaving his beard, Yuuto also took the time to tidy up his long, unruly bangs. The change must've been pretty drastic as some of the inmates he passed by even asked Dick if Yuuto was a new guy.

"BB's apparently bragging that his eye for beauty was spot-on,'" Dick said.

"That bastard," Yuuto scowled, a deep crease forming between his brows.

"Fortunately, BB's got his hands too full these days to chase after you," Nathan said.

"Yeah," Mickey nodded knowingly. "The Black Soldiers have split into BB's faction and Choker's, and there's some serious infighting going on. BB's hell-bent on taking down Locos Hermanos, so he's been trying hard to win over Choker's crew. I bet BB wants to get all that crap wrapped up so he can get back to chasing after you."

Yuuto shot Mickey a sharp glare, and Mickey hurried to defend himself.

"No, but seriously," he said, "You've really changed. With your beard gone and your hair all neat, you look like some classy prince or something. Wouldn't be surprised if you were descended from Japanese royalty."

"There's no royalty in Japan. They're called the Imperial Family."

Mickey grumbled, "What's the difference?" but Yuuto didn't bother explaining.

The conversation died down after that until Nathan broke the silence.

"Matthew sure is late," he said, glancing around the dining area. "He's usually the first one to show up for meals."

At Nathan's comment, Mickey's expression turned concerned. "Yeah. That little glutton skipping lunch? Doesn't add up."

A heavy, foreboding tension settled over their table—the same grim thought crossing everyone's mind. Mickey snapped out of it first, and just as he began to rise to go look for him, a friendly inmate from Block A named Osborne walked over.

"Yo, Mickey. I saw your cute little buddy earlier; he was with Bernal from Block C."

"What?" Startled and alarmed, Mickey shot up, grabbing Osborne by the front of his shirt. "What do you mean, 'with Bernal?'"

Osborne stepped back, flustered.

"H-Hell if I know!" he stammered. "I just saw the two of them going into the linen room together."

"Shit!" Cursing, Mickey stormed off, face twisted in anger.

Nathan quickly thanked Osborne, then turned to Dick and Yuuto. "Let's go too."

Since running was against the rules, the three of them walked briskly out of the cafeteria, heading straight for the linen room.

"Who is Bernal?" Yuuto asked as they moved down the hallway at a quick pace.

Dick's expression turned grim. "He's a good-looking Chicano, friendly on the surface and all, but inside, he's absolute filth, a true bastard," Dick said, spitting out insults. "A hardcore pedophile who raped a young White brother and sister. And he's also a sadist, to boot. Word is, he mutilated their genitals with a knife after the assault."

Sex offenders were hated in prison, but those who targeted children were the most despised of all. Yuuto felt sick just hearing it. It wasn't even logical—it was a visceral, instinctive disgust.

"That sick fuck." Yuuto said. "You don't think he'd go after Matthew, do you?"

"It's very likely. There aren't any kids in here for him, so he probably went for the next best—" Dick clamped his mouth shut, as though the thought alone was unbearable.

A moment later, they reached the linen room. The door was slightly ajar. The three of them carefully pushed it open and crept inside. It was dark, the lights were off, and no one else was around. Floor-to-ceiling shelves were crammed with sheets and towels.

"Mickey, where are you?" Nathan called out.

"Over here, damn it!" Mickey's voice was coming from the adjacent room.

Mickey's voice rang from the adjacent room. Nathan rushed over and flung the door open. It seemed to be a sheet-packaging area—giant burlap sacks were stacked high, blocking their view. Yuuto and the others slipped through the narrow spaces between the bags, and what they saw left them speechless.

Matthew lay unconscious and limp on the floor. His face was grotesquely swollen, and his shirt was soaked with blood from his nose, so red it was frightening. At a glance, he was unrecognizable.

His pants had been stripped off, his lower half completely exposed. Blood dripped from between his legs, leaving no doubt about what had been done to him, but what enraged Yuuto most of all was seeing Matthew's arms tied behind his back.

He hadn't even been able to defend himself.

"Goddamn it! That bastard Bernal!" Mickey choked on the words, his throat tight with grief and tears. "I'll fucking kill him! Oh, Matthew… What the hell did he do to you, you poor bastard?"

Mickey fumbled frantically to untie the coarse rope around Matthew's wrists. His hands trembled uncontrollably, and his tear-blurred vision made it impossible to do anything.

"Move, Mickey. I've got it," Dick muttered. "Lennix, cover Matthew with a sheet. Nathan, go get a guard. We'll need a stretcher to get him to the infirmary."

Dick worked quickly and skillfully to loosen the knots. Matthew's wrists were rubbed raw, blood seeping from the torn skin.

"Matthew, come on, hang in there!" Mickey called out, but Matthew didn't stir.

Dick quietly checked for injuries. When he gently touched Matthew's shoulder, the boy let out a low moan, and Dick's brows drew tight in pain and fury. "His shoulder is dislocated. We'll lay Matthew face down on that table. Help me out."

The three of them carefully carried Matthew over. Dick let the dislocated arm hang loosely over the table's edge. He lifted the arm and let it fall under its own weight about ten times. Then, after feeling along the shoulder, he nodded.

"That should do it." nodded Dick.

Yuuto was impressed. *So he knows how to reset a dislocated joint, huh*, he thought, curious. *Maybe he learned it in the infirmary?*

"Just hang in there a bit longer, Matthew. We'll get you to the infirmary soon," Mickey said.

At his words, Matthew's eyelids fluttered, and he barely opened his eyes. His lips trembled, as if he wanted to say something, but he couldn't seem to produce a sound. When Mickey asked if Bernal had done this to him, Matthew's face twisted in pain, and he nodded.

A moment later, two guards rushed in carrying a stretcher, with Nathan close behind. One of the guards was Guthrie, the chief officer who was known for being relatively decent toward the inmates.

"Jesus Christ," Guthrie muttered, shaking his head before turning to Yuuto. "Who did this? Did any of you see the bastard?"

"When we got here, there was no one left. B—" Yuuto opened his mouth ready to say Bernal's name, but Mickey shoved his shoulder—*Don't say it*. The message was clear, and Yuuto quickly held his tongue.

"Guthrie, get him to the infirmary, please. Make sure a real doctor checks him out," Mickey pleaded.

Guthrie gave a firm nod. "Yeah. Let's get him on the stretcher. Dr. Spencer should still be here."

While the guards loaded Matthew onto the stretcher, Yuuto and the others cleared the path by moving the burlap sacks filled with sheets to either side.

"I'm going with you," Dick said firmly. Guthrie granted him permission and handed him one side of the stretcher.

"Damn it. Why the hell wasn't the linen room locked?" Guthrie cursed. "Whoever was supposed to do that's in deep shit."

Once everyone was outside, Guthrie locked the linen room door with an angry grunt. "You three, back to your cells. I might come ask questions later, so you better stay put. Move it! Make way!"

The prisoners in the hallway began to crowd around, curious about the commotion. With Guthrie leading the way, the stretcher carrying Matthew disappeared down the corridor.

“Come on, Mickey. It’s almost time for headcount,” Nathan said gently to Mickey, who was still staring down the hall where Matthew had vanished.

Mickey didn’t move.

“That fucking bastard,” his voice came out in a low growl, barely above a whisper. “I’ll never forgive him.”

His little brother figure had been brutalized in the worst possible way. He had to be burning with rage—so much that it must’ve felt like his insides were boiling. Of course, Yuuto felt the same, but no one had looked after Matthew more than Mickey had. It wasn’t hard to imagine the depth of his sorrow and fury. After all that care, he’d still been powerless to protect him.

At a loss for words, Yuuto reached out and gripped Mickey’s shoulder, tense with anger.

CHAPTER 12

Matthew's condition was more serious than they had expected.

Dr. Spencer, the on-duty physician who examined him, determined that the injuries clearly required surgery and immediately ordered the prison to transfer Matthew to a nearby hospital. In addition to an anal tear and full-body contusions, he had a depressed fracture in his cheekbone, as well as fractures in his collarbone and fingers. On top of that, there was damage to his right eye. Though a detailed examination would be conducted once his condition stabilized, it was already likely that his vision would be significantly impaired.

When Dick relayed this report, Mickey's anger deepened.

Yuuto suggested that they should tell the guards that Bernal was the perpetrator, but Mickey stubbornly shook his head.

"Matthew followed the inmates' code and didn't say who did it. We can't go ratting him out now," he argued. "Besides, nobody saw it happen. Even if we scream it was that bastard, it won't amount to much. Maybe they'll throw him in solitary for a bit. That's it. The guy's doing a hundred and twenty years. You think he gives a shit if they tack on a couple more? That's why I'll be the one to get revenge for Matthew."

"Don't do it, Mickey," Nathan warned, trying to reason with him. "If something happens to you, Matthew would feel responsible."

Mickey wouldn't listen. "That bastard knew Matthew was like a little brother to me, and he raped him anyway. So this isn't just about Matthew. It's my problem too. Please, I need your help."

Dick and Nathan exchanged glances before sighing in resignation. Mickey was completely consumed by vengeance and wouldn't calm down until he struck back somehow.

Mickey had already devised a plan. Bernal always spent time at the weight training area in a corner of the yard before dinner. Being a muscle freak, he never skipped his daily bench presses.

"At dinner time, all the inmates gather at the central gate—the only entrance to the West Wing. I'll use the crowd as cover to get close and stab Bernal from behind," he explained, then locked eyes with each of them as he continued. "Nathan, you take the knife from me and pass it to Dick. Dick, you toss it into the gutter next to the basketball court. There's a spot where the grate's lifted about five centimeters. Below that is a sloped tunnel that connects to the sewage drain. Drop the knife there, and no one will ever find it. Yuuto, you stand behind me and form a human wall to block the view."

"How are you planning to take a knife out in the yard?" Yuuto asked.

"I'll hide a small folding knife in my underwear," he answered. "The guard in charge of the checks out there lately is a damn rookie. He used to get real handsy with the frisking, but after inmates started calling him a faggot, he doesn't do such thorough checks anymore. And the metal detector at the central gate's busted. A small knife like that won't set it off."

Mickey's bloodshot eyes and deadly serious expression made him look completely different from the usually playful man he was.

"We'll do it tomorrow," he mumbled, sounding defeated. "I'm counting on you."

When the meeting ended, Yuuto and Dick left the cell together. As they walked down the catwalk, Yuuto spoke to Dick in a low voice. "Is this really okay?" he whispered. "Shouldn't we try harder to talk him out of it?"

"Stopping Mickey when he's this fired up? No way. All we can do now is hope he doesn't screw it up," Dick said with a sigh, then his tone shifted. "More importantly, are *you* okay with this? Turning a blind eye to what he's planning means you're basically an accomplice, even if you don't get your hands dirty."

They had arrived at their cell. Yuuto strode to the end and stopped. "I'm not worried about myself. I'm more worried about Mickey. I can't forgive Bernal for what he did either. If he can't be punished by legal means, then I have no qualms with Mickey taking things into his own hands."

By accepting Mickey's revenge, Yuuto was aligning himself with the kind of justice that existed behind bars, not the one recognized in the outside world. To answer Dick's question… he couldn't say that he didn't have any doubts, but living in this place, he didn't feel it was entirely wrong either.

Weird.

It really struck Yuuto as strange. Not too long ago, he'd been someone who arrested criminals, and now he was willingly playing a role in a planned assault. And surprisingly, he wasn't all that hesitant about it. Maybe it was because he could now feel, not just understand, that this place was a lawless, dog-eat-dog jungle.

At that moment, he wondered what Dick would say if he revealed he used to be a DEA agent. The thought passed through his mind as he sat down on the bed. He was tempted to tell him, but stopped just short. He didn't need Warden Corning's warnings to know—it was a secret he had to keep at all costs.

Dick sat down beside him. "Lennix. I went too far about the Lindsay incident. I'm sorry," Dick apologized, but Yuuto shook his head.

"It's fine. I dragged you into it. It's my fault I followed Galen."

"Don't blame yourself. I was just taking my frustration out. I'm the one who should be sorry."

Despite Dick's words, something didn't sit right with Yuuto. If that debt to Galen really didn't matter, why had Dick been so upset? He'd said something about all he'd built up being destroyed in an instant. What exactly did he mean by that?

Yuuto studied the side of Dick's face, searching for clues, when Dick glanced over. "What?" he asked, tone tinged with suspicion.

"No, it's nothing. Just… you have really clear blue eyes," he said. "And your blond hair—it's striking. Do you have Scandinavian blood?"

He deflected with something he'd always been curious about.

"Who knows? Maybe I do," Dick shrugged. "But if I had the brains to match this packaging, I could probably sell my sperm to a bank for a good price. Too bad."

Yuuto chuckled at the joke. He'd heard that young White men who were tall, blond, blue-eyed, and highly educated could sell their sperm for a high price.

"But if you ask me, your black hair and dark eyes are far more striking, beautiful. Your hair is sleek like silk, and your jet-black eyes have this mysterious depth. I feel like I could get lost in them."

Dick suddenly reached out and gently stroked Yuuto's hair.

"D-Dick…" Yuuto stiffened, sucking in a sharp breath. "What are you doing?"

"And your skin…it's so smooth, like ivory," Dick continued, ignoring Yuuto's question. "Can I touch you?"

Dick leaned in so close their lips nearly brushed. His rugged fingers traced lightly along Yuuto's collarbone.

"Dick!" Unable to take it, Yuuto shouted, and Dick smirked, stifling a laugh.

"You always react so honestly."

Realizing he'd been teased again, Yuuto flushed red with anger and punched Dick's stomach and shoulder. Dick let out an exaggerated groan and collapsed backwards onto the bed. Overly dramatic, he cried, "Mercy! I surrender!"

"If you do that again, I'll hit you for real. I may not look it, but I have a black belt in karate."

"Really? That's impressive. Let me see your hands."

When Yuuto held out his right hand, Dick took it as naturally as if it were the most casual thing in the world. It was an innocent gesture, yet for some reason, it made Yuuto's heart skip a beat.

Unaware of Yuuto's inner turmoil, Dick gently traced the back of his hand with the pad of his thumb. It was such a soft touch, like how one would treat a woman's hand, that it stirred something in Yuuto's chest and even made his cheeks flush.

Yuuto subtly pulled his hand back. "O-Okay, that's enough."

Dick nodded with an unusually serious expression. "You really do have calluses on your knuckles," he acknowledged. "You should teach me karate. I'm interested."

"Do you even know what karate is?" Yuuto asked, raising a brow. "It's not the same thing Bruce Lee does."

Americans often lump all hand-to-hand martial arts under the term karate, treating karate, kung fu, taekwondo—even Bruce Lee's Jeet Kune Do—as if they're all the same thing.

Dick raised a brow, clearly irritated.

"I *do* know," he said, and Yuuto could practically hear him roll his eyes. "Karate originated in Okinawa, Japan. Have you ever lived in Japan?" Dick asked, still sprawled out on the bed.

"When I was little, yeah. My dad's work had us there for a year. I spoke enough of the language to attend a regular elementary school, but I never fit in. I couldn't wait to go back to the States," Yuuto recounted, lost in the memory. "Such a beautiful country. In spring, cherry blossoms bloom everywhere; you'd see the branches heavy with flowers, white petals drifting down like snow—it was so dreamlike, so beautiful. That image is still burned into my memory."

"Cherry blossoms, huh?" Dick propped his cheek on his hand and murmured quietly. To Yuuto, it seemed like Dick, too, was remembering something from long ago, something nostalgic.

"You'll go back to Japan someday. I'm sure of it."

Dick's gentle tone was comforting, and Yuuto felt a pang in his chest. Dick had no family—no home to return to. The thought of that kind of loneliness, of living on with no one, stirred a deep, inexplicable sorrow in Yuuto.

Dick stared out the window, his gaze distant; a small patch of blue sky framed in the square of glass. What was he thinking about, looking at it?

Even sitting so close they could touch, Dick still felt far away. Yuuto didn't know why, but that was how it felt. He couldn't quite put it into words—Dick's heart was like a mirage. You could see it, but it had no substance. The more you tried to grasp it, the more it slipped through your fingers.

He could be cold one moment and strangely considerate the next. He seemed aloof, but he could joke and tease. He had the strength to snap a man's neck like a bear, and yet carried the hollow solitude of someone teetering on the edge of isolation. There was something inside Dick's heart—something Yuuto couldn't stop thinking about. It wasn't mere curiosity. It came from somewhere deeper, something earnest and sincere.

He wanted to know the real Dick, to peer into the depths of his heart. This baffling, powerful yearning left even Yuuto unsure of himself.

CHAPTER 13

"You're late."

As Dick appeared in the cell, Mickey let out an exaggerated sigh, clearly irritated. "For fuck's sake, Dick. We've got to hit the yard now or we'll run out of—"

"Sorry, Mickey. Call it off for today," Dick interrupted quickly. "There was a huge brawl between Black and White inmates in the East Wing. Tons of injuries and the infirmary's a damn mess. I've got to get back and help Spencer right away."

Mickey looked up at the ceiling and shook his head. "Come the fuck on, man," he said exasperated. "There's gotta be other staff around. You don't need to be the one to go back."

"Nowhere near enough hands. Listen, Mickey. We do Bernal tomorrow. A day won't change anything. He's not going anywhere. Got it?" Dick emphasized firmly before striding out of the cell.

Nathan patted Yuuto on the shoulder. "It is what it is," he said. "Let's put it off."

"No," Mickey said. "We do it today. Even without Dick."

Nathan and Yuuto tried to reason with him, but Mickey wouldn't budge, and he shot to his feet with stubborn resolve. "If you two won't help, I'll do it myself."

There was no talking him down. Mickey's mind was made up, and Nathan and Yuuto, unwilling to let him do it alone, eventually gave in. The plan was adjusted slightly: Yuuto would take the knife first and then pass it to Nathan.

With that, they were on the move.

Mickey made it through the central gate without anyone noticing the knife he had hidden. The three of them stepped onto the yard and stopped near the training area.

Standing between Yuuto and Nathan to stay out of sight, Mickey pulled the knife from his underwear. It was a small blade, about ten centimeters long. He wrapped it in a black handkerchief and stuffed it into his pocket.

Bernal was lying on a weight bench, pressing a heavy barbell over his chest—the sight of that powerful, well-built body suddenly filled Yuuto with unease.

"What if he fights back after you stab him?" he whispered.

"I'll be gone before he can," Mickey said. "Besides, no one reacts instantly after getting stabbed in the back."

If Mickey, the one doing it, was that confident, Yuuto couldn't argue.

As the clock neared five, inmates on the yard began heading to the dining hall. Bernal finished training, threw on his shirt, and started walking without showing any signs of caution.

Yuuto and the others kept their distance, trailing behind him. Near the central gate entrance, the crowd grew denser, and the flow of bodies naturally slowed down.

"All right, let's go."

The three of them slipped through the crowd, closing in on Bernal. Mickey pulled the knife from his pocket. Yuuto's tension spiked. He moved in behind Mickey, trying to block the scene from view.

Taking a deep breath to steel himself, Mickey slammed into Bernal and, with all his strength, drove the knife into his back.

Bernal let out a scream. Mickey yanked the knife out and quickly wrapped it in the black handkerchief, handing it off to Yuuto. Keeping a blank expression, Yuuto stepped back and passed it to Nathan behind him. Nathan took the knife and vanished into the crowd in an instant.

According to plan, Mickey was supposed to slip through the

central gate before the guards caught on. But despite being stabbed deep in the back, Bernal's reaction was shockingly fast. Like a bull enraged by an attack, he grabbed Mickey's shirt and slammed him to the ground.

Just as Yuuto had feared, things went off-script.

"You fucker!" Blood pouring down his back, Bernal snarled and wrapped his thick fingers around Mickey's throat. Mickey glared up at him, refusing to back down.

"Serves you right, you perverted piece of shit!" Mickey glared up at him, refusing to back down. "That's for Matthew!"

Bernal's grip only tightened. Mickey's face began to swell and darken as he choked, arms flailing as he struck the ground, the air, and the immovable body pinning him down to no avail. The surrounding inmates started to panic. If this kept up, the guards would be on them any second.

Desperate, Yuuto kicked Bernal in the head with full force. Caught off guard, Bernal groaned and collapsed. Yuuto seized the moment to drag Mickey up.

"You little..." Bernal shook his head and staggered to his feet. "You're with that brat, too, aren't you? If you're so desperate for my attention, and want me to fuck you so badly, I'll grant your wish. You can cry and scream just like he did, with tears and snot pouring down your face."

At that moment, the crack of a rifle rang out across the yard—warning fire from a surveillance tower.

The guards had finally noticed the commotion.

Inmates hit the ground en masse, scrambling to lie flat. But Bernal didn't move. He glared at Yuuto with a face twisted in fury, unmoving, and Yuuto stood his ground, meeting that glare head-on.

"He made the sweetest noises," Bernal sneered. "Fucking him wasn't fun enough. So I switched to the handle of a mop halfway through. Want to see what that feels like for yourself?"

In that instant, Yuuto felt an overwhelming surge of hatred. This man was filth, and even in a cesspit like this prison, he had no right to exist. It wasn't rage—it was something colder. A quiet, bone-deep fury that filled Yuuto's entire being.

"What the hell are you standing around for?" Bernal bellowed, pounding his chest with a fist. "If you're not coming, I'll start things myself!"

Bernal charged at him.

Yuuto didn't panic—he sidestepped swiftly and, as they passed each other, struck the back of Bernal's neck with a precise knife hand blow. The hit landed squarely on a vital point, stopping Bernal cold and dropping him to his knees. But Yuuto didn't let up; he followed it with a sharp kick to the temple, using the edge of his foot. That final strike did it. Bernal's knees buckled like a marionette with its strings cut, and he collapsed face-first to the ground.

A shrill whistle pierced the air. Several guards came sprinting over. Though Yuuto didn't resist, he was tackled roughly and beaten with batons.

"Yuuto Lennix! You heard the warning shot, didn't you?" the guard pinning him down yelled. "Why didn't you drop to the ground like everyone else?"

"He charged at me," Yuuto choked out, his face pressed to the ground as he spat dirt. "I was defending myself."

One of the guards, clearly fed up, kicked him hard in the ribs. "Watch your damn mouth!" he said, clearly not having expected an answer. "Take him to interrogation. Bernal goes to the infirmary—he's foaming at the mouth!"

As they shackled Yuuto's wrists and ankles, a pale-faced Mickey stumbled toward him. Yuuto gave him a firm look and nodded as if to say, *"It's okay."* Mickey shook his head, distraught.

No need for both of them to get caught. Even if Yuuto confessed that Mickey had stabbed Bernal, without the knife, there'd be no proof, and he wouldn't be punished.

"All of you, move it!" bellowed the guard behind them as he herded the inmates inside. "Get to the dining hall now or you'll miss your damn meal!"

With the guards screaming at the others, Yuuto was hauled away to the central building, shackled like a dangerous criminal caught red-handed.

The interrogation was relentless, but Yuuto stuck to the same story: he'd been heading toward the central gate when Bernal, walking ahead of him, suddenly screamed and spun around. When Yuuto got closer to check on him, Bernal attacked in a frenzy. Yuuto acted purely in self-defense—no malice, no premeditation, and certainly no knife involved. That accusation was completely baseless.

No matter how hard they pressed him, Yuuto gave the same calm, repeated answer, eventually wearing down the interrogators.

"Lennix. This whole thing, it's related to Matthew Kane's rape case, isn't it? If you didn't stab Bernal, then it had to be Michele Ronini. You three were always together with that Kane kid. If you come clean now, we'll return you to Block A," one of the guards said, all pretense gone. "You've been a model inmate. You don't want to screw up your sentence over this, do you?"

Yuuto froze for a split second, his resolve wavering at the threat of a longer sentence. The guard saw it and went in for the kill. "Just be honest. Ronini did it, right? No one will know you ratted him out."

Words rose in Yuuto's throat, but he forced them down. He couldn't betray Mickey.

"I don't know who stabbed him," Yuuto mumbled.

"So that's how it is," the guard said. "If you're going to keep playing dumb, you're going to the hole. And your sentence will be extended. Get ready."

The interrogation ended. Yuuto was thrown into solitary confinement.

Even though he was new to the place, the other occupants barely paid him any attention, casting dull, lifeless glances within their cramped, dark cells. The smell was overpowering—a choking mix of mildew, human waste, body odor, and rotting food that clung to every inch of the building.

Anyone locked in here long enough would have their spirit sucked out—even the strongest young man, Yuuto thought.

When ordered to approach the door, he did as told, and his cuffs and shackles were removed through the bars; no matter how many times it happened, he could never get used to them. The cold touch and the grating metal sounds all made him feel less than human.

"Cool your head in here. When you're ready to confess, we'll be listening."

After the guard left, Yuuto looked around the cell, which was about four feet wide and eight feet deep. At the very back, like some twisted centerpiece, stood a yellowed, exposed toilet. There was no bed, just a folded blanket laid out on the floor.

Yuuto curled up under the blanket like a dog and eventually fell asleep. He was awakened by noise from the hallway—it was breakfast time. A food cart clattered past the cells.

He shivered under the blanket. His muscles were stiff, his joints aching. This region didn't have much temperature fluctuation, and daytime was usually mild, but mornings and nights were freezing around this time of year. Sleeping on a cold floor with only a blanket was sheer torment.

More than the physical, it was the mental toll that wore him down, and the cold made everything feel more miserable. As much as he hated to admit it, he had regrets. Not about covering for Mickey, but about letting things escalate with Bernal. Getting locked up like this meant he couldn't continue his investigation.

Yuuto was serious about finding Corvus and getting out of here, but that didn't mean he would succeed. He should have avoided trouble, racked up good behavior, and earned early release. He'd lost his temper and acted impulsively.

Now, he was wrestling with a tangle of conflicting emotions: guilt over his mistake, justification that what he did was right, fear of how prison life was already starting to infect him, and resignation that this was simply how things worked here. It all swirled inside him, keeping him restless through the cold night.

The food cart stopped in front of his cell. There was a small sliding slot at the bottom of the door. A guard unlocked it, and an inmate slipped a tray through. Yuuto recognized him; it was Park, a Korean from Block A.

Park gave him a quick wink, then dropped his gaze to the plate. Yuuto gave a small nod and accepted the tray. Once the cart and guards had moved on, he quickly inspected the food.

Beneath the shriveled pancake was a small, folded scrap of paper.

Tear this up and flush it after reading.

Living alone isn't so bad, huh? At least you don't have to look at your grumpy roommate's ugly mug. Just think of it as a little vacation. Take it easy.

Looking forward to having you back.

-D

The message was written in tiny, cramped letters. It was from Dick. The content was trivial, but it was more than enough to lift Yuuto's darkened spirits.

Looking forward to having you back. Yuuto reread that part over and over. Those words encouraged him in a way that felt oddly powerful. He wanted to keep the note with him forever, but it would be troublesome if a guard found it. Following Dick's instructions, Yuuto tore the letter into tiny pieces and reluctantly flushed them down the toilet.

After he finished eating and washed his face, he found himself with nothing to do. The small window, set so high in the wall that he couldn't even reach it, didn't allow even a glimpse of the outside world. The sheer emptiness of having nothing to do was more painful than he had imagined. He couldn't help wishing he had at least a newspaper to read.

As Yuuto leaned against the wall, lost in thought, someone knocked on the wall. Two knocks in quick succession. He figured it must be the prisoner to his right trying to say something, so he moved to the front of the cell.

"What is it?" he whispered, pressing his face against the bars.

When he had passed by the neighboring cell earlier, the prisoner inside had been wrapped in a blanket and asleep. He hadn't seen his face at all.

"How are you holding up, newbie?" the voice was calm and low. It was hard to tell whether the man was young or old, but the Spanish accent made it clear he was Latino.

"Not bad," Yuuto answered nonchalantly. "What about you?"

"Can't complain," the man shot back in the same tone. "You're that Japanese guy from Block A, right? Heard you laid out Bernal."

If this man were Chicano, he might not be too happy that one of his own had been taken down.

"What if I did?" Yuuto replied cautiously.

"Taking down a big guy like that—pretty impressive, if you tell me!" the man laughed, probably imagining the whole thing. "I would've liked to see that kick of yours in action."

Hearing the man's unguarded laugh put Yuuto a bit more at ease. But how had he learned all that, stuck in a solitary cell?

"How did you find out?" Yuuto asked curiously.

"My man delivers the day's news with every meal—three times a day," the man joked in reply.

The man said his name was Neto, and indeed, he was Chicano. To Yuuto's surprise, he'd already been in solitary for a month. Probably bored out of his mind, Neto started talking to Yuuto whenever he could. His stories were interesting, and at times even philosophical. Inmate-to-inmate conversations were banned, but the guards only made rounds once an hour. Yuuto found himself listening intently to the deep, resonant voice coming through the wall.

On the third day, after lunch, Yuuto was doing push-ups to kill time when he heard Neto humming faintly. The melody was nostalgic, something he recognized. He knocked twice on the wall. At some point, two knocks had become their signal for *"Let's talk."*

"Neto, you're in a good mood. That was *La Golondrina*, right?"

When he pressed his face closer to listen, Neto replied, "That's right."

La Golondrina was a well-known Mexican folk song. His stepmother, Leti, used to hum it sometimes, too.

"Today's the fifth of May," he added. "I'm celebrating."

"Oh, it's already the fifth? *Cinco de Mayo*, huh?"

Cinco de Mayo, formally known as the anniversary of the Battle of Puebla, is a Mexican holiday. Strangely, it's celebrated more in the United States than in Mexico itself. Back home, Yuuto used to enjoy Leti's festive cooking or go out partying with Paco.

"I'd kill for some chicken in mole sauce right now," Yuuto murmured, thinking fondly of Leti's cooking.

"You like Mexican food?"

"Yeah," he sighed longly. "My stepmom is Chicana, so Mexican food is what I grew up on—it's my comfort food."

"Really?" Neto sounded surprised. "Can you speak Spanish?"

"I can. I'm fluent in Spanglish, too."

At that, Neto suggested they talk in Spanish instead.

"*Órale, amigo*," responded Yuuto with a laugh, and Neto immediately continued in his native tongue.

"Yuuto, do you know what *La Golondrina* is really about?"

Golondrina means swallow—a bird. It's a melancholy song that tenderly longs for the freedom of the swallow while lamenting the singer's own inability to return to his homeland. Despite its sadness, the melody is gentle and never feels tragic.

"I heard it's a metaphor for migrant workers," Yuuto said.

"Yeah," he hummed, "but really, it's a song about a man imprisoned during the revolution, longing for freedom. Pretty fitting for us inmates, don't you think? The swallow symbolizes freedom, unbound, able to fly wherever it wants."

Now that it was said out loud, it made perfect sense.

"I celebrate *Cinco de Mayo* with a free spirit, even behind bars. I honor the pride of the small Mexican army that defeated a French force twice its size at Puebla. Even locked in this tiny cell, no one can imprison my heart. Right?"

Yuuto could feel Neto's deep pride in his Mexican identity in every word. It was more than patriotism; it felt like a firm defiance against the social oppression he'd surely faced.

Even as the largest minority group in the United States, Mexicans still face heavy discrimination. For many, the term "illegal immigrant" is often synonymous with "Mexican." But, if you thought about it, much of the American Southwest used to be part of Mexico—El Paso, Los Angeles, San Francisco. All Spanish names. Some say the mass immigration movement is not just economic but also a kind of unspoken land reclamation.

"How long is your sentence, Neto?"

"Three years for a minor assault."

"I see." Yuuto trailed off, thinking. "Hey, Neto, did you know that Mexico has the lowest suicide rate in the world?"

Yuuto's words made Neto let out a faint chuckle. "That's good to hear. Suicide doesn't suit us, cheerful, resilient Mexicanos. How about the Japanese?"

"Pretty high," he confirmed. "Japan's suicide rate is double that of the United States, but its homicide rate is only one-tenth of America's."

"So, the Japanese are gentle-hearted pessimists?"

"Maybe they're just weak. I don't really know—I was born and raised in the States."

"Same here. But I understand Mexicans better than someone born there," Neto replied instantly, and Yuuto gave a wry smile.

Even as an immigrant, Neto had grown up surrounded by others like him, immersed in his culture from birth. A person like that probably couldn't relate to someone like Yuuto.

Yuuto lacked any real sense of identity when it came to race or ethnicity. Being called Japanese never quite felt right, and being called American only registered as a technicality—something on paper. Despite having multiple cultural backgrounds, he didn't fully belong to any of them. He always carried a vague discomfort, as if he fit nowhere.

"To me, Japan feels really distant," Yuuto muttered, the weight of the conversation pressing down on him. "Not just in terms of geography, but emotionally too. Honestly, I feel closer to Mexico. When I was a kid, I used to wish I could be Chicano like my mom and brother."

"Then be one," Neto said lightly. "From today on, you're a yellow Chicano."

Yuuto knew it was a joke, but it felt like Neto was telling him, "You're one of us." The thought brought a slight warmth to his chest.

"Neto. *Muchas gracias.*"

When Yuuto thanked him, Neto replied in a slightly exaggerated tone, "*De nada.*"

Being locked up in a place like this, with no contact from anyone, could've driven him crazy. But having Neto in the cell next door was a huge comfort.

In this unlikely place, Yuuto had found a good friend. Leaning his back against the cold wall, he silently gave thanks for this unexpected encounter.

CHAPTER 14

A week had passed since Yuuto was thrown into solitary confinement. *When the hell was he going to get out?* The thought echoed with every breath he took, making him desperate. With no way to continue searching for Corvus, his mental state grew more and more strained by the day.

Frustrated, he punched the wall.

Then punched it again. And again.

Only when he heard the now-familiar knock coming from the other side did he stop.

"Calm down, Yuuto," Neto said in a comforting tone. "Getting pissed won't change a thing. You should be getting out soon."

"How do you know?"

"If it was just a fight, they'll hold you for a week at most. And Bernal's already out of the infirmary."

Hearing that only made Yuuto more anxious. What if Bernal tried to get revenge on Mickey? "Is Bernal the vengeful type?"

"Yeah. Like a goddamn snake," Neto spat. "You worried about that Mickey guy? He's the one who stabbed Bernal, right?"

Yuuto froze. Even though he knew Neto couldn't see him, he still found himself staring toward the voice in shock.

"Your info network's insane," he said slowly, the cogs in his brain turning. "What, do you just know everything?"

"Pretty much," he said nonchalantly. "I know you're sharing a cell with that Dick guy. I know that bastard BB tried to sweet-talk you on your first day. Oh, I even know the Sisters shaved your beard."

“Geez. How the hell do you know all that?”

“Yuuto, don’t worry about Bernal,” Neto said firmly, ignoring his question. “He won’t lay a finger on you or your crew.”

The certainty in Neto’s voice struck Yuuto as odd. There *had* to be a reason behind that kind of confidence, right? He needed to know.

“How are you so sure?”

“Right after Bernal landed in the infirmary, a top guy from Locos Hermanos paid him a personal visit and made it clear—told him to keep his mouth shut, or we’d come for him. I also told him that if he snitched to the guards about what happened, we’d make sure he’d regret it. Besides, he doesn’t have the balls to go up against us.”

It was only then, stupidly late, that Yuuto finally put it together.

The friendly Chicano who chatted with him every day, sharing stories like an old friend, who seemed to know about everything. Who exactly was he? What was his real identity? Could it be…

“Are you Rivera?” he asked, even though he already knew the answer. The pieces had all clicked into place. “The boss of Locos Hermanos?”

“Yes. I am Ernesto Rivera,” Neto said promptly, throwing Yuuto off guard with how easily he gave himself away.

Who could have guessed that charismatic Neto was the Rivera of Locos Hermanos?

“Why keep it a secret all this time?”

“A secret?” he said, amused. “I wasn’t hiding anything. You just never asked.”

Ah.

“I mean… yeah. You’re right.”

Neto was short for Ernesto. Yuuto had just never connected the dots. From the start, Neto had introduced himself openly. And it’s not like he had any reason to hide it from Yuuto; he wasn’t Black or one of Rivera’s enemies after all.

"But why would you threaten Bernal? He is a Chicano, isn't he?"

"I know he raped one of your friends. Of course, he got what was coming. He's a disgrace to the Chicano name," Neto spat the words with clear disgust.

"I see." Yuuto hummed, taking everything in. "So, when do you get out?"

"No clue. They said ten days at first, but it's been dragging on. The Black Soldiers are still having internal beef, so the guards are scared shitless about letting me out too soon."

Despite knowing full well how dangerous his presence was and how easily he could spark a riot, Neto stayed composed. He never let anger or frustration get the better of him, not even when he was stuck in here with no end in sight.

The leader of Locos Hermanos wasn't just dangerous; he was tough as hell and had a will of steel.

"If the Black Soldiers come for you, will you fight back?"

"If shit comes flying, you swat it away," Neto answered. "I'll try to avoid a war, but if it comes down to it, I won't back down."

Out of nowhere, Henry Galen's face popped into Yuuto's head. If Neto were the leader of Locos Hermanos, maybe he'd know something about the head of a rival gang.

"What about ABL? Are they keeping quiet?"

"They're sneaky as hell. Probably hoping the Chicanos and the Blacks will wipe each other out. They'll sit back, enjoy the show, and then stomp on whoever's left."

"What kind of leader is Galen?"

"He's smart. But he's hard to read. He doesn't let anyone—even his top guys—know what he's really thinking. Even Tonia, who was with him for a while, said she never understood the guy."

The sudden mention of the leader of the Sisters reminded Yuuto that Neto and Tonia were lovers. Or so he was told.

"Oh, right. I forgot to thank you. For helping Tonia."

It took him a second to realize what Neto meant when Giverny had nearly assaulted Tonia. So even that had reached his ears? Yuuto couldn't help but feel a little stunned.

"It was nothing. The guy is a coward. Just threatened him with the guards watching, and he froze."

"Still, it takes guts to face off against someone with a weapon. If you hadn't stepped in, she might've gotten hurt. I mean it—I'm grateful."

"You say thanks one more time, and I won't know where to put myself." Yuuto joked before sobering up. "You must miss Tonia."

"Of course. She's my only little brother, after all."

Yuuto jerked toward the bars. "Wait, what?" he exclaimed. "Did you just say brother? I heard you two were dating!"

"That's just what she wants people to believe," Neto said. "Our parents split when I was seventeen, and we got separated. We've even got different last names now. I never thought we'd end up in the same prison, let alone be able to live together again. I am happy, but she's ashamed. Says someone like her shouldn't be related to someone like me."

Neto sighed, pausing before continuing.

"So she doesn't want anyone to know. Stupid, isn't it?"

There was something in Neto's voice—part pity, part deep affection. Yuuto thought he could understand how Tonia felt. She was proud of her brother but afraid of tainting his image, of being seen as the stain on someone so admired.

"That was supposed to be a secret, wasn't it? Was it okay to tell me?"

"I told you because I trust you. Tonia said she likes you, and I feel the same. You're my friend now." Neto's voice was firm, unwavering.

This wasn't some naïve guy handing out trust for free—he was a survivor. A man who had lived through hell, in a world where trust could get you killed. If he trusted someone, it was because his instincts told him he could.

And trust had to be answered in kind.

Yuuto felt the weight of it and decided to respond in the only way that made sense to him: confiding in him about his search.

"Neto, do you know if Galen has a burn scar on his back?"

"A burn scar? Why?"

"I'm looking for someone. I can't explain why, but I have to find him. No matter what, because whether I find him or not, my whole life depends on it. I think Galen might be the guy. If he's got burn scars on his back, that could be the proof I need."

"I see," Neto said, then gave a short snort. "You've got your reasons, then. I don't know anything about burn scars, but I've heard he's got a gunshot wound on his lower back."

A gunshot wound…

A bullet could leave a burn depending on the angle, or if it was a big enough caliber, it might've torn the skin in a way that looked like a burn. It was a bit of a stretch, but it was something.

"When you get out, ask Tonia about it. I'll let her know to help you if she can."

"Thanks, Neto. Really—"

"Shh." Neto cut him off. Yuuto hadn't noticed, but footsteps were approaching. He backed away from the bars and moved quickly to the back of his cell. In the next second, the guard stopped in front of his door and barked in a gruff voice, "Yuuto Lennix, get up. You are going back to your cell."

CHAPTER 15

Mickey was the first one to welcome Yuuto back to Block A. "Yuuto! Welcome back!"

He'd gone straight to the showers to scrub away the grime. Freshened up, he barely had time to settle back into the cell before Mickey stormed in. His face raw with emotion, Mickey pulled Yuuto into a fierce embrace. Yuuto held on just as tightly, the weight of everything pressing between them.

"I'm really sorry, man," Mickey burst out. "It was my fuck-up. I felt so bad I couldn't even eat. Look at me, I've lost weight, haven't I?"

Yuuto pulled back and gave Mickey a once-over from head to toe, raising an eyebrow. "Where?" he asked flatly. "You don't look skinnier at all. Still running your mouth, I see."

"Are you blind or what?" Mickey laughed and ruffled Yuuto's hair, clearly happy to see him.

As they chatted, other inmates began to come by, one after another, to say hi, pat him on the back, and engage in small talk, even those whom Yuuto had never spoken to before.

"What's going on?" he asked.

"They're showing respect," Mickey explained. "You got thrown into the hole for sticking up for a friend—everyone's heard about it! And they want to see with their own eyes the guy who took down Bernal. Your name's been buzzing around for days. That kick was fucking epic, man. Some people are saying maybe you're actually a ninja or something."

Yuuto let out a half-laugh. *A ninja,* seriously? He never meant to get involved and hadn't even planned to touch Bernal. All this hero talk made him uncomfortable.

"I only jumped in at the last second. You're the one who avenged Matthew, Mickey."

"Yeah, well, you're the one who got caught. I owe you for that, and I'll pay it back someday. I promise," Mickey said with rare seriousness, then urged Yuuto toward the dining hall. It was almost dinner time.

Even there, more inmates approached him, smiling and welcoming him back.

"Feels like you're a damn hero now, huh?" Mickey teased, which only made Yuuto more embarrassed and self-conscious.

They had just taken their seats when Nathan and Dick walked into the cafeteria.

"Yuuto!" Nathan lit up as he approached. "You are back!" Yuuto stood up to greet Nathan, who placed his tray on the table and pulled him into a tight hug.

"I'm so glad you're alright. Everyone's been worried sick, wondering when you'd get out. Right, Dick?" Nathan looked over his shoulder, prompting Dick to speak.

"Yeah. No kidding." Dick gave a short nod and locked eyes with him.

Yuuto's chest warmed at the sight of his cellmate. For a second, he thought Dick might hug him too, but instead, Dick extended his right hand in his usual cool manner. Yuuto felt a tiny pang of disappointment but shook his hand all the same and sat back down.

"How was life in the hole?" Nathan asked as they started eating.

"Cramped and maddening," Yuuto answered, shaking his head. "Made the regular cells feel like paradise. But I was lucky, the guy in the cell next to mine was a decent dude. We talked through the wall, behind the guards' backs. It helped a lot."

"I'm glad," Nathan said, nodding solemnly. "Solitary confinement is one of the worst forms of abuse in prison. It's a barbaric tradition, nothing more. Even psychiatrists admit it causes serious psychological damage to be locked up alone with no contact. Being able to talk to someone should have made a huge difference for you."

He paused, then continued with a heavy expression. "This country's prison system is in the worst shape it's ever been. As a place for rehabilitation, it's totally dysfunctional—it's nothing more than a warehouse for people. Yuuto, do you know how many people are locked up in the United States?"

"No idea."

"2.2 million. The United States has the highest prison population in the world. Thirty years ago, there were only about six hundred prisons. Now there are around fifteen hundred. That kind of growth isn't normal, is it?"

"Well, maybe crime has gone up too," Yuuto said.

"Not really." Nathan shrugged. "According to one legal scholar, crime rates haven't increased that much—but the rate of incarceration has. On top of that, sentences are getting harsher. And what's fueling this trend is the privatization of prisons. Back in the 1980s, before privatization took off, there were 800,000 prisoners; in just two decades, that number shot up to 2.2 million."

"So, you're saying they're locking people up just to feed the prison business?"

"Exactly. Prisoners are raw materials, profit generators, for corporations. Even Schelger Prison, though it's technically state-run, is operated by Smith-Bucks Company, the biggest private correctional corporation in America—"

Yuuto was listening with interest, but Mickey cut in. "Give it a rest, would you? I don't wanna hear heavy shit during dinner. This food's already crap, don't make it worse."

"My bad," Nathan said with a shrug and a laugh.

Just then, a stir ran through the cafeteria. Everyone's attention turned toward the front. Yuuto followed their gaze, and there they were: members of Locos Hermanos. They walked in formation, sharp eyes sweeping the room, surrounding a man at the center with a dark, black scruff.

"It's Rivera! He's finally back!"

Shouts rose from the murmuring crowd—it was the Chicanos. Their voices swelled into cheers, followed by clapping and pounding on tables, until the whole cafeteria erupted with excitement.

The guards stood by, visibly unsure of how to respond. They knew all too well that if they tried to shut down the celebration with brute force, the joy could flip to violence in a heartbeat, but it didn't come to that. With a simple hand gesture, Neto signaled his men to settle down, and they obeyed. Their leader's will was enough to quiet the crowd.

Yuuto watched as Neto passed by, surrounded by his people, moving with quiet confidence. Though he looked only in his early thirties, he carried himself with the presence of someone much older, someone with importance and dignity.

His body was muscular, and his face fierce and striking. On his left arm, just visible under his white T-shirt, was a black tribal tattoo, and on the right, the colorful image of the Virgin of Guadalupe, Mexico's holy mother, had been inked into his skin.

Neto was more formidable than Yuuto had imagined, and now he was free, finally released from solitary confinement.

Yuuto wanted to congratulate him, but the man walking past wasn't just the friendly voice from the next cell over. It was Ernesto Rivera. He was not just the head of Locos Hermanos, but the leader of the entire Chicano faction inside Schelger Prison. He was no longer someone whom Yuuto could approach easily.

Maybe they'd cross paths again. Maybe he'd get the chance to say something next time. For now, Yuuto averted his gaze.

"So that's why there were so many guards around today," Mickey muttered beside him. “Rivera’s back. Oh, look at BB’s crew, the way they’re glaring at him, it’s like they’re ready to explode.”

Sure enough, in the back of the cafeteria, the Black inmates, especially those from the Black Soldiers, were shooting daggers at Neto’s table, tension thick in the air.

“Damn. This place feels like it could go up any second,” Mickey muttered, then turned back to them. “Hey, Dick, how’s Choker doing?”

“He’s still lying in bed, giving orders through his guys,” Dick replied. “But he could lose consciousness any day now. Last December, Spencer said he’d be lucky to last three months, so at this point, he’s hanging on by sheer willpower.”

“If BB takes over, this place’ll get even worse than it is now.” Nathan sighed and shook his head.

For a while, Mickey and Nathan exchanged thoughts about how far the rift between the Black and Chicano groups might go, what moves ABL might make next, and what it would mean for all of them. Yuuto listened quietly, pressing his palm to his forehead. He felt hot, his temples throbbed with a dull pulse, and his whole body ached with fatigue.

Even just sitting still was becoming painful.

“Let’s head out,” Dick said, cutting through the conversation. Yuuto, relieved by the suggestion, promptly stood up. All he wanted now was to lie down in his cell. But as they walked out into the corridor, a voice with a Spanish accent called from behind.

“Rivera, you did your time. We’ve been waiting for you.”

Yuuto turned and saw Neto walking a few paces behind, surrounded by Chicano inmates. Everyone seemed eager to say something to him, and Neto gave each of them a respectful nod in return.

Yuuto watched without thinking—until Neto’s eyes met his.

They were several meters apart, but at that moment, their gazes locked. Neto narrowed his eyes slightly, as if trying to confirm something, then began pushing through the crowd toward him.

"Yuuto, what's up?" Mickey asked, frowning at Yuuto's sudden stop. But Yuuto didn't hear him; his attention was fixed entirely on Neto.

Neto stepped up and stopped in front of him. "Yuuto? That's you, right?"

There was no doubt. It was the same voice he'd listened to through the wall, day after day in solitary.

Yuuto smiled.

"Yeah. It's me," he said. "I'm surprised you recognized me."

Neto let out a small laugh and grinned widely, an unguarded, genuinely happy smile he only showed to those he trusted. "Of course I recognized you. I knew the moment I saw you. Man, I've been wanting to meet you."

He opened his arms and pulled Yuuto into a firm hug. The man was big, and Yuuto practically disappeared into his chest.

"Me too," he said, his voice muffled against the man's chest. "I'm glad you're out. Congrats."

"Yeah. Right after you were released, they moved me out," Neto explained. "It would've been better if we came out together, then we could've celebrated properly."

Neto pulled back and studied Yuuto's face for a moment. Then, without warning, he reached out and cupped Yuuto's cheek, running his thumb along his narrow jaw.

"So it's true," he said, half to himself. "Tonia was right. You've got a face that's way too refined for a place like this."

"Cut it out." Yuuto gave a sheepish laugh and gently pushed his hand away.

"Let's talk more later," Neto said quietly. "We still have that thing to deal with. Come to my cell anytime, you're always welcome."

He was referring, of course, to hearing from Tonia about Galen.

"Got it." Yuuto nodded gratefully.

Noticing Dick nearby, Neto lifted his fist in a casual greeting. Dick responded without a word, raising his own and tapping it lightly against Neto's. To Yuuto, it looked like mutual respect: two men, vastly different, recognizing something in each other.

Once the Locos Hermanos crew had moved on, Mickey turned to Yuuto with a look of utter shock.

"Yuuto, what the hell was that?" He gaped. "You know Rivera?"

When Yuuto explained that Neto had been in the next cell during his time in solitary, Mickey's eyes widened, and he nodded slowly in realization.

"Damn…"

Back in Block A, Yuuto was at a headcount in his own cell for the first time in a while and let out a deep sigh. His head was spinning, probably from the fever. He thought about lying down to rest, but the moment he sat on the bed, Mickey showed up again, inviting him to head to the rec room with them.

"Sorry, I'm gonna sit this one out," Yuuto said.

"What? Come on, there's still plenty of time before lights out," Mickey insisted. "Just come for a bit—"

"Mickey," Dick said, stepping in gently but firmly. "Lennix isn't feeling well. Let him rest."

Yuuto was genuinely surprised; he hadn't expected anyone to notice he was unwell. Dick always acted like he didn't care about anyone, but he was sharper than he let on.

Once Mickey was gone, Yuuto lay down on the bed. The moment his body hit the mattress, the fever seemed to spike higher, and he felt a wave of heat wash over him.

Dick sat down on the edge of the bed and placed a hand on Yuuto's forehead.

"You're burning up. Open your mouth a second." Yuuto obeyed, allowing Dick to peer inside his mouth. "Your tonsils aren't swollen."

He then proceeded to ask a few quick questions: how he'd been feeling in solitary, whether he'd had any diarrhea or nausea, and so on. When he was done, he fetched a damp towel and placed it gently over Yuuto's head.

"Doesn't look like an infection," he concluded. "Probably just stress and exhaustion."

"It'll go down soon."

"Hope so," Dick murmured, and picked up a book to read beside him. From time to time, other inmates came by to check on Yuuto, but Dick turned them all away with a simple, 'He's not feeling well.'

"Dick…" When Yuuto called out to him, Dick looked up with a questioning glance. "The letter… *thanks*. It meant a lot."

He finally got the words out, and with them came a sense of relief, like something heavy in his chest had finally lifted, giving him the courage to continue. "What you wrote, *'Looking forward to having you back'*, that line really kept me going. I wanted to thank you right away, but… I didn't know how to say it."

Maybe it was the fever, but for once, Yuuto could speak from the heart. Still, Dick didn't say anything. Maybe he thought it was no big deal and felt awkward being thanked so seriously.

Yuuto looked away, suddenly embarrassed.

"It wasn't all bad in the hole, huh? Since Rivera was there." Dick's voice was cold, almost accusatory.

Yuuto was confused by the sharp tone. Why did it feel like Dick was blaming him for something?

"No way!" he said, dismissing the accusation. "Sure, talking to Neto helped keep me sane, but I wanted out of there so badly. I was thinking about getting back here the whole time."

What about you?

Were you waiting for me too?

Was that line in your letter just something you wrote to be nice?

Yuuto wanted to ask many things, but he couldn't. It sounded too much like something a clingy, insecure boyfriend would say.

He brushed the thought aside, trying to reason with himself. It had to be the fever, the relief of finally being back. Sure, the cell was still cramped and miserable, but compared to that hole, it felt like paradise. Maybe that's why his emotions were all over the place.

"Yuuto," Dick's voice, barely above a whisper, broke his thoughts.

Yuuto's eyes shot open. It was the first time Dick had ever called him by his first name. Mickey and Nathan had used it from the start, but Dick had always stuck to Lennix.

"I'm glad you're out," he continued. "Welcome back, Yuuto."

His voice was flat, as usual, but his eyes were warm, Dick's gaze, which always felt cold, now seemed unbelievably warm. As those vividly blue eyes stared into his, Yuuto felt like his whole being was being gently enveloped by Dick, and a bittersweet ache stirred in his chest.

Why was it only with Dick that his heart felt so unsteady? What was it about this man that pulled him in so strongly? No matter how much he thought about it, he couldn't find the answer.

"Get some sleep. I'll stay right here and keep watch so no one bothers you."

Being cared for by Dick made him happier than he wanted to admit; probably happier than if anyone else had done it. He couldn't explain it, but he knew that much was real.

Despite the fever still burning through his body, Yuuto closed his eyes, feeling strangely at peace. Since arriving at Schelger Prison, he had never fallen asleep feeling so safe and calm.

CHAPTER 16

Yuuto awoke to the sensation of someone changing the towel on his forehead. At some point, lights-out had come and gone. The world around him was already steeped in darkness, and Block A had fallen completely silent.

As his eyes adjusted to the dimness, he could make out Dick's face, faintly illuminated by the pale moonlight. He was sitting at the edge of the bed in the exact same posture as before Yuuto had fallen asleep.

"What about the final headcount?" Yuuto asked. Normally, no one was allowed to skip it, and everyone had to stand before the bars for inspection.

"I asked them to overlook it and said you had a fever. Guthrie was on duty, so he let it slide."

The fever showed no signs of breaking. Yuuto's entire body felt like it was burning, and even his breath came out searing hot. Dick reached out to touch his cheek, checking his temperature.

"If only I had something to bring the fever down…" He stood and went to the sink, filling a cup with water. "Can you sit up?"

Yuuto gave a small nod, but his head felt so heavy he couldn't lift it.

"If it's too much, don't worry—I'll help you drink."

Yuuto had assumed Dick would lift his head for him, but instead, Dick brought the cup to his own lips and took some water into his mouth. Then, he leaned in closer. Yuuto was taken aback, shocked at what he realized Dick intended to do, but Dick's face kept drawing nearer.

"Di—"

Their lips met, swallowing Yuuto's voice, and cool water smoothly flowed into his mouth. Reflexively, Yuuto swallowed, and the sound of him gulping echoed unnaturally loud in the silence. He stared in a daze as Dick calmly repeated the action. The confusion of why was drowned out by the unexpected softness of Dick's lips, leaving Yuuto's mind a total blank.

"Want another drink?"

For some reason, it felt like he was being asked if he wanted another kiss. Still dazed, Yuuto looked up at Dick and their eyes met and locked in the darkness, the gaze growing deeper, more entangled. Yuuto wanted to say he'd had enough, but instead, his body betrayed him and gave a slight nod. Dick leaned over him again, passing the water mouth to mouth.

The water tasted like ambrosia, like the sweetest of nectars. It caressed his tongue gently and flowed to every parched corner of his body. It was as if that sweetness was rehydrating each cell. But it wasn't enough. He wanted more.

More of that water. More of those lips.

Unconsciously, Yuuto's tongue flicked out and traced Dick's wet lips, hungry for another drop, *hungry*. Dick's body stiffened for a moment—but quickly responded to Yuuto's silent plea and gave him more. Yuuto drank deeply, enraptured.

When Dick's lips finally pulled away, Yuuto was surprised by the pang of loneliness he felt. He knew it was strange, but couldn't stop the feeling from rising.

Dick wiped Yuuto's damp lips with a finger and let out a deep sigh.

"You know…" he said with a rough voice. "Even if you've got a fever, aren't you being a little too careless?"

"What do you mean?" Yuuto asked with a hazy look on his face, fighting the urge to touch his lips.

Dick sighed again. "If you really don't get it, then never mind."

He sounded annoyed, and Yuuto was left wondering why Dick seemed so upset out of the blue.

"Dick. I'm fine now," he said. "You should get some sleep."

"Don't worry about it. I can go one night without sleep."

Yuuto let out a faint laugh, and Dick furrowed his brow.

"What's so funny?"

"I was just thinking how much you've changed," Yuuto answered, recalling his first night in prison. "You once said you had no intention of taking care of me. That you 'got no interest in cleaning up after some dumb newbie.' Remember?"

That was what Dick had told him, clear as day, that first night, when Yuuto had been beaten to a pulp by BB's goons.

"You've got a hell of a memory," Dick said, sounding exasperated.

Yuuto's mouth curved into a wry grin. "I may not look it, but I can be pretty tenacious… that's why I still can't shake how cold you were to me in the beginning."

He knew it sounded petty, but it was something he couldn't let go of. Yuuto had misunderstood Dick at first, thinking he was simply unfriendly. But over time, he'd realized Dick wasn't someone who was cold-hearted. Distant, maybe, but not cruel. Which only made him want to understand why he'd been pushed away so deliberately.

"Did I do something to rub you the wrong way? Was there something about me that annoyed you?"

"No. It wasn't you. It's just…" Dick paused. "I've always had a stubborn personality. I can't bring myself to trust anyone until I know exactly what kind of person they are… If it's been weighing on you, then I'm sorry. I mean it."

Dick's tone was calm and sincere. Yuuto didn't get the sense that he was lying, but he still wasn't fully convinced. Back then, Dick's eyes had carried more than just caution; there had been something sharper, almost like hostility. It hadn't felt like he was simply being wary. There had to be a more specific reason he had kept his distance.

"Dick..." Yuuto hesitated for a second before continuing. "Before I came here, I worked for the Department of Justice—at the DEA."

It was a secret Yuuto had intended to take to the grave while in prison. But somehow, he found himself wanting to tell Dick. Maybe it wasn't so different from what Neto had done—entrusting him with the truth about Tonia. Revealing a secret was a way of showing that someone mattered. Somewhere in his heart, Yuuto wanted Dick to understand that.

"Wow. Impressive."

"I'm not joking. It's true. I arrested a lot of drug dealers. Put them behind bars."

"The DEA, huh?" Dick showed no particular shock; his face stayed calm and unreadable. "So you were an agent?"

"Yeah. Mostly undercover work. Stings and buy-bust operations. It was dangerous, but I had a solid partner. His name was Paul. He was the best partner I could've asked for..." Yuuto paused to steel himself. "But he was killed. I'm convinced it was someone connected to one of the dealers we took down, but the police arrested me based on nothing but circumstantial evidence. I was framed, and I walked right into their trap."

"That's why you said you were innocent."

"Yeah. Paul was a good man, and I trusted him more than anyone. I looked up to him," Yuuto said through gritted teeth, his voice low. "They say I killed him."

Take it easy, Yuuto. You act all calm, but you get fired up way too fast. You'll never live long like that. Paul's words echoed in his mind. Whenever Yuuto let his emotions get the better of him, Paul would always tease him like that. He had guided Yuuto through so many things, grounding him when he couldn't keep himself steady.

"I didn't even get to attend his funeral. Didn't even get to say goodbye..." his voice trembled, and his chest tightened.

Now that he thought about it, everything had happened so fast after his arrest: The shock of Paul's death, the endless interrogations, the trial, the conviction, the FBI's approach. Fear, anger, despair—it had all hit at once. He'd been so consumed with his own survival that he never had time to grieve.

But now, finally, the weight of Paul's death hit him with full force. The realization that someone irreplaceable was truly gone. That there was no corner of this world where Paul still existed. The pain clenched tightly around his chest.

He tried to steady himself with a deep breath, but it was no use. The heat behind his eyes spilled over, and tears slid down his temples.

"I'm sorry..." he choked out, past the knot in his throat.

"Don't be. I know what it's like to lose someone close. Mourning a friend's death isn't shameful. I cried my eyes out when I lost a friend too."

Dick stroked Yuuto's head gently, soothingly, like comforting a child. Again and again, over and over. "Think you can sleep now?"

Gentle eyes. Gentle hands. A gentle voice.

Yuuto gave a small nod and closed his eyes. As he drifted off once more, one wish settled deeply in his heart. He hoped that one day, he could reach the sorrow buried in Dick's heart too. That when that day came, he could be the one to comfort him. He meant it, from the bottom of his heart.

He wanted to be the one to wipe away Dick's tears.

CHAPTER 17

Yuuto's fever remained high the next day as well, and it wasn't until the third day that he was finally able to sit up. Even then, his temperature hadn't fully gone down. Concerned, Dick suggested that he see the doctor and took him to the infirmary.

Normally, they would've had to file a request with the guards, wait for approval, and then patiently stand in line until it was Yuuto's turn, but thanks to Dick's connections, they were granted a special consultation after regular hours.

As they left Block A and walked down the corridor together, they happened to run into Neto.

"Yuuto. You don't look so good," he said, stopping right before him. "Are you sick?"

"He's had a persistent fever. I'm taking him to the infirmary," Dick answered.

Neto reached out and touched Yuuto's neck with a worried expression. "Solitary must've taken a toll on you. Make sure you get checked properly."

"Thanks, Neto," Yuuto said, nodding.

Just then, a sharp whistle pierced the air behind them. When they turned around, they saw BB standing there with his crew. The sight of him instantly drained Yuuto, like all the energy had been sucked out of him and his stomach dropped.

BB was, without a doubt, the last person he wanted to see.

"Rivera, that's my bitch," he said while leering at Yuuto. "Don't touch him like it's nothing."

"Don't be fucking stupid, BB. Yuuto's my friend," Neto shot back. "And I don't take orders from you."

Tension crackled in the air as the men from Black Soldiers and Locos Hermanos squared off, each side flanking their leader with hostile glares. The standoff was on the verge of exploding when a passing guard blew his whistle sharply.

"What's going on?" the guard shouted, striking the cell bars with his baton to punctuate each word. " No loitering in the hallway! Move it!"

BB ignored the guard's swinging baton, fixing Neto with a fierce glare before spitting in contempt, "Rivera, don't think you're getting away with this. I'll settle this properly—and with you too, Yuuto."

Once the Black Soldiers had left, Neto turned to Yuuto with a stern expression and warned him to be careful. Then, with his crew in tow, he walked off.

"You're like the Helen of Schelger Prison," Dick muttered sarcastically once they were alone.

"Helen?" he asked before it dawned on him. "Wait… you mean *Helen of Troy*?"

"Yeah. Watching BB and Rivera glaring at each other over you made you look like some fabled beauty who launches wars. Helen brought down Troy, and you… Your presence might very well spark a hell of a fire in this place."

"Don't be ridiculous and stop making weird accusations," Yuuto snapped, glaring at Dick. "The gang rivalry's been going on long before I got here. And BB aside, Neto's just a friend."

Dick raised an eyebrow but didn't say anything and just started walking again. He had been so gentle when nursing Yuuto, but now that he was feeling a little better, Dick had returned to his usual blunt self. Yuuto sighed quietly. *This man really did have two sides to him.*

While Yuuto was bedridden in his cell, Dick had snuck away from work multiple times to check on him. He had brought back medicine from the infirmary, delivered meals to his bed, and even helped him change his sweat-soaked shirts. He had taken care of him so attentively that Yuuto had felt a little guilty.

But now that he was recovering, Dick had become cold again and Yuuto couldn't help but feel a strange kind of irritation. *You even fed me water mouth-to-mouth,* he thought with a huff. The shift in attitude was almost insulting.

Perhaps Dick was simply the type who couldn't help but care for those in need. If that were the case, it would explain why he was so devoted to his work in the infirmary.

That realization that he wasn't special gave Yuuto a ridiculous sense of betrayal. It was a childish feeling, like a kid vying for a parent's affection. He knew that, but he couldn't help it. And he found himself resenting Dick. The frustration even dulled the special fondness he had started to feel for him.

As they made their way to the infirmary on the third floor of the central building, Yuuto refused to say a single word out of pride. Dick didn't seem to notice or care. The fact that he was the only one fretting over their dynamic made Yuuto feel all the more foolish.

When they reached the infirmary, Dick knocked on the door to what looked like an exam room on the right. "Spencer, it's me. I'm coming in."

Inside, a White man who looked to be in his mid-forties was sitting at a desk, studying an X-ray with intense focus. His hair was a mess, and his stubble was unkempt. Yuuto recognized him as the doctor who had handled his medical check when he was admitted. Without the white coat, he wouldn't have looked like a doctor at all; he just had that worn-out vibe.

"Oh, Dick. That you?"

"That X-ray—Jason's leg?"

"Yeah," the doctor confirmed. "The part that was surgically fixed at the outside hospital. Looks like the bone still hasn't healed. I'm guessing the surgeon was a real quack. Poor guy might need another operation."

"Try not to get too excited," Dick deadpanned. "Anyway, take a look at him. He's my cellmate."

Dick guided Yuuto into a chair.

"You're Yuuto Lennix?" The doctor looked at him kindly.

"Yes. It's nice to meet you," Yuuto said. "Sorry for bothering you so late."

"Oh? A polite young man in prison, now there's a rare sight. I've been working at this place for five years, and this is the first time I've heard so much as a hint of consideration from an inmate."

Spencer motioned for him to unbutton his shirt and placed the stethoscope hanging from his neck into his ears.

"Living with Dick must be tough, huh?" Spencer said playfully. "He's a stubborn guy with no charm, always acting so high and mighty. I can't count how many times he's called me an incompetent, third-rate hack."

Yuuto smiled faintly.

"You've got some nerve saying that, after working me like a dog," Dick retorted. "I'm going to check on the others."

Once Dick had left, Spencer began the examination. Yuuto's only symptom was a fever, and even that had started to go down, so there didn't seem to be anything to worry about. Still, Spencer offered to take blood and urine samples just to be safe and send them off for testing.

"Since you're here anyway, how about an IV?" Spencer asked, smiling casually, like he was offering a cup of tea. When Yuuto lay down on the examination bed, the doctor himself prepared the drip and inserted the needle.

"Don't you have a nurse?" Yuuto asked.

"I do. But he's on his lunch break," Spencer explained. "And that guy acts like he owns the place, it's a pain. Even though I'm the doctor, I've got the lowest status around here. Pretty tragic, isn't it?"

Yuuto found himself liking Spencer's cheerful and easygoing manner. He couldn't speak for the man's medical skills, but he certainly had a personal charm.

"Dick's been checking in on you a lot lately," Spencer remarked slyly. "Thought he was being sneaky and all."

"I'm sorry… I must've been a bother to you, too, Doctor."

"Not at all," he said, waving a hand to dismiss the apology. "Honestly, it was pretty entertaining seeing that usually ice-cold bastard rushing back and forth between the cellblock and here, all out of breath. I teased him, said maybe he had some secret kid stashed away in the ward, and he looked totally flustered. Gave me a bit of satisfaction, really. He's always giving me hell, you know?"

Spencer's words were harsh, but his eyes were gleaming with amusement. It was obvious he didn't take Dick's rude attitude to heart—he had the kind of temperament that just let things slide.

When the IV finished, Yuuto thanked him and slipped his arms back into his shirt. He said he wanted to talk to Dick before heading back, and Spencer, as friendly as ever, told him to check the room next door.

Yuuto did as instructed and headed to the adjacent room. He gently opened the door and saw rows of beds separated by curtains. He couldn't see the patients directly, but it was clear they were inmates recovering from injuries or illness.

From the bed closest to the door on the right, he heard voices. It was Dick.

"Don't start giving up," Dick said, his voice full of compassion and warmth. "A guy like you? This isn't you. Everyone's waiting for you to come back."

Yuuto couldn't help but eavesdrop.

"That's enough, Dick. I'm done," the man said. "No one knows me better than I do. I just want to see Rivera one last time. I am sure he knows I no longer hold any power, but I want to explain it to him properly, with my own words."

The voice was frail, and judging from the conversation, it was probably Choker.

"Alright. I'll tell him. Anything else you want?"

"Let's see… ask Nathan to bring me a book. Something calming, a novel or whatever."

"Got it. I'll stop by again later to check on you."

The curtain opened and Dick stepped out. Behind him, Yuuto caught a glimpse of a thin, emaciated Black man lying in the bed. When Dick noticed Yuuto, he gave a small nod and quietly drew the curtain shut.

"Was that Choker?" Yuuto asked as they stepped out of the infirmary.

"Yeah. He's in bad shape—physically, mentally, and he's starting to lose hope," Dick sighed. "Back in the day, even Rivera gave him respect. He used to be one of the most feared guys in this place, but now he's just a shadow of his former self."

Dick shook his head slightly, a look of pity on his face. Even Yuuto, who didn't know the whole story, could sense that Dick had some kind of personal connection to Choker.

"Are you heading back to the cell?"

"Not yet. I want to stop by the library and see Nathan first." He felt bad for not helping out lately and wanted to say sorry. "Alright. I'll see you later, then. Thanks for everything."

Yuuto turned and started walking, but after a few steps, Dick called out to him.

"Yuuto."

He turned around, but Dick only stared at him silently. His expression was strangely tense, as if he had seen something dangerous lurking behind Yuuto, and it made Yuuto feel an urge to glance over his shoulder.

"What is it?" Yuuto asked, puzzled.

"Be careful," Dick finally spoke. "Don't let your guard down with anyone in here."

Yuuto found the warning odd, especially now, as it has been over a month since his arrival.

"No matter how trustworthy someone seems, no matter how friendly they act or how big their smile is… never trust them completely," Dick said this flatly, then disappeared back into the infirmary.

Yuuto didn't understand why Dick was suddenly giving him this warning, but he figured it probably had to do with people letting their guard down once they start to feel comfortable, and getting burned for it. With that thought, he made his way to the library.

The library was divided into two sections: one for general books, and the other a law library stocked exclusively with legal materials. Maybe because lunchtime was near, the place was deserted. Yuuto walked between the bookshelves and stepped into the law library at the back. That room was also empty.

A small room was adjacent to the law library, and Yuuto continued toward it. It was the same room Nathan always used to meet with inmates one-on-one.

Just as he raised his hand to knock, he heard voices arguing inside, and his hand stopped instinctively.

The door was slightly ajar.

"Don't get full of yourself," someone said. "Not everything goes the way you want. Just returning Rivera to the general population was already a major concession on our part."

It was a haughty-sounding man's voice. Though he was keeping it low, the anger was obvious in his tone.

"Mr. Corning," Nathan replied calmly. "I've explained many times that releasing Rivera, in the long run, will lead to positive outcomes for the prison as well.

"If anything happens, I'll be the one held responsible."

"There are more important things to worry about than your position," Nathan said enigmatically. "Come now, it's time you left. For a warden to be seen negotiating directly with a mere inmate like me… people will have a good laugh."

Yuuto sensed that one of them was about to stand, and quickly stepped away from the door, slipping into the space between the bookshelves. A moment later, the door opened, and the man who had been speaking with Nathan stepped out.

It was indeed Richard Corning, the warden of Schelger Prison. Aside from the brief conversation they had when Yuuto was first admitted, he had only ever seen the man posturing during large assemblies.

Once Corning was out of sight, Yuuto waited a beat before knocking on the door to the small room. "Nathan," he called. "It's me."

"Ah, Yuuto. Come in."

Nathan was seated at his desk, flipping through a stack of documents. Yuuto hesitated for a moment, then brought it up as casually as he could. "I just passed the warden, and he didn't look happy. Did something happen?"

Nathan gave a bitter smile and let out a small sigh. "I've clashed with him more than a few times," he began. "You know I deal with inmate rights and lawsuits, right? Sometimes I negotiate better treatment for inmates in exchange for dropping a case. When there's guard abuse that could explode if it got out, I've used that as leverage. Yeah, it's dirty and borders on blackmail—I *know*. But I do it to force the warden's hand. It's not about winning in court, my goal is to protect the inmates."

Yuuto hadn't realized Nathan was taking such an aggressive stance against the prison system. Seeing that he wasn't just kind but also fiercely principled deepened Yuuto's respect for him.

"Law libraries in prisons everywhere are shrinking," Nathan continued, clearly wanting to get something off his chest. "The Federal Bureau of Prisons and some politicians want to curb the so-called 'frivolous lawsuits' that inmates file. They see law libraries as giving prisoners too much knowledge, too much power, so they're getting rid of them. Inmate rights are progressively diminishing.

Nathan tossed the documents onto the desk, then slowly stood up. With a heavy expression, he walked over to the window and stared out, as if burdened with some unspoken weight.

Watching the lonely figure of his back, Yuuto felt a desire to understand Nathan more deeply and to support him in some way.

"Nathan…" Yuuto said. "About what you said in the cafeteria before. That stuff about prisoners being intentionally increased for the sake of the prison business. If you don't mind… I'd like to hear more."

"You're interested?"

When Yuuto nodded, Nathan smiled faintly and took a file from one of the cabinets. Inside were various charts and columns of neatly compiled data.

"The details are all in here. 2.2 million, isn't that absurd? The number of prisoners in the United States is honestly abnormal. The country has less than 5% of the world's population, but 25% of the world's inmates. Hearing that stat… you'd think America must be drowning in crime, right? But the actual crime rate here isn't off the charts. There are plenty of countries with higher crime rates, and yet, only in America does the number of prisoners keep rising at a terrifying pace. They can't even build new prisons fast enough to keep up."

"So it's the incarceration rate that's abnormal?"

"Exactly. A rising inmate population should be a red flag for any country. You'd expect policies aimed at reducing it. But here, they

flipped the problem on its head and turned mass incarceration into a massive industry—a money-maker. Private companies started jumping into the prison business. They get a fixed management fee per inmate from the government and then work those inmates for slave wages—sometimes less than a tenth of a cent an hour."

Nathan was deep into his explanation, and Yuuto listened attentively, wanting to understand his interest in this topic.

"And it doesn't stop there. Food, medical care, essentials, transport—all those auxiliary services also grow and profit from prisons. You also need loads of security gear: high-voltage fences, handcuffs, stun guns, bulletproof vests, you get the gist. The 'prison-industrial complex' is a gold mine, but it's not just companies that profit. Local governments benefit too."

"When a prison is brought into a state, there's construction work, and after that, jobs inside and around the facility. Plus, inmates get counted as residents of the town, which means more funding from the state and federal governments. To the state and to corporations, prisoners are both raw material and golden eggs. They've become absolutely indispensable."

Yuuto had heard about the increase in private prisons, but had never really considered it a problem. But now, hearing that the prison industry had become a core component of America's economy, he couldn't help but feel that Nathan was right—it was abnormal. It was one thing for companies to profit as a side effect of inmate growth, but growing the inmate population *for the sake of profit* was completely backwards.

"Of course criminals should be punished," Nathan clarified, perhaps misunderstanding his silence. "But if they're just thrown into some isolated place with no meaningful education or rehabilitation, how are they supposed to feel remorse or reflect? If anything, prisoners who suffer unfair treatment and abuse end up growing even more hostile and antisocial than before."

"Sadly, the human heart is just like the brain; it's soft. Put it in a round mold, and it turns round. Put it in a square mold, and it turns square. People are shaped by their environment. Yuuto…" he muttered. "Living here, don't you feel like your mind's started to warp a little? Even someone like you, who's always lived properly, don't you think you've been influenced by how prisoners think and act? Can you honestly say the atmosphere here hasn't gotten to you?"

"Honestly, no…" Yuuto answered in a small voice. "I don't think I can say it hasn't changed me. Right now, I feel like I'd do just about anything to protect myself."

"That's only natural," Nathan looked at Yuuto and gave a faint, weary smile. "If you knew someone was planning to hurt you, you'd have no choice but to strike first. This place is no different from a battlefield and trying to live true to yourself is damn hard. Maybe all the work I do for inmates, all the studying… Maybe I'm just trying to run away. It helps distract me from thinking about how hopeless my future is."

"That's not true, Nathan. You're doing something incredible. I really respect you, sincerely," Yuuto spoke firmly, and Nathan gave him a light pat on the shoulder.

"Thanks, Yuuto," Nathan sighed. "I'm glad you listened. Not many inmates take an interest in this kind of thing."

Suddenly, Dick came to mind. Nathan often had one-on-one conversations with him, too.

"What about Dick? Don't you talk to him about this stuff?"

"Dick doesn't care about things like this. If anything, he sees society itself as the enemy from the start. He thinks wanting anything from it is already a mistake. His worldview is a bit warped. Well… given what he did, I can't say I blame him."

Yuuto felt his chest tighten. Nathan knew what Dick's crime was. Confronted with the truth he'd always wondered about, Yuuto felt a strong, undeniable temptation.

What crime had Dick committed? He wanted to know.

"What did Dick do?"

Nathan showed an uncharacteristic moment of hesitation. A sudden sense of unease crept over Yuuto, and he began to tense up. Was it really something that difficult to talk about?

On edge, Yuuto waited anxiously for Nathan's next words.

"He killed a cop."

"What?" Thinking he had misheard, Yuuto asked again. "What did you just say?"

"He killed a police officer," Nathan repeated, his eyes shadowed. "Dick murdered a cop. Killing a law enforcement officer carries a heavy sentence. He got thirty years."

CHAPTER 18

A cop killer.

Dick murdered a cop.

Dick's crime echoed in Yuuto's mind the entire walk back to Block A after parting with Nathan. He, of course, didn't know the full circumstances, but the crime Dick had committed struck him harder than any other. Maybe it was because of his own past as an investigator, or maybe it was because the pain of Paul's murder was still a raw wound, aching in his chest.

What had Dick thought when Yuuto confessed that his partner had been killed? Had he looked back on his own crime and felt a stab of guilt? Or had he coldly thought that a man in that kind of job had it coming?

I know what it's like to lose someone close.

Yuuto wanted to believe those words had been sincere, yet he couldn't shake the feeling that something didn't sit right. Irritated with his own narrow-mindedness, he stepped into Block A.

As he took a deep breath to shake off his bad mood, his eyes landed on Hawes's thin shoulders. He was trudging into his cell, shoulders slumped. Seeing his dejected back, Yuuto was reminded of what Mickey had said—Hawes hadn't been the same since Matthew left.

Yuuto walked over to the front of Hawes's cell and stood at the entrance, peering inside. Hawes was sitting on the edge of his bed, staring blankly at a spot on the wall.

"Hawes. How're you holding up?"

Yuuto tried to speak as gently as possible, but Hawes still flinched, his shoulders jerking.

"Oh, Yuuto…" he said, exhaling a shaky breath. "I'm alright, more or less. Heard you were down with a fever. You doing better?"

"Much better. I heard you're getting released by the end of the week? Just a little more to go."

Hawes nodded in small, slow motions. Even though his long sentence was finally coming to an end, there wasn't a trace of joy on the old man's face. He was probably still worried about Matthew.

"Hawes, Matthew's going to be fine," Yuuto reassured the old man. "He's young, he'll bounce back before you know it."

"Y-yeah. That's what I think, too... But it's hard leaving this place without even saying goodbye to that boy."

"When he gets back, I'll tell him you wanted to say goodbye. I promise."

Hawes gave a frail smile, and Yuuto turned to go, relieved, but Hawes stopped him. "Yuuto. Could you give me a hand with my bath before lunch tomorrow? These old arms don't work like they used to. I can't even wash my own back."

Yuuto knew Matthew had helped Hawes bathe from time to time. Without him, the old man was probably struggling.

"Sure."

"Thanks. Around eleven-thirty, then?"

Yuuto returned to his cell after agreeing to the time and lay down on the bed. The fever hadn't fully passed, and even small movements still left him drained.

"Yuuto. Are you asleep?" A husky voice whispered near his ear, just as he was about to drift off, and he jolted upright in surprise.

It was Tonia, and she was sitting at the edge of his bed.

"Sorry. Didn't mean to wake you."

"It's fine. Just startled me, that's all. You came alone?"

"No. One of Neto's guys is with me. He's waiting outside."

Yuuto glanced toward the hallway and saw a member of Locos Hermanos standing there with his back turned.

Thinking about it, there was no way Tonia, known to be Neto's girl, would've come alone into another block.

"I heard you've been running a fever. Neto was worried."

"It's gone down. I just got checked out in the infirmary," Yuuto answered. "Why are you really here?"

"Oh? Was it so wrong to come just because I wanted to see you?"

Tonia smiled with a flirtatious glint in her eyes, and Yuuto instinctively looked away. It felt almost like he was alone in a bed with a woman. Whenever he was face-to-face with Tonia's stunning, natural beauty, he found it dangerously easy to forget the simple fact that she was, in truth, a man.

"No, of course not," Yuuto amended. "I'm really glad you came all this way to see me."

"I'm glad to hear that. Oh, and about Galen," she added in a low voice.

Yuuto nodded. "Yeah?"

"There are no burn scars on his back."

"But I heard he has a gunshot wound?"

"He does, but it's barely noticeable. It's old, and unless you're really looking for it, you wouldn't even notice."

Yuuto felt a twinge of disappointment. Galen's gunshot wound wasn't distinctive enough to count as a reliable identifying mark.

"Did he keep in touch often with anyone outside?" Yuuto asked, unwilling to give up.

"No," Tonia shook her head without hesitation. "He cut ties with his old crew a long time ago. As far as I know, he has zero contact with anyone on the outside—no letters, no phone calls, no visitors. Nothing."

The possibility that Gaelen was Corvus seemed to shrink further.

He had been Yuuto's prime suspect, but at this point, it might be best to cross him off the list entirely.

"I don't know what's really going on," Tonia said gently, tapping Yuuto on the knee. "But I hope you find the person you're looking for soon."

"Thanks," he said genuinely. "You've been a big help."

With that, Tonia left, escorted by one of Neto's men.

The Corvus investigation was back to square one, but Yuuto couldn't afford to let frustration slow him down. Three suspects remained. So far, he hadn't gotten a strong gut feeling from any of them. He lay back on the bed, mentally reviewing the names:

Edward Perry, the former mechanic.

Carl Bizon, a low-ranking member of ABL.

Michael Becks, who worked in the cafeteria.

He closed his eyes and pictured each of their faces, one by one. Which of them could be Corvus? Who should he target next? But no matter how hard he tried to focus, his thoughts kept circling back to Dick. *Cut. It. Out!* Annoyed with himself, he reprimanded himself, but the command had little effect.

The desire to confront Dick about the truth behind the cop killer label grew stronger by the day. There must be a compelling, undeniable reason for what had happened.

Dick wasn't the kind of man to kill a police officer without just cause. Yuuto wanted to believe that. He tried desperately to convince himself of it. But even he could recognize that this line of thinking wasn't about justice but self-preservation. About comforting himself.

To feel disgust toward Dick's crime meant feeling disgust toward Dick himself.

Yuuto didn't want to hate him. He wanted to believe in him. He *needed* to believe in him. Not for Dick's sake, but for his own—for the part of himself that was undeniably drawn to him.

"Hawes, let's head to the showers."

The next day, Yuuto kept his promise and invited Hawes to bathe. The old man emerged slowly from his cell, towel in hand.

"After the shower," Yuuto said animatedly, "let's have lunch together."

"Yeah… Sure," he mumbled. Just like the day before, Hawes looked far from well. His distracted, heavy expression suggested his thoughts were elsewhere.

But truthfully, Yuuto was the same.

The question of Dick's past was gnawing at him, but he didn't have the guts or gall to ask him outright. All he could do was stew in uncertainty.

As they walked down the hall, he heard Nathan's voice from behind.

"Yuuto, heading to the showers?" A voice called out from behind him in the hallway. It was Nathan, carrying a few books under his arm.

"Yeah," Yuuto answered. "Are you heading to the library again?"

"Stopping by the infirmary first. Dick asked me to lend some books to Choker. He's quite the reader—reads something new every day, even from his sickbed. Pretty impressive mental strength."

After parting ways with Nathan, Yuuto suddenly remembered. Yesterday, Choker had told Dick he wanted to read a novel that would bring him peace. Words that revealed his desire to live out the rest of his days in quiet reflection. Choker, having no one on the outside, had refused to be transferred to a hospital. Maybe this prison really was the closest thing to home for him.

Shower time rotated weekly by block, and today's morning slot belonged to Block A. With lunchtime approaching, the place was unusually empty. As Yuuto and Hawes undressed in the changing room, a guard named Cowen walked over and patted Hawes on the shoulder.

"Hawes. I hear you're getting out the day after tomorrow. Congratulations." Cowen's voice was syrupy and insincere. Hawes mumbled a nervous thanks, looking confused.

Yuuto didn't like Cowen. He wasn't violent, but his perpetual eerie smirk and snide remarks made his presence uncomfortable. Despite acting like he looked down on inmates, Cowen took bribes from the gangs and helped with their gambling. Yuuto would've preferred one of the stricter, more overbearing guards instead.

"Don't cause any trouble before then. Keep your head down, for your good."

With that, Cowen strolled off in a good mood. Yuuto sighed in relief that he wasn't being hassled, then wrapped a towel around his waist. He took Hawes by the hand to help him walk without slipping and led him into the shower room. He turned the faucet, and hot water burst from the wall-mounted showerhead. Yuuto held out his hand to check the temperature, then turned to Hawes.

"Do you want me to wash your hair first? Or your back?"

"Want me to wash your hair first? Or your back?"

"Yuuto. I… I…" Hawes murmured in a hoarse, broken voice, shaking his head like a broken doll. His face looked like death.

"What's wrong?" Yuuto frowned. "Are you feeling sick?" Worried by his abnormal state, Yuuto reached out to his shoulder.

But Hawes stumbled back, as if trying to escape him.

"I'm sorry… I really am. But I had no choice. If I didn't do this, I'd never get out of here."As he spoke, Hawes opened the door to the changing room with trembling hands—

—and in the next instant, several men burst in, fully clothed.

Yuuto's heart froze, and a wave of terror seized his body. They were all Black, and they were members of the Black Soldiers.

"I'm sorry, Yuuto! Please, forgive me!" Hawes shouted, his face twisted in pain, and fled into the changing room. Replacing him was BB, wearing a triumphant smile, eyes locked on Yuuto.

At that moment, Yuuto understood everything. He had been set up: Hawes and Cowen had been in on it from the start.

"Well, Yuuto. Looks like we finally get to have our date." BB said, grinning darkly as he approached.

Yuuto knew there was no escape, so without hesitation, he lunged at BB. But BB's lackeys were on him in an instant, pinning his arms and legs and rendering him completely immobile, completely helpless. No matter how desperately he struggled, the muscular men overpowered him and forced him face-first against the wall.

"Let me go! Don't touch me!" he yelled.

"Hold him tight. He might look like this, but he dropped Bernal with one punch. Don't get cocky." BB moved behind him, grabbing a handful of Yuuto's hair and yanking his head back. "You've got some nerve. Didn't think you'd try putting the moves on Rivera… So? Has he fucked you yet? What's his cock taste like?"

"Fuck you," Yuuto spat. "There's nothing between us!"

"We'll see about that," he sneered. "I'll ask your body myself."

Yuuto was grabbed around the waist, and his earlobe was slowly, wetly licked. Disgust surged through him, making his skin crawl. Reflexively, he jerked his head and smashed his forehead into BB's face.

BB grunted and staggered back.

"You bitch!" The man on Yuuto's right immediately grabbed his hair and smashed his head against the tiled wall. His forehead split open, and blood sprayed down his face, blinding his vision in red. The shock hit harder than the pain, and his consciousness started to slip.

"You think you can act tough just 'cause I showed a bit of

kindness," BB said directly into his ear. "Cocky piece of shit, you will learn."

He heard the metallic clink of a belt being undone. Yuuto froze in terror.

No.

Anything but that.

He could handle being beaten. He could survive getting kicked around. But not this—

Yuuto let out a strangled scream of pain.

BB's hard cock was jammed into Yuuto's tight hole. It was forced in without mercy, sending a bolt of searing pain through him, so intense he forgot how to breathe, stealing the air from his lungs. BB began to move immediately, every thrust violent and punishing, using the full weight of his powerful body. Yuuto clenched his teeth and bore it. He swore he wouldn't make a sound, but the pain broke through, and broken cries slipped out from between his lips.

Yuuto tried to muffle his pained groans.

Blood must've started to flow from the rough assault, because after a few thrusts, he felt a slick wetness between them. Ironically, it made the movements smoother, easing the pain just a little. But the pressure, the nauseating sensation of having his insides churned like they were being stirred with a burning rod, only grew worse. He felt like he was going to be sick.

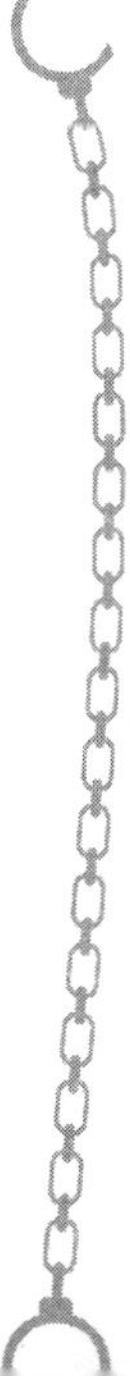

As Yuuto arched back in pain, the men grinned and pinned him down.

"Hey BB, how's that little yellow bitch's hole?" One of them asked in a filthy tone.

"Tight… Fuckin' perfect," BB groaned. "If Choker hadn't been bitching, I could've had some fun with him way earlier." BB rammed into him even harder. Trapped between the cold wall and BB's pounding body, Yuuto could only keep letting out moans of anguish.

"Ahh, fuck, I can't hold it anymore—"

Letting out a bestial growl, BB came inside him. He exhaled, satisfied, and slowly pulled away. Then, as if Yuuto were no more than garbage, the men shoved him to the ground.

"If you behave, I'll be sweet to you next time. But if I catch you giving Rivera those eyes again and making a fool out of me, next time we'll all take turns. Got it?" BB spat the threat at Yuuto's crumpled body and left the shower room with his crew.

Even after they were gone, Yuuto couldn't move.

More than his body, it was his heart that had been shattered. Beaten down to nothing, he didn't even have the strength to lift a finger. The crushing weight of defeat and humiliation wrapped around him like chains. It felt like his soul was slowly dying.

The shower kept beating down on the floor, spraying water that splashed over Yuuto's body. As if surrendering to warm rain, he let go of consciousness and sank into deep despair.

CHAPTER 19

Someone's hand gently stroked his cheek.

Lured by that tender touch, Yuuto awoke from his sleep. When he tried to open his eyes, his eyelids twitched slightly, and his head throbbed with a splitting pain.

"Yuuto, you're awake."

Dick's face was right next to his. Yuuto gazed into his blue eyes, then looked around. White walls. Partitioned curtains. Clean sheets. "Is this… the infirmary?"

"Yeah. We found you collapsed in the shower room," Dick said gently. "Do you remember being brought here on a stretcher?"

"Sort of," Yuuto answered in a hoarse voice. "It's all fuzzy. Just fragments."

When he touched his head, feeling something off, he realized it was wrapped in bandages.

"You had a cut on your forehead," Dick explained, eyes following him. "Took three stitches."

"My head feels really foggy."

"That's probably because Spencer gave you a tranquilizer. You were a little delirious when you got here," he said, trailing off as if weighing his words. "Yuuto, was it BB who attacked you in the shower room?"

Yuuto nodded. There was no point in lying to someone who already knew. "I was set up. Hawes and the guard, Cowen… they were in on it."

"Hawes too? Why?"

"They must've threatened him," Yuuto said without emotion. "Told him if he wanted to get released safely, he had to trick me and lead me to the showers."

"Yuuto," Dick shut his eyes, as if trying to suppress his rage as he spoke. "If you don't want to answer, you don't have to. But was it only BB who raped you?"

He understood the intention behind the question. Dick wanted to know whether Yuuto had been assaulted by multiple men. If it had been a gang rape, the risk of HIV infection would skyrocket. With unprotected sex and shared drug needles, AIDS was rampant in prisons.

"BB was the only one, but I'd like to get a blood test anyway," he said. He had meant to sound calm, but his voice came out shaky. He berated himself with a wry smile, but right then, he felt a surge of emotion rise uncontrollably in his chest.

He had been *raped*.

No matter how much he hated acknowledging it, he could not avert his eyes from reality. He knew he had to come to terms with it. He knew he couldn't run away. But the incident was much too painful to accept wholeheartedly.

"Dick, I—" His words trailed off, and tears welled up in his eyes. He didn't want to cry, not over this, but the anger and frustration rising from deep within him twisted together and spilled out as tears.

"I'm sorry, Dick," Yuuto said through gritted teeth. "You warned me, and… I guess I got complacent. BB hadn't made a move in a while, and I let my guard down. It's my fault. I brought this on myself."

He'd just been warned not to trust anyone, and here he was like this, in such a pathetic state. The depth of his own foolishness pierced him to the bone, and even his excuses sounded hollow.

"Stop it. You're the victim here. Don't you dare blame yourself like that," Dick said firmly, reproaching him.

"You must think I'm an idiot. Like, 'I warned you again and again.'"

"No. I don't think that," Dick said vehemently. "All I'm thinking about now is how I will make BB pay. I'll get revenge for you."

"Dick?"

"I'll take the pain and humiliation you went through and return it to that bastard a hundredfold."

There was a dangerous glint in Dick's eyes. Beneath his calm expression, Yuuto sensed an unfathomable fury. He'd never seen Dick like this before, and it took his breath away.

"If you want him dead, I'll do it," Dick said.

"Dick, what are you saying?"

"I wouldn't feel a shred of guilt killing someone like him. If it would ease your pain even a little, I'll take care of him. Don't worry about it. My hands have been stained with blood for a long time. Getting some fresh blood on them now wouldn't mean a thing—"

"*Dick!*" Unable to take it anymore, Yuuto grabbed his arm. He couldn't let him say another word.

"Stop. That's enough. I'll be okay."

What frightened him wasn't Dick's words. It was the shadow he saw behind them, the depth of the darkness inside him that spilled through with every word. Until then, Yuuto hadn't realized just how deep it ran.

"That's a lie!" Dick snarled. "You're a proud man, more than you let on. Someone like you, being violated like that, there's no way it didn't hurt. You're dying inside, aren't you? You hate BB, don't you? Then get revenge. There's no law in here to punish him; the only justice is payback. So use me. I'll be your hands. All you have to do is say the word."

Listening to Dick, Yuuto felt himself start to unravel. What was right? What was wrong? Did justice even exist? What was evil? But this confusion didn't begin today; it had started long ago, back when he was first arrested.

Yuuto should never have been sent there in the first place. And yet, he'd fallen into the trap of a false accusation, branded a criminal, and unjustly imprisoned. He hadn't done a single thing wrong. So then, who was at fault? The police? The real culprit who set him up? The jury that declared him guilty?

Back when he was still on the outside, Yuuto had never questioned the system—the idea that the law judged people. He'd believed without hesitation that those who broke it should be punished, that society required justice to maintain order. Criminals belonged in prison, where they would reflect on their crimes and work to reform themselves to reenter society. It had all seemed so obvious.

But the reality was different: this wasn't a rehabilitation facility. As Nathan had said, it was merely a place of containment. And even though Yuuto had only been here a short time, he could already say with confidence—no one here truly changed. Instead of repenting, they learned to hate society more and vowed that next time, they'd be smarter about their crimes.

Deep in his own heart, Yuuto was also filled with hatred. He hated those who hurt him, oppressed him, abandoned him, and ignored his suffering. Why was he the only one who had to endure so much pain? That question fanned the flame burning inside his chest, a flame fueled by rage, despair, and sorrow.

But if he gave in to that flame and let it consume him, it would be the end, and he would lose himself completely. Once that darkness took over, he'd never be able to return to the person he was before.

Nathan had said that people were shaped by their environment. Yes, Yuuto believed that too, but that's exactly why he had to stay strong, not for anyone else but himself.

"Dick. I'll endure this," Yuuto began, his voice fervent, desperate. "I'll get through it, no matter how hard it is. That's why I don't want you to do anything. Please, don't do something you'll regret. If you killed someone for me, I'd never be able to forgive myself. And if I ever do get revenge on BB, I'll do it with my own hands. I won't let anyone else clean up my mess."

At Yuuto's plea, Dick's hardened expression finally softened.

"That's just like you," he said with a sigh. The usual sarcastic glint returned to his face, and Yuuto felt a wave of relief wash over him.

"I'll be fine. I'm not going to lose to something like this."

As he said it to Dick, he was saying it to himself, too.

"I can't lose," he whispered it again and again, and Dick clasped his hand tightly, enveloping it with his own. The warmth of Dick's grip, the raw compassion flowing through his skin, offered more strength than any words ever could.

At that moment, Yuuto noticed something. There was a wall to his left, and just beyond it, a door. That meant this was the bed closest to the entrance, on the right side. Choker had occupied this bed when he came here yesterday.

"What happened to Choker? He was here yesterday, wasn't he?"

When Yuuto asked, Dick's eyes widened slightly, then he slowly shook his head. Now it was Yuuto's turn to be stunned.

"It cannot be."

"Yeah," Dick shook his head. "He didn't make it. Just before you were brought in, he breathed his last. Nathan happened to be visiting at the time."

Imagining the pain Dick must be feeling, Yuuto couldn't find any words. Even if he had known this day would eventually come, after caring for Choker so devotedly for so long, it must have felt like a bitter end.

Yuuto felt more anxious than sad about Choker's death. With him gone, there was no one left who could keep BB in check. The Black Soldiers were now completely under BB's control, and depending on what he decided to do next, a storm of unrest could sweep through the prison. Yuuto's mind flashed with an image of Neto and Tonia, and he silently prayed nothing would happen to them.

Beyond that, all Yuuto could do was wait and see.

On a brighter note, Yuuto's time in the infirmary was remarkably comfortable, thanks to Dick's attentive care. But his special treatment didn't go unnoticed—bored inmates took every chance to tease them about their closeness.

The patients constantly complained about how Dick was rough or uncaring and never failed to bring Yuuto into it. They would say things like, 'What, is Yuuto the only one you're gonna be nice to?' or 'Hey, I want VIP treatment like the newcomer over there.' Dick didn't seem to care at all, but Yuuto was mortified.

Mickey and Nathan were the first to visit. Mickey was furious and itching to do something to punish BB, but Yuuto repeatedly told him he appreciated the thought, so long as he didn't do anything stupid. He said it so many times it bordered on nagging. Mickey knew full well that it was too reckless to go after a gang leader like BB, so though he was clearly unhappy about it, he eventually relented. Yuuto was deeply relieved.

After they left, Chief Guard Guthrie came by to hear Yuuto's side of the story. But no matter what he was asked, Yuuto simply said he'd been attacked from behind and didn't see who did it. As Guthrie was leaving, he quietly told Yuuto that Cowen claimed the attack happened while he was in the bathroom.

And that was the end of it.

That afternoon, Tonia and Neto also came to see him. Neto gave Yuuto a pained, sorrowful look, then murmured something about needing fresh air before quietly rising from his chair and stepping out.

"I'm sorry, Yuuto," Tonia said, gently stroking his arm with a sympathetic touch. "It really hurts him to see you like this and to think about how much you must've suffered. That bastard BB—he's unforgivable."

"Thanks," he answered softly. "But I'm okay now."

As Yuuto held her hand, Dick came in. Seeing them hand-in-hand, he squinted playfully. "Well, excuse me," he said, raising both hands. "Should I come back later?"

"What the—? Don't be stupid."

"Stupid? That's harsh." While swapping out Yuuto's IV, Dick kept teasing the now-flushed Yuuto. "You two were having such a moment, I thought I'd give you a little privacy."

"Dick!"

Tonia giggled and gave Dick a gentle glare. "Dick, are you jealous or something?" she shot back. "Don't worry, I'm not about to steal your precious Yuuto away."

Dick just shrugged and said nothing. The fact that he didn't even try to argue back made Yuuto more flustered than anything.

"Oh, right," Tonia added. "I talked to that sister who used to be involved with BB—about *that* thing."

"What did she say?" Dick asked.

"He seems to be extremely cautious when it comes to sex. She said he always used condoms, even during oral."

Yuuto was surprised by the nature of the topic, but after Dick explained the reason, it made sense. When Spencer examined Yuuto while he was unconscious, a rectal test found no trace of semen. Suspecting that the rapist may have used protection, Spencer had mentioned it to Dick, who then turned to Tonia to confirm the theory.

"BB voluntarily requested a blood test six months ago, and at the time, he wasn't infected with anything," Dick informed them. "He's a careful guy, so it's safe to assume he used protection when he attacked you too."

There was still the risk of a latent infection, but Yuuto felt genuinely relieved by Dick's words. This had been the part weighing most heavily on him.

"Rivera's furious about what happened to you," Dick added. "He's been pacing the halls like a caged bear, looking like he's about to explode."

"Of course he is," Tonia said with a shrug. "Neto's a man of deep loyalty, and last night was rough. He went on a rampage in the cell and shattered every last one of my favorite teacups. I thought he would storm into Block D and take on BB right then and there."

She noticed Yuuto's worried expression and gave him a gentle smile.

"Don't worry," she said. "Neto is smart. No matter his anger, he won't act on emotion alone."

"I'm glad to hear that," Yuuto said with a sigh.

"But even if Rivera doesn't start anything," Dick said. "It's only a matter of time before BB makes a move."

Tonia nodded, her expression hardening.

"That's right. Now that Choker's gone, it wouldn't be surprising if a war breaks out at any moment."

"You and Neto, please be careful. I'm really worried about you."

"Thank you, Yuuto. You just focus on getting better, okay?"

After a little while, Neto returned.

"Tonia, let's go. Yuuto is a patient, not your lunch date. Don't wear him out."

"Alright, alright. Men are always so impatient," Tonia said with a dramatic sigh.

The way they acted reminded Yuuto of a wife chatting too long and a husband waiting restlessly to go home. He couldn't help but smile.

"Neto, thanks for coming all the way."

"Take your time recovering," Neto said sternly. "And when things get tough, sing a song. It helps lift the weight."

Hearing that, Yuuto remembered the song Neto had sung in

solitary, *La Golondrina.*

"Yeah," Yuuto said. "Maybe I'll try singing *La Golondrina* too."

"You do that. Even swallows rest their wings in the middle of a long journey. No need to rush. You'll make it to your destination."

Yuuto understood. What he really meant was: *You'll find the one you're searching for*. It was just the kind of encouragement Neto would give: quiet, grounded, and full of hope.

CHAPTER 20

Yuuto's injuries weren't too serious, so during the fifth-day checkup, Spencer told him he'd be cleared to return to his cell the next day. At the same time, he was permitted to take a shower, so Yuuto approached Dick and asked if he could bathe. There was a shower room next to the infirmary, reserved for patients.

Dick placed a waterproof bandage over the wound on Yuuto's forehead, which hadn't had the stitches removed yet, and then escorted him to the shower room.

"Thanks, Di—wait, huh?"

Yuuto blinked in surprise. For some reason, Dick had untied his hair and was now stripping off his clothes.

"I'm getting in too. I always take my bath here before dinner."

"Wait, getting in? This is a one-person shower, isn't it?"

"It's built spacious for assisted bathing, two men can fit easily. Come on, hurry up and get undressed. And for the record, you're the one interrupting my routine," Dick said arrogantly, with a towel wrapped around his waist.

What a selfish guy, Yuuto thought indignantly, but arguing would just waste time. Still pouting, he began undressing and followed Dick into the shower room.

"Yuuto. Sit in that chair. I'll wash your hair." Dick held the showerhead with hot water running and motioned with his chin to a shower chair with a backrest.

Yuuto tensed. "I-I can do it myself."

"You still have a slight fever. What if you get dizzy and fall? Just stay put and let me care for you until you're back in your cell."

Yuuto gave Dick a baffled look. In the end, this was part of Dick's 'caregiving.' They had never used the shower in their block together, so it might really be true that this was Dick's regular bathing spot—but still, he must've insisted on joining him out of worry.

What a caring guy, Yuuto muttered internally as he lowered himself into the chair. Dick began washing Yuuto's hair efficiently. Yuuto closed his eyes and let himself feel Dick's fingers moving across his scalp. The firm but gentle pressure felt nice.

"Hawes was released yesterday," Dick said.

"I see," murmured Yuuto.

"Are you okay with that?"

Still with his eyes closed, Yuuto responded softly, "It's fine. He was a victim too. I'm sure he struggled with it, and it must've weighed heavily on his heart."

"You're too forgiving," Dick said.

It wasn't entirely true that Yuuto felt no anger toward Hawes, but the man was a skinny old guy who'd spent twenty years in a hellhole like this and had finally regained his freedom. Getting revenge on someone like that wouldn't bring Yuuto any satisfaction.

Once the hair-washing was done, Dick told him to stand up so he could wash his back next.

"I can do that much myself," Yuuto said.

"Just your back. The rest you do yourself."

"Okay, Mom." Grumbling, Yuuto stood up from the chair. To steady himself, he placed one hand on the wall. Dick lathered a sponge and began scrubbing Yuuto's back.

"You're way more overprotective than you look," Yuuto mumbled, almost like talking to himself.

"Not with just anyone," Dick replied, and Yuuto's heart skipped a beat.

The way he said that, was he implying that Yuuto was special to him?

"You've got bruises," Dick's arm came from behind and gently traced Yuuto's wrist—the one he was bracing against the wall. Faint bruising could still be seen around both his wrists—marks from when he'd been pinned down during the rape.

As Yuuto stared at the bruise, memories started surfacing. He didn't want to remember, but the rising steam and sound of the shower summoned the nightmare back: Black hands gripping his wrists; lips curled in a sneer; pink-tinged blood mixing with water and flowing across the tiles; blinding pain as he was penetrated by brute force—every scene flashed through his mind in an instant like a series of jolting flashbacks.

His heart began to race. His breathing grew ragged. His hands trembled.

The present dissolved underneath his feet.

"Yuuto?" Dick's chest touched his back. The moment Yuuto became aware of the man's solid, muscular body behind him, he panicked. The terror of being raped by BB from behind came rushing back in vivid detail.

"No!" Reacting instinctively, Yuuto twisted away from Dick and pressed his back against the wall, covering his face with both hands. Even though his vision was blocked, even with his eyes closed, the fear that had taken hold of him wouldn't leave. It chased him relentlessly.

"No… stop… please, don't…"

"Yuuto, listen to me. Calm down." Dick grabbed his wrist, and Yuuto flinched hard.

"Let go. Stop it!" he yelled, breaking free with a forceful tug.

"Yuuto, look at me!" Dick seized both of Yuuto's arms and shook him with undeniable strength. "Look into my eyes. Who's standing in front of you? Say it."

Blue eyes stared earnestly into his own. Eyes like they could pull him in—Dick's eyes.

The nightmare finally faded.

"Dick," Yuuto whispered. "Dick Burnford."

"That's right. It's me. I'd never hurt you. You know that, don't you?" Dick smiled gently. It was a warm, enveloping smile; with it, the tension melted from Yuuto's body all at once.

"Dick, I was so scared," Yuuto leaned his forehead against Dick's broad shoulder and confessed in a trembling voice. "When I was raped, more than anger or frustration, it was fear that overwhelmed me. I was paralyzed by it. My body went numb. I couldn't fight back. BB just—" he couldn't finish the thought. "I couldn't do a damn thing. It makes me sick how helpless I was. I hate myself for it. I'm such a coward. I'm weak. Completely useless."

He hadn't wanted to admit it, had tried not to think about it, but seeing how easily he'd lost control like this forced him to face reality. No matter how much he tried to act tough, this was all he was.

"Dick, I'm a failure. I can't do this anymore."

A myriad of emotions invaded him at once, flooding his chest. He couldn't find the words. Shaking his head in frustration, Yuuto didn't even know what he was trying to say, but still, he wanted Dick to understand. He wanted him to know the kind of person he really was. All the chaos and confusion swirling inside him.

"Yuuto," Dick said gently. "Anyone would feel fear if they went through what you did. It breaks your heart and makes you feel weak, but that doesn't mean you have to hate yourself. It's okay to fall apart sometimes; it doesn't make you any less of a person."

Yuuto lowered his gaze, watching the water swirl down the drain as Dick continued to talk.

"You seemed so calm, I convinced myself you were fine. But of course, no one could bounce back from that so easily. I'm sorry; I didn't realize." Dick hugged Yuuto and whispered gently into his ear.

His deep voice had a strange power, and it always eased Yuuto's mind and brought him peace.

"Dick," Yuuto breathed.

Dick eyes' twinkled as he gently brushed the wet hair away from Yuuto's forehead. With Dick gazing into him like that, all the emotion that had been weighing so heavily on Yuuto's chest seemed to dissolve. Just moments ago, he'd felt like he'd be crushed unless he let it all out—but now, it felt like he didn't need words anymore. Like he didn't need to say anything at all.

And being wrapped in the warmth of another human for the first time in so long, that comfort, that sense of safety, made his body and heart relax so much it felt like he might melt.

Dick softly pressed his lips to Yuuto's forehead. It was a gentle kiss full of compassion. Even though they were both men, there wasn't the slightest hint of disgust; on the contrary, Yuuto found himself wanting Dick to do it again and again. Their skin pressed together was hot. The raw feeling of wet flesh touching wet flesh stirred something deep inside Yuuto—something delicate, something dangerous.

He felt heat rise in his lower belly and was suddenly overwhelmed with panic. The lower halves of their bodies were pressed tightly together, and if this kept up, Dick was bound to notice. Yuuto instinctively tried to pull back, but his back hit the wall. There was nowhere to run.

In a panic, Yuuto shoved Dick's chest with both hands.

"Yuuto?"

"I-I'm fine now, I want to get out," he tried to make an excuse and twisted away desperately, but the towel wrapped around his waist was starting to rise from his arousal. Dick's eyes dropped to it, and a flicker of surprise crossed his face. He'd noticed.

Yuuto was so mortified that he wanted to disappear. He was just being comforted, nothing more, and yet here he was, getting hard like some shameless idiot. Dick must be disgusted. Maybe even looking down on him now.

"I'm gonna go," Yuuto repeated, unable to take it anymore. He tried to move away from Dick, but Dick quickly pushed him by the shoulder, pinning his back against the wall again.

"I'm not done washing you yet."

Dick picked up the sponge that had fallen to the floor and slid it from Yuuto's neck down to his chest. Even though it was obvious what was happening in Yuuto's crotch, Dick continued to wash him without a change in expression.

"Dick, that's enough. I—"

Without warning, Dick tugged the towel away from Yuuto's waist and he gasped. Dick dropped the sponge and instead wrapped his soapy fingers around Yuuto's now fully hard cock.

"Dick! What are you—" Yuuto grunted, his words interrupted by a moan escaping past his lips.

"It's fine. Just stay still. I'm not gonna hurt you," Dick whispered hotly against his ear. "Trust me and don't think. Just leave everything to me."

He began to stroke with slow, deliberate movements. A jolt of pleasure surged through Yuuto's body, and he arched back slightly. His words dissolved into incoherent groans. "Dick, you shouldn't—ah!"

Wrapped in that large hand, stroked gently from base to tip, Yuuto felt all the blood in his body rush to that one spot. Dick's hand stirred the heat even further, and any shred of reason he had left slipped away. His mind was going blank.

"It's okay," Dick said. "This is nothing. Don't be embarrassed, just relax. It's probably been a while since someone touched you, huh? Just focus on how good it feels. Loosen up. There's no one else here. Just me. I'm the only one looking at you."

Dick's lips brushed against Yuuto's earlobe. Each hot breath sent a deep shiver racing down his spine. Dick's hand moved skillfully, taking Yuuto higher and higher, closer and closer to the edge.

Yuuto panted loudly. It felt so good that tears welled up at the corners of Yuuto's eyes.

In prison, where privacy was nonexistent, even jerking off was nearly impossible. But Yuuto had always had a pretty low sex drive, so it hadn't really bothered him, and more than anything, it was a mental thing—he just hadn't felt the desire.

But being touched like this, all the forgotten cravings came flooding back. Even though he knew it was wrong, he wanted more of this sweet stimulation and wanted to drown in it. His hips threatened to move on their own, seductively.

"Feels good, doesn't it?" Dick pressed his forehead to Yuuto's and asked in a low voice. Yuuto gave a trembling nod. "You don't have to hold back. Just let it all out."

Dick's lips were right there, so close their breath mingled. Yuuto wanted them.

He wanted Dick's sweet lips. He didn't know why; maybe it was just lust, or maybe it was something more. But whatever the reason, he couldn't stop himself from craving that kiss. Reason was useless against this burning desire.

Yuuto's lips parted slightly, inviting. His eyes pleaded silently: *come here*. Dick, ever perceptive, responded right away, granting his wish.

Their lips met softly, deeply. The moment Dick's tongue slid in, a sweet tingle spread through Yuuto's whole body, and he let out a muffled moan against the kiss, the sound swallowed by Dick's insistent mouth.

Under the stream of the shower, they hungrily tangled their tongues together. Even as they kissed, Dick's hand never stopped moving, steadily pushing Yuuto closer to the edge. It didn't take long, Yuuto came while still locked in Dick's kiss, his breath hitched with a moan.

The pleasure was so intense that his body trembled in small spasms before going limp. Dick wrapped his arms tightly around Yuuto to keep him upright, and Yuuto could only gasp helplessly, still in a daze. Dick huffed and pressed a soft kiss to his cheek.

As the high faded, only the awkwardness remained. Yuuto grew increasingly uncomfortable, but before he could completely come back to his senses, he noticed something strange about Dick. And then a fresh wave of embarrassment struck.

"Dick?"

Something hard was pressing against his stomach. It was Dick—and he was fully erect.

"Should I?" Yuuto asked. "I mean, I could do it for you—with my hand."

His voice was barely audible, like it could vanish at any second. Just saying it was mortifying. But it felt wrong for him to be the only one getting off.

"You would?" Dick pressed his hips into Yuuto with amusement. Yuuto instantly stiffened.

"O-Only if you want me to," he blurted the words out in a rush, and Dick gave a dry chuckle before pulling away.

"Don't force yourself. I'm not expecting you to do anything. That was just me acting on my own. I'll take care of myself later."

Yuuto felt a bit relieved, though guilty about it. Maybe it was unfair after initiating the kiss, but even if he could handle being touched, actually wrapping his hand around another guy's cock was something that still took an insane amount of courage.

"You should get out. You'll get lightheaded here."

Dick gave him a gentle push on the shoulder, and Yuuto nodded, still feeling a flicker of guilt.

As Dick immediately began washing his hair, Yuuto turned to leave. But just as he was about to close the shower door, he glanced back—and his eyes were drawn to Dick's back.

It wasn't the exaggerated, showy musculature of someone trying to impress. It was practical, balanced, and clearly the body of someone who had been naturally and consistently trained. Yuuto stared a moment longer than he meant to, and then saw it.

His breath caught in his throat.

"What's wrong?" Dick had noticed Yuuto standing there, unmoving, with the door still open. He turned around.

"Your back."

"Hm? Oh, that," he said dismissively. "Burn scar."

Dick rinsed the soap off under the shower, revealing the mark clearly. It was a wide, puckered scar near his lower back, large and obvious, unmistakably the result of a severe burn.

"Was it from a fire or something?"

"Back when I was in the military I screwed up during a mission. It was a rough unit, full of hard-ass commanders. Got banged up all over."

Yuuto felt like he'd been struck by lightning. He grabbed the bath towel with a trembling hand but was too stunned even to start drying off. A burn scar. Military background. White. Around thirty. Serving time for murder.

Dick matched every one of the conditions for Corvus.

And then there was the fact he'd killed a cop, his antisocial mindset, the coldness with which he'd said that killing a person didn't mean anything to him. Weren't all those traits perfect for a terrorist?

It wasn't confirmed yet, not even close. Yuuto wouldn't make such hasty conclusions, but all the strength drained from his body.

His knees gave out, and he collapsed onto the cold floor, catching himself with both hands.

CHAPTER 21

After finishing breakfast in the infirmary, Yuuto gathered the few personal items he had—a spare shirt, a towel, a toothbrush, and a magazine Mickey had brought for him—and tossed them all into a plastic bag before sitting down on the bed and letting out a long sigh.

Yuuto was tired; he hadn't gotten a wink of sleep last night. Ever since seeing the burn scars on Dick's body in the shower, his mind hadn't been able to rest. It had been a shock to realize that Dick met all of Corvus's criteria, but even more troubling was the fact that Dick's name hadn't appeared on the FBI's list.

At first, Yuuto thought maybe the FBI had overlooked him. But they'd supposedly conducted thorough checks on every inmate's background and physical features. So why had Dick slipped through the cracks?

As Yuuto sat in gloomy silence, waiting for Spencer's rounds, a sudden commotion came from the direction of the examination room. The door swung open violently, and a nurse named Russell poked his head in.

"There's an injured man in Block D of the West Wing," he informed them. "Looks like he's in no condition to be moved, so I'm heading over with the doctor. Rounds will have to wait."

"Who got hurt?"

"Was it a fight between the Black guys and the Chicanos?"

The other patients in the infirmary asked eagerly, but the short-tempered Russell snapped back, "How the hell should I know?"

Spencer appeared behind him, adding, "I'll let you know when we return, so behave yourselves. Dick should be coming around soon."

Once Spencer and Russell had left, the inmates immediately began speculating that war had finally broken out between the Black Soldiers and Locos Hermanos. Yuuto, however, wasn't in the mood to join the chatter. He quietly slipped out of the infirmary and sat on a bench in the waiting area, lost in thought.

Now that suspicion had taken root, every mysterious aspect of Dick seemed somehow connected to Corvus. Dick's cold profile, and the gentle smile he showed only to him—they were like two sides of the same coin. Which was the front and which was the back, it didn't matter.

What mattered was that Yuuto had come to accept this duality in Dick, and because of that, he couldn't bring himself to trust him completely.

No. Dick couldn't be like that. He wasn't the kind of man who'd get involved in cowardly acts of terrorism.

Frustrated, Yuuto began pacing around the waiting room.

"Damn it!" he cursed, slamming his fist against the first hard surface he saw, which was the examination room door.

To his surprise, it creaked open. It seemed that, in their rush, Spencer and Russell had forgotten to lock it.

A sudden realization struck Yuuto like divine inspiration, and he slipped into the examination room. At the back of Spencer's desk was a large filing cabinet that should contain the personal medical records of the inmates. Yuuto yanked open drawer after drawer, checking the contents in each one.

Until—*Bingo!*

There it was: the files organized by inmate number. He quickly found a white plastic folder with Dick's ID number containing health check results and other medical records. At the very front was the initial admission medical form listing height, weight, blood type, medical history, and any tattoos or scars.

Yuuto stared at it, wide-eyed.

The section for scars was completely blank. No mention of the burns. Not even the scar on Dick's forehead. The attending physician's signature was Spencer's. There was no way Spencer could have missed such prominent injuries.

Yuuto put the file back where it belonged and stepped out of the room.

There was only one conclusion: for some reason, Spencer had deliberately omitted Dick's physical characteristics from the initial admission report. That's why the FBI hadn't been able to identify him. But what kind of relationship did Spencer have with Dick? If there was a connection beyond that of doctor and inmate, what exactly was it?

Yuuto's thoughts kept drifting to the worst-case scenario. According to the FBI, Corvus had been giving instructions to his allies from inside the prison. Still, with all inmate communications monitored unless directed to an attorney, it would've been nearly impossible to hint at terrorist activity. As such, the most reasonable explanation was that he had a special means of communication. If Dick was Corvus, then Spencer may have been acting as his go-between. Through him, staying in touch with outside conspirators would've been easy.

If that were true, Yuuto should contact Heiden at the FBI right away and have them launch a full investigation into Dick Burnford, who had been left off the suspect list. But before doing that, Yuuto wanted to confront Dick himself. He needed to hear the truth, from Dick's own voice, through his own words, while looking him in the eye even if it turned out to be a lie.

Unable to sit still any longer, Yuuto ran out of the infirmary.

If he waited, Dick would come eventually, but he wanted to catch him first, somewhere quiet, where they could talk alone.

The corridor in the West Wing was packed with inmates, now

free from headcount. As Yuuto pushed against the flow of people, a sudden emergency siren blared through the facility.

Something had happened somewhere, but Yuuto didn't stop. He kept walking until someone suddenly grabbed his arm.

"Well, look who's out of the infirmary already," a voice said. "Hey, Yuuto. Missed me?"

His heart nearly stopped. The hand clutching him belonged to BB.

"Let go," he rasped, his throat dry.

BB saw through Yuuto's fear and leaned in slowly, like a predator closing in on its prey.

"No need to be so scared," BB whispered. "I told you, didn't I? Next time, I'll be really gentle with you. You're my girl now, after all."

The lewd words made Yuuto's blood boil, his fear overwhelmed by sudden, explosive rage. He slapped BB's hand away and shoved his massive chest with all his strength. BB's huge frame staggered backward, and his underlings rushed to steady him.

"Don't screw with me!" Yuuto shouted, his fury on full display. "There is no 'next time,' you piece of shit!"

BB's eyes flared with a dangerous glint.

"So you wanna get hurt again, huh? These bitches never learn," BB spat before turning to his men. "All of you, get him!"

BB's men swiftly closed in, surrounding Yuuto. Towering Black inmates tightened the circle, and Yuuto dropped his stance, ready to fight.

"Send him back to the infirmary," BB snarled with a cruel smile.

But just as he grinned, an arm suddenly looped around BB's neck. His face twisted in pain. "*Ghh!*"

"You're the one going to the infirmary."

It was Dick. His arms were clamped around BB's thick neck with crushing force, as if he might snap it on the spot.

"Don't worry," Dick whispered, hatred dripping from his voice. "I'll take good care of you."

Yuuto watched in shock as Dick raised his free hand and stabbed something into BB's ear.

BB's blood-curdling scream tore through the corridor. Dick sprang back, shoving past the stunned Black Soldiers and grabbing Yuuto by the arm. "Let's go!"

"Dick! Dick Burnford!" BB was writhing on the ground in pain, yelling Dick's name. Something strange was protruding from his ear—upon closer examination, it was a pencil. BB was bleeding profusely from his ear, and the blood quickly colored his shoulder crimson.

The Black Soldiers stared in shock at their writhing leader, then snapped out of it and charged after Dick and Yuuto. The two ran with everything they had, but the surge of inmates in the central hall slowed them down, and it wasn't long before the men were on their heels again.

The air turned murderous as the group of Black inmates closed in, step by step.

"Yuuto, shall we?" Dick asked, eying the crowd. His question almost sounded like an invitation to dance.

But he understood: they would have to fight their way out of there.

"Yeah," Yuuto answered without hesitation. There was no way they could win against more than a dozen men, but the thought of fighting with Dick by his side made him strangely unafraid.

But just as the two steeled themselves, another group of men appeared from down the hall, shifting the balance in an instant.

It was the Locos Hermanos.

Without hesitation, they charged into the Black Soldiers, starting an all-out brawl.

In an instant, the corridor erupted into a storm of shouting.

Ordinary inmates fled in all directions while others jumped into the fray to support their factions, and before long, chaos had engulfed everything.

"Yuuto!" Neto came running up to him. "Head for the Central Wing! Go with Dick!"

"Neto!" He exclaimed, surprised. "No way! I'm staying to fight!"

"This is between us and the Blacks. You need to go."

"But—"

Dick tugged at Yuuto's arm. "Come on. If you stay, Rivera won't be able to move freely. He'll be too worried about you," he said, then turned to Neto. "Rivera, take care of yourself. I'm praying you make it out of this."

Neto gave Dick a firm nod, then gripped Yuuto's shoulder tightly.

"BB's going to hunt you and Dick down no matter what. So go find someplace safe," he said. "I'll be fine, don't worry about me, and if you were wondering, I already got Tonia evacuated with a guard."

With a heavy heart, Yuuto let himself be pulled away by Dick. As they moved, he turned to look back and Neto gave a salute, as if to say 'don't worry,' before disappearing once more into the fray.

The emergency siren kept blaring as guards rushed to contain the outbreak. But the chaos was spreading too fast. The prisoners' excitement was contagious, a true domino effect, igniting violent flare-ups throughout the facility; soon, the situation became beyond what a few guards could handle.

Once a riot broke out, it stopped being just a racial issue. All the pent-up frustration the inmates had been holding in finally found an outlet, and it was akin to an erupting volcano.

"This is my fault."

"No. This was going to happen sooner or later," Dick answered. "Just now, in Block D, one of the Black inmates aligned with Choker's old faction was thrown from the third-floor walkway. He was a moderate, one of the ones trying to negotiate with the Chicanos after

Choker died. His death was probably BB's doing. Rivera must've found out and decided to act."

As they made their way back toward the infirmary, Guthrie came running from the administrative wing.

"Burnford," he barked. "What the hell happened in the West Wing?"

"The Blacks and the Chicanos are at war," he said. "Guthrie, give me the master key. I need to get that package."

Dick held out his hand, and Guthrie inhaled sharply.

"Hurry. I want to settle this while I still can. This is the only chance we'll get."

"Fine." With a pained expression, Guthrie gave a solemn nod and removed a key from the bundle hanging at his waist, handing it to Dick.

"Yuuto. I've got something I need to take care of. You go on ahead to the infirmary. BB might send someone after you. Lock the door from the inside and stay hidden. Got it?"

With a firm shove from Dick, Yuuto took off running, not entirely sure what was going on, but he knew he had to get moving. When he reached the stairs, though, a thought hit him.

Nathan. He might be in the library, unaware of the potential danger.

Every morning after headcount, Nathan always went straight to the library. If he was there now, it would be safer to bring him along to the infirmary. Yuuto dashed up the stairs and threw open the library door.

Just as he'd expected, Nathan was there, standing by the window, gazing outside.

"Nathan!" Yuuto called out, and Nathan slowly turned around, wearing the same gentle smile as always.

"What's wrong, Yuuto?" Nathan said, cocking his head. "You look like you've seen a ghost."

"There's a riot in the West Wing—a full-blown war between the Blacks and the Chicanos! The guards probably won't be able to contain it. Come with me, we're going to the infirmary to take shelter."

"Ah, I figured something was going on. That siren's been blaring nonstop. And look, you can see smoke out there. I guess the inmates got carried away and set fire to some mattresses or something. Not much in here that'll burn, though, so I doubt we need to worry about a real fire."

Nathan's laid-back tone only irritated Yuuto further.

"What are you doing being so calm about this? The rioting inmates might rush this way, too! We have to go—now!"

Yuuto grabbed Nathan's arm, but Nathan only gave a sheepish smile.

"Can you give me a second? I want to take some important papers and books. If someone sets a fire here, that would be a real disaster. I'll be quick."

Yuuto let out a heavy sigh at Nathan's maddening composure. "Nathan—"

"All right, I'll behave. No need to look at me like that." Shrugging, Nathan patted Yuuto on the back. "Let's go."

"What about Dick and Mickey?" Nathan muttered quietly as he locked the library door behind them. "I'm worried about them."

"I don't know about Mickey, but I was just with Dick a moment ago. I think he's fine."

"Where is he now?"

"No idea," Yuuto replied as they started walking. But before they could get far, both of them came to a sudden stop.

Dick had appeared at the top of the staircase, carrying a large backpack he hadn't had before.

"Yuuto? What are you doing here?" Dick asked, stunned. "I told you to go to the infirmary!"

Clearly, he hadn't expected to find Yuuto here, and his last words came out harsh and reprimanding.

"But, I thought Nathan might still be in the library, so—"

"Get over here. Now!"

Dick's expression tightened, his voice sharp with urgency. Yuuto, caught off guard, nodded hastily.

"A-Alright," he muttered, confused. But just as he started to move, Nathan grabbed his arm.

"Don't go, Yuuto. Dick has a gun."

"What?"

That can't be true. Yuuto looked at Dick in disbelief. Dick's right hand was suspiciously hidden behind his back.

"Dick, show me your right hand," Yuuto said, his voice trembling.

As always, Dick complied without a word, slowly raising his right hand into view. He was holding a black automatic pistol, and without a moment's hesitation, he lifted his arm and leveled the gun directly at them.

"What, what is this?" Yuuto stared, stunned, into Dick's cold, distant eyes. "Dick, what are you—"

A dry gunshot cut through his trembling voice.

Yuuto's eyes widened. Dick had fired straight into the ceiling. It was clearly a warning shot, but knowing he'd actually pulled the trigger made Yuuto's shock that much deeper.

"No sudden moves, Nathan," Dick warned. "Yuuto, you're coming with me. Step away from him. Now!"

The way Dick aimed the gun so deliberately at Nathan made Yuuto panic. Why? Why is he pointing a gun at Nathan, of all people? Has he lost his mind? Or is Dick really Corvus, finally revealing his true, ruthless self?

No. That's not possible. Dick isn't Corvus. He can't be.

"Dick, stop! Put the gun down!"

Yuuto instinctively stepped in front of Nathan. But Dick didn't lower the pistol—instead, he stepped closer.

"Yuuto. *Move*."

"Well, well. So it really was you," Nathan said, his voice carrying a sharp edge Yuuto had never heard from the usually refined man. "I can't say the thought never crossed my mind, but you really had me fooled. So you've been watching me for a whole year? That's some remarkable patience."

Just as Yuuto registered how jarringly cheerful Nathan's voice sounded, a sudden coldness kissed his cheek. He went still.

Nathan was holding a slender knife.

"Nathan?"

"Sorry, Yuuto. I'm going to need you to be my hostage. He seems to care deeply about you, so there's no one better suited for the role." Nathan's voice was almost gentle as he pressed the blade firmly against Yuuto's throat. "Dick, hand me the pistol. Try anything at all, and I'll slit his throat clean through."

The blade dug into Yuuto's neck. Everything was happening so fast that his mind could no longer keep up. Confusion overtook him—he had no idea what was going on.

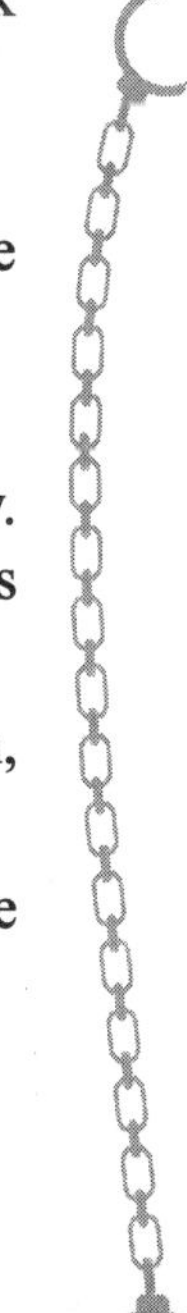

"Do it, Dick. Or do you want to see Yuuto die?"

Dick remained motionless, his gun still aimed, but he didn't move a muscle.

Nathan pressed harder. Yuuto felt a sting when his skin was cut.

"Stop!" Dick barked sharply, his voice laced with urgency. Nathan's hand hovered, trembling on the edge of killing. "I'll do as you say. Just don't hurt him."

With a bitter, pained expression, Dick slowly crouched down, placed the pistol on the floor, and slid it toward Nathan.

Yuuto obeyed. Nathan took the pistol from him and swapped the knife for the gun, pressing the barrel against Yuuto's head.

"Pick it up, by the barrel," Nathan ordered, gesturing with the knife.

"Tell me one thing. Was it you who killed Choker?"

Dick's quiet question hung heavy in the air. Nathan tilted his head, almost playfully.

"Killed him? Ha! That's such a dramatic way to put it. I merely silenced him—for his sake, of course. He was suffering, and I just wanted it to end quickly for him. He died without much struggle, really. Peaceful. It was so peaceful, and I almost felt relieved while I watched him. No need to read a soothing novel, he passed on in peace."

Nathan continued speaking in that same gentle tone, and Yuuto felt like he was trapped in a nightmare. With that soft, innocent face, Nathan had murdered Choker. He could've just waited for him to die naturally, but instead he'd chosen to end it with his own hands.

"Don't twist it into some noble act. You wanted him gone!" Dick yelled. "You knew that with Choker out of the way, the Blacks and the Chicanos would undoubtedly start a war. You were just waiting for that to happen."

"I'm not sure what you mean," Nathan replied with a mocking smile.

"Were you ordered to start the riot? Or is all this your own plan?"

"Your intuition is impressive. Really, I'm in awe, but your follow-through is lacking." Nathan's tone was condescending. "You can't beat me, Dick."

With that, Nathan shoved Yuuto hard in the back, sending him tumbling to the floor. Dick rushed to his side instantly.

"Such a shame, Dick. I thought we could've been good friends."

Nathan lowered the gun and aimed. Dick stepped in front of Yuuto, shielding him with his body.

"Don't," he said in a low, firm voice.

Nathan smiled softly, as if he were greeting an old friend. His eyes were tender, angelic even.

"What a beautiful friendship," he said, watching them. "Or is it love? Either way, it's touching. It makes my chest ache. So I think I'll let you die together… after all, no one should die alone."

"Nathan, stop! Please!" Yuuto cried out from behind Dick's shoulder. "What's gotten into you? You're not this kind of person!"

Even now, Yuuto couldn't believe what was happening. Part of him still clung to the hope that this was all some kind of mistake. "You were always trying so hard—for everyone. You were kind. A good man!"

"I wanted to try being that kind of person," Nathan hummed softly. "Someone completely unlike myself. But I'm tired of playing the part, and I've had my fun. The Nathan Clark you knew is gone. It's time to take off the mask, Yuuto."

"Then, was the story about your false charge a lie, too?" Yuuto clung desperately to hope.

"Yeah. It was just to gain your trust. Well, I guess not everything was a lie. I did kill Nathan Clark's mother. That part's true."

Yuuto couldn't make sense of what that meant. But there was no time for more questions. Nathan raised the gun and pointed it squarely at Yuuto's forehead.

"Goodbye, Yuuto. I really did enjoy our little friendship game."

Nathan gave a wistful smile, as if he were genuinely mourning the farewell, all while his finger tensed on the trigger.

A voice rang out through the hallway, shattering the tension. "There he is! There's Burnford!"

Immediately after, a group of Black inmates, all members of the Black Soldiers, rushed up the stairs and into the scene, cutting between Nathan and his would-be victims.

"Lennix is with him! Kill them both!"

The gang's unexpected arrival gave them a split-second opening and Dick reacted instantly.

"Now!"

He grabbed Yuuto's arm and broke into a run down the hall, away from Nathan. The Black Soldiers shouted and gave chase.

Gunfire rang out behind them. Yuuto turned and saw one of the men collapse, blood spraying from his chest.

"What the fuck?"

"It's Nathan! He's got a gun!"

Panic swept through the Black Soldiers. Nathan showed no hesitation, and no mercy; he kept firing, cutting down anyone in his way. Soon, the narrow corridor turned into a bloody massacre.

Dick and Yuuto ran for their lives, bolting down the emergency stairwell at full speed.

On the first floor, two more Black inmates appeared, but Dick struck one down with a clean punch before they could react. Yuuto put all his strength into a kick, sending the second one flying.

"This way, Yuuto!"

They sprinted through the hallway, following Dick's lead. He made a beeline for a storage area behind the cafeteria. Using the master key he'd gotten from Guthrie, Dick unlocked a heavy iron door and shoved Yuuto inside.

Once they were in, he locked it from the inside and finally let out a relieved breath.

"What is this place?" Yuuto asked, looking around.

"A secondary food storage. They keep non-perishables and stuff with a long shelf life here."

The room was packed with towering shelves, boxes, and crates stacked tightly. Dick moved deeper into the space and opened a door to an adjacent room.

Inside, a small break room about the size of two prison cells had been set up. A sink, a small cupboard, a table, and some chairs filled the space. Dick dropped his backpack on the floor, then pushed the table and chairs to one side.

"This is the kitchen staff's break room. It's small, but there's a toilet. We'll hole up here for now."

"Won't the guards come looking?"

"The riot in the West Wing's probably spread to the East Wing by now. The staff will be too busy trying to get things under control. With how bad it's gotten, it might be days before this settles down." Dick found a few folded cardboard boxes and laid them on the floor like makeshift mats.

Once they both sat down, Yuuto let out a heavy sigh.

"Dick. Explain this to me. I don't understand any of it. At one point, I really thought you might be Corvus."

When Yuuto looked at him, Dick gave a faint smile. A knowing smile. He knew exactly who he was referring to.

"That's a terrible misunderstanding," he scoffed. "So you really are FBI, after all."

"No. I told you, didn't I? I was a DEA agent. Everything I said about my partner being killed, about being wrongfully arrested, was all true. I never lied to you. The FBI came to me after my conviction. They offered me a deal—if I could find Corvus in this prison, they'd let me go."

"That does sound like the kind of stunt they'd pull," Dick hummed, pensive. "I'll be straight with you: I'm not Corvus. Corvus is Nathan."

Yuuto bit his lip. After what he'd seen from Nathan earlier, the thought had crossed his mind. But even then, it had seemed too absurd—too outlandish to accept that the gentle, universally beloved Nathan could be the leader of a terrorist organization. Hearing it now from Dick, with such certainty, was the only way Yuuto could finally believe it.

"But the FBI told me Corvus had burn scars on his back. I've showered with Nathan a few times, and he didn't have anything like that."

"He had cosmetic surgery before entering this prison. Probably had the scars removed. And the real kicker? He's not even the real Nathan Clark. He stole his identity to infiltrate Schelger Prison."

Yuuto's was spinning. Was the Nathan he knew just a mask? Nothing more than a disguise for Corvus? Then what had happened to the real Nathan?

"Is it really that easy to impersonate someone else?"

"It is, if you've got the backing of a powerful organization. Just look at me. I came here as Dick Burnford, the man convicted of killing a cop, to find Corvus."

Yuuto stared at Dick, stunned into silence. Not just Nathan—Dick, too, was wearing a mask?

"Yeah, I know. That one's a shocker. But for now, just keep calling me Dick like always," he said with a wry smile, flicking Yuuto lightly on the cheek.

"Then who the *hell* are you, Dick?"

Dick fell quiet, hesitating, as if weighing whether to say more. But then, perhaps deciding there was no longer any point in hiding it, he met Yuuto's gaze and spoke calmly.

"I'm a CIA contract agent."

The CIA, the Central Intelligence Agency, reporting directly to the White House. The name hit like a slap. Yuuto's eyes widened in disbelief.

"Up until two years ago, I was in Delta Force."

"Delta Force?" Yuuto repeated, disbelieving. "As in *the* Delta Force? The Army's elite counter-terrorism unit?"

"Yeah. My connection to Corvus goes all the way back to those days. Want to hear the full story?"

Yuuto nodded without hesitation. He wanted to know. Everything about Dick's past. Everything that had led to this moment.

"Then, let's have some coffee first."

Noticing a jar of instant coffee on the sink, Dick stood up. Yuuto followed, helping him out by preparing cups while Dick filled a kettle with water. They used a small gas stove to boil it, poured hot water into the mugs, and sat back down on the cardboard-covered floor.

Dick took a few quiet sips, saying nothing for a while. Yuuto didn't rush him. He could sense that Dick was wrestling with something—something too heavy to bring up easily. This wasn't a story that could be told lightly.

Finally, Dick placed his empty cup on the floor, gave a small breath, and spoke.

"It's a long story…"

CHAPTER 22

Dick's story was fascinating in every way.

An orphan raised in an institution, Dick received a military scholarship and entered a military academy. While still a student, he began training and, upon graduation, enlisted in the Army. He joined the Green Berets and eventually became a member of Delta Force. Officially known as the 1st Special Forces Operational Detachment-Delta of the United States Army, Delta Force is, as the name implies, an elite unit specializing in special operations.

Its members undergo rigorous training not only in combat but also in tank and aircraft operations, explosives disposal, breaching tactics, VIP protection, first aid, and hostage rescue—preparing them thoroughly for any battlefield scenario. After completing the harsh training, Dick began undertaking covert missions abroad.

Yuuto didn't know the details, but he had heard unsettling rumors that Delta Force sometimes carried out illegal activities, such as overseas assassinations of high-value targets. Perhaps for that reason, even though it's considered one of the world's top special forces, the Department of Defense does not officially acknowledge Delta Force's existence.

"We operated in four-man teams in Delta, and our team was really close. Frank, Jonathan, and Noel. They were dependable and full of life. With them, even the hardest missions were bearable," Dick recounted tenderly, his voice wistful. "At that time, we were based out of Fort Bragg, North Carolina, but at one point, we pooled our money and bought a beach house together. During breaks, we'd head there to shake off the grime of work and relax until the next mission. They were the best friends I ever had, truly irreplaceable.

And Noel… Noel was especially important. He was my lover."

Yuuto's chest tightened at the unexpected confession. He had known that Dick had once had a lover, but hearing the name and the specifics suddenly made that presence very real.

"Noel was two years older than I, and we clicked right from the start. He was kind to everyone, a warm and gentle soul. But one day, when I told him I was gay, his behavior suddenly changed. I thought he hated me, but that wasn't it," Dick chuckled. "Turned out he was gay too, and he'd liked me for a long time. From there, it all just came naturally. We started dating. Frank and Jonathan accepted us without issue. They treated our relationship as perfectly normal. And for the first time in my life, I had both a kind lover and understanding comrades. I finally felt like I had a family. But my happiness didn't last. One day, Corvus took it all away."

Dick abruptly fell silent and stared at his palm, as if trying to find what he had lost within it. Then, slowly curling his fingers into a fist, he continued speaking. What followed was difficult even for Yuuto to hear.

Two years ago, in February, Dick and his team received an emergency deployment order. Their mission was to rescue hostages and neutralize a heavily armed cult group called White Heaven, which had barricaded themselves in a standoff. Since Delta, whose operations are typically overseas, had been deployed, the team suspected that the government wanted to suppress the incident before it became public.

"We weren't given any real details, but that wasn't unusual. We don't ask why, we just go where we're told and do what we're ordered."

That night, they headed out from Fort Bragg to the mountain lodge in South Carolina where the standoff was taking place. But when they arrived, military negotiators were already speaking with the suspects, and it seemed a violent breach might be unnecessary.

Before long, the suspects began surrendering one after another, hands in the air. Following their commanding officer's orders, Dick and his team cautiously entered the lodge to search for a reported injured hostage. They found him unconscious and wounded in a room on the second floor.

"Frank, our team leader, told me to get a stretcher. I was the only one who left the building," Dick's voice was full of regret. "That's when it happened. A deafening explosion went off, and I was blown away by the blast. My eardrums ruptured, and shards of glass and splinters pierced my face and hands. Dazed and bleeding, I looked back at the lodge. I couldn't believe my eyes. The second floor had been completely blown away, as if it had never existed. The three of them were killed. Their bodies were torn apart beyond recognition. It was a horrible way to die."

Dick's voice trembled slightly. The precious friends he had come to think of as family, the peace he had found after a lifetime of loneliness, his lover—everything had been ripped away in an instant. The depth of the pain Dick had endured was beyond anything Yuuto could imagine.

"I wished I'd died with them," Dick mumbled.

Overcome with emotion, Yuuto grabbed Dick's arm. In turn, Dick grasped Yuuto's hand and gave a small nod, as if to say he was okay.

"But why did the explosion happen?" Yuuto asked.

"It was on Corvus's orders. After the surrender, he called in and gave instructions to the remaining cult members. He wasn't even there; he'd fled the scene already. He told them to set a time bomb just before surrendering, supposedly to destroy evidence. But I think he did it for fun—to blow up his own people and the hostage along with them. Corvus, White Heaven's leader, is a psychopath."

As expected, a heavy feeling settled in Yuuto's chest. So Corvus was the leader of that cult group.

"I'd always been prepared for the dangers of a job where death is a constant companion. But Corvus's cowardly methods are something I could never forgive. I writhed in frustration and rage throughout my time in the hospital. I genuinely wanted to find Corvus and take revenge. But I had no way of doing so," Dick spat, frustrated. "Eventually, I fell into the depths of despair, lost all will to live, and left the military. I spent my days in a downward spiral, drowning myself in alcohol, thinking about Noel and the others. After that, well, my path became the same as yours."

"The same as mine?"

Dick nodded. "The CIA got in touch, apparently, they'd been monitoring Corvus for years as a dangerous figure. He's a creepy man who excels at brainwashing young people and forming fanatical groups. But he's not just your typical cult leader. He has connections with several terrorist organizations, funding them, even assisting their operations. Word is, even fundamentalist terror groups rely on Corvus when they want to enter or hide in the United States."

After the White Heaven siege, the CIA desperately hunted Corvus, who had vanished without a trace. Eventually, they learned he had assumed the identity of a man named Nathan Clark and was hiding out as an inmate in Schelger Prison. That's when the CIA scouted Dick as an agent and sent him in.

"The CIA wanted to use my military background, that and my desire for revenge. And to be honest, it was just the lifeline I needed."

What shocked Yuuto more than anything was the sheer volume of information the CIA had on Corvus. While the FBI had also been tracking him, they were clearly lagging far behind. When Yuuto pointed that out, Dick gave him one of his signature sarcastic smiles.

"The CIA and FBI have always been rivals," he said. "They don't share intel. In fact, they're constantly trying to outmaneuver each other. It's absurd. Even before 9/11, both agencies had picked up on warning signs, but because they kept secrets from one another, they failed to prevent the attacks.

"And they didn't learn a damn thing," Dick muttered angrily. "The CIA's fixation on Corvus isn't about justice—it's about survival. They've been under fire for years, blamed for 9/11, for Iraq, for everything the Department of Defense and the public are furious about. This is just their way of proving they're still relevant.

"As for the neocons in the White House… that's a whole other story. One that has nothing to do with you or me. I agreed to be a contract agent because the CIA promised me the legal clearance to eliminate Corvus. I wanted the right to take him out, legally."

Dick's sole mission was revenge on Corvus. He was living only to settle the score for his fallen comrades.

"So you were planning to kill Corvus from the start?"

"Yes. But the CIA had conditions. I was told to get close to him and extract as much intel as possible. They wanted to know about the organizations backing him. I gained Corvus's trust, and after a year of work, I managed to gather some decent intel. I finally convinced the CIA that I had enough, and they gave me the green light for the assassination," Dick said, his voice tinged with an emotion Yuuto couldn't quite place. "Just when I thought I could finally end it, *you* showed up. And then the CIA called it off."

"Because of me? Why?"

"Because of the string of terrorist incidents Corvus had directed through White Heaven survivors, the FBI finally started connecting the dots. When the CIA realized that, they began suspecting you might be an FBI agent. They ordered me to keep an eye on you. They were also curious how much the FBI knew about Corvus. From your behavior, I could determine that the FBI had no solid leads. Honestly, I was relieved. If you'd turned out to be a threat to my mission, I would've had to deal with you."

Yuuto stared at Dick, realization dawning. So that's why Dick had been so cold toward him in the beginning.

"Then, it wasn't a coincidence that we ended up as cellmates?"

"Of course not," Dick chuckled. "Two people with ties to the CIA and FBI ending up in the same cell by chance? Doesn't add up."

"But how? Could the CIA even interfere with internal prison

logistics like that? If so, why not just have Corvus arrested directly instead of going through all this?"

"It wasn't like that. It was Guthrie. He's a CIA collaborator. As head of security, he manipulated the cell assignments. And while we're at it—Spencer, too. He was the CIA's liaison for me."

"So, Corvus being nice to me, that had a purpose?"

"Yeah. He always greets newcomers kindly, sizing them up with his own eyes. He was a bit suspicious of you, especially because of how sneaky you were acting."

"Wait, is that why you got mad during the Lindsay incident?"

"Pretty much. If you started chasing the wrong target, and that made Corvus suspicious of your true identity, it could've blown everything. He might've run."

So that was why Dick had been so mad that time. Yuuto grimaced, realizing now what an annoying pain in the ass he must have been in Dick's eyes.

"I never suspected Nathan was Corvus. He completely fooled me," Yuuto mumbled. "I even respected him."

"No wonder. Even I, knowing his true identity, almost believed in the persona he crafted—model prisoner, upstanding man. Sometimes, there are people like him, not just good at pretending, but able to truly become someone else. Almost like a split personality."

Yuuto felt a crushing wave of exhaustion and rested his head on his knees.

"What's wrong?" Dick asked.

"I'm just drained. I feel like a complete fool—like I've been dancing in the palm of your hands this whole time. I was chasing Corvus with everything I had, relying only on the tiny scraps of information the FBI gave me. My whole life was on the line." Yuuto didn't know whether to laugh or cry. "And yet, Corvus was right beside me the whole time. And on the other side of me was the man watching both him and me. From your perspective, I must have looked like some pathetic, reckless idiot. It's so humiliating."

"Don't beat yourself up," Dick said, ruffling Yuuto's hair. Annoyed, Yuuto slapped his hand away.

"Whose fault do you think this is?"

"Don't be mad. I owe the CIA nothing, but once I agreed to work for them, I was obligated to keep secrets. And let's not forget—technically, you're the enemy. I've already told you more than I should."

He was right. Yuuto had no right to blame him. If anything, he should be grateful Dick had finally told him the truth.

"What about Nathan—no, Corvus? What do you think he did after everything that just happened?"

"He knew staying in prison kept him safe from law enforcement's radar. But once he found out someone was sent to assassinate him, of course he ran," Dick said, casually. "He's got connections with the warden. He might already be out by now."

Yuuto was stunned. Because of his interference, Dick's year-long mission had failed. No, more than just a mission—this had been his personal crusade, something he'd staked his entire life on.

"Dick, I'm sorry," Yuto blurted, his face pale. "It's my fault. Corvus got away because I got in the way."

But Dick shook his head. "It's not your fault. I was the one who hesitated. If I'd just taken him out the moment he killed Choker, we wouldn't be in this mess. I knew things would get complicated once the riot broke out. I guess I let this cushy prison life dull my instincts."

Dick gave a self-deprecating laugh and pulled a small radio from his backpack. "Sooner or later, the news of the riot will get out, and they'll start broadcasting it. Judging from past prison riots, I'd say it's only a matter of time before the National Guard gets called in. You and I are both on BB's hit list, so we should stay hidden until then."

Yuuto agreed and leaned back against the wall, completely drained. Now that he understood what was going on, his body finally let go of the tension.

"Yuuto," Dick called his name, and Yuuto turned his head slightly without lifting it from the wall. "When the National Guard arrives, I'm going to escape in the chaos. Once I'm out, I'm going after Corvus."

Yuuto was shocked, but managed to keep his composure. "I see," he murmured. If it was Dick, he'd pull it off. He had probably made all the preparations already. There was no need to worry. "You'll be fine, and you'll find Corvus. I'm rooting for you."

Dick had spent a whole year getting close to Corvus. He must have collected valuable intel, such as potential hideouts and the organizations backing him.

"Why don't you come with me?" Dick asked. There was a kind of fervent intensity in Dick's eyes.

"Huh?" Yuuto couldn't hide his surprise at those words.

"I can get at least one person out with me. You found Corvus, but he got away. Can you really count on the FBI to keep their promise? Are you going to spend years here for a crime you didn't commit? Don't throw your life away behind bars." Dick pressed on, and Yuuto faltered in confusion.

Escaping with Dick…

It was an unbelievably tempting offer. But not something he could answer immediately. Once Dick got out, he could return to his old life. But for Yuuto, escaping meant gaining freedom at the cost of being branded a fugitive—a new stain on top of the one he already carried.

"Come with me, Yuuto."

The firm invitation made his heart waver. He wanted to go with Dick. He didn't want to be separated from him, not like this. Even if it meant breaking out of prison, he wanted to get away from this place and taste real freedom, even just for a second.

That word 'freedom' carried a sweetness that made Yuuto's chest ache. But becoming a fugitive meant he could never see his family again. He'd spend his life looking over his shoulder. Could that truly be called freedom?

—But if he refused, he'd lose Dick. He might never see him again.

His thoughts churned wildly. After much inner turmoil, Yuuto made a bitter, painful decision.

"I really appreciate your offer, but I'm staying here."

"You sure about that?"

"Yeah," Yuuto said, nodding firmly. "But I'm not planning to stay here forever. I've got the fact that I made contact with Corvus, and I'll use that as leverage with the FBI. I'll find a way to work something out."

Yuuto forced a note of optimism into his voice, and Dick gave a bitter smile and shook his head.

"What is it?"

"I can't believe how stupid I've been. You turning me down snapped me out of it. I'm honestly relieved." He gave a twisted, self-mocking smile. "Even if I had gotten you out, I wouldn't have been able to stay by your side. It was a reckless offer. Just forget I said it."

Yuuto quickly shook his head. "No way."

"Yuuto?"

"I'll never forget it. That you asked me to come with you—I'll remember it forever."

Even if it was just a fleeting whim, even if it was an irresponsible offer, he was deeply moved by Dick's feelings. It was far better than being coldly told goodbye.

"Even if I never see you again, I'll never forget you."

Dick looked down and muttered just one word, "Yeah."

CHAPTER 23

About four hours after the chaos began, a news report about the Schelger Prison riot aired on the radio.

"Breaking news from Schelger Prison, California, where a fight between Black and Latino inmates has erupted into a full-scale riot. Authorities have initiated a full lockdown, but tensions remain high. Reports indicate that multiple guards are currently trapped inside the affected cell blocks, and concerns for their safety are mounting. The entire facility is now effectively paralyzed as emergency protocols remain in effect."

"At this rate, the National Guard's going to be deployed sooner than expected," Dick said after hearing the news.

The two of them went to a storage room and gathered canned food and drinks at random to secure supplies, then brought everything back to the small room. Neither of them had much of an appetite, but Dick told Yuuto to eat while he still could, so Yuuto reluctantly agreed to have lunch.

Dick had made porridge of sorts by boiling oatmeal and Spam in a kettle. The container, a coffee cup, left much to be desired, but the taste wasn't half bad.

"This makes me feel like I'm out camping," Yuuto said. "If we had sleeping bags, it'd be perfect."

Dick gave a faint smile as he scooped up the porridge with a teaspoon. "Reminds me of army field training."

"For me, it brings back memories of summer camp as a kid. Every year, my dad forced me to go, and I hated it. I was terrible at group activities."

Dick gave Yuuto a curious look.

"But you're good at getting along with others."

"I just make it look that way. I can get by on the surface, but I'm no good at forming deep bonds. That's why I've never been good at making friends or dating."

"It's not like you never had a lover, though, right? When was your last relationship?"

"About two years ago. I dated a pretty brunette Paul introduced me to, but she dumped me after three months. Said I cared more about work than her, that I was boring."

Dick raised a brow slightly and shook his head with a touch of sympathy. "The classic 'Which is more important, your job or me?' line. I never understood why people feel the need to compare. It's like asking someone to choose between bread and water—you need both."

"You've never had any of your boyfriends say that to you? That you loved your job more than them?" Yuuto asked jokingly.

"Nope," Dick said in all seriousness. "In fact, Noel always told me to choose the mission over him if it came down to it. I think he meant that, given the nature of our work, we couldn't let personal feelings get in the way."

Every time Dick mentioned Noel, Yuuto felt a quiet ache in his chest.

"Did you date anyone besides him?"

"There were a few I just slept with, but Noel was the only one I'd call a lover," Dick answered. "Before I met him, I didn't really understand romantic feelings. He taught me a lot."

No matter what Yuuto asked, Dick's answers always came back to Noel. Whenever he praised him, Yuuto felt he was being denied, even though it wasn't a comparison.

He knew the reason: he was in love with Dick. Not just as a friend, he was genuinely drawn to him.

He didn't know when it started, and the reason didn't matter. Even if he didn't want to admit it, it was an undeniable fact. He wasn't gay, but he was definitely feeling romantic emotions for Dick, and in his heart, he longed to be wanted in return.

Wanting to change the subject, Yuuto said, "Once we get out of here, if you find Corvus again, are you going to kill him?"

"Yeah. That's practically the only reason I'm still alive." His voice carried not even the slightest hesitation.

"You spent a whole year getting close to him. Didn't your feelings ever waver? From where I stood, you two looked genuinely close."

"I was acting to make him let his guard down. If I'd let even a hint of hostility show, he'd have noticed. Just like he was pretending to be the honorable Nathan, I was pretending to be 'Dick: someone who only opened up to Nathan.'"

The willpower it took to suppress that hatred and befriend the man he wanted to kill was nothing short of incredible.

"Do you think less of me, knowing I can kill so easily?" Dick asked.

Yuuto shook his head weakly. He couldn't bring himself to condemn Dick, not after Corvus had killed his lover and friends. Besides, Dick had surely taken lives during his time in the military. If one were to judge him on ethics alone, then all the killings committed in the name of justice and the governments that ordered them should also be condemned.

"I don't. I don't have the right to," Yuuto began softly. "But, if I could choose, I wouldn't want you to kill anyone else. Not because life is sacred or because it's a sin or anything like that… I just feel like every time you hurt someone, it wounds you too."

Dick said nothing. His silence made Yuuto feel as if he were silently asking, 'What do you think you understand about me?' The oppressive silence weighed heavily on the room. Feeling suffocated, Yuuto stood up.

"Where are you going?" Dick asked.

"I'm just going to check the storage room. It gets cold at night, and maybe I can find something to use as a blanket—"

Yuuto's excuse was cut off when Dick grabbed his hand.

"Don't go."

"I-I'll be right back."

"No." Dick yanked his arm forcefully, and Yuuto lost his balance, stumbling forward. He ended up dropping down right onto Dick's lap, straddling his knees without meaning to.

"The hell was that for?" Yuuto exclaimed.

"Stay here. I want you here," he pleaded. "Don't leave me."

Dick said it with a serious face, and Yuuto was shaken. He thought for a moment he was being teased again, but his gaze remained entirely sincere. Dick reached out gently. His large hands cupped both of Yuuto's cheeks, and Yuuto's heartbeat quickened.

"Yuuto." Dick pulled his face closer, and their foreheads touched. Yuuto's face was slightly higher than Dick's. Looking up at him, Dick swept back his black hair with an impatient hand. "Stay with me. I am begging you."

Those words were so unlike him. His eyes looked pained, and his breath was hot. Dick's conflict came through naturally. It was easy to understand because Yuuto felt the same impulse.

He also wanted to touch. To feel.

A man's desire can peak in an instant with no warning, triggered by something small: a look, a glance, a careless word, a tone of voice, a scent, the color of skin. Something about him had flipped Dick's switch, and knowing Dick wanted him made Yuuto unable to hold himself back. He pressed his lips to the bridge of Dick's nose in a hesitant kiss.

"Yuuto. Don't tempt me," Dick's raspy voice was full of desire. "I'm already at my limit."

Yuuto wanted him to cast off restraint. Growing impatient, he kissed him on the lips this time.

"Yuuto."

"Don't you get that I'm at my limit too?" He pleaded desperately. Dick looked surprised and gave a small shake of his head.

"You're not gay. You're just getting swept up by me," Dick groaned. "You'll regret it."

"It's true I'm not gay. I've never once wanted to sleep with a guy before," Yuuto said with a quiet intensity. "But I want you. I want to touch you. I want you to touch me. Because I love you, isn't that enough? Am I not good enough for you?"

Dick reached out and caressed Yuuto's cheek with the gentleness of someone handling something fragile.

"No, it's *me* who's not good enough. The way I am now, I can't promise you anything. I don't have the right to hold you."

Yuuto pondered the word "right." Perhaps Dick still held onto Noel's memory in his heart, and felt that embracing Yuuto would be a betrayal of that.

"I don't want anything. I won't ask for promises. Just think about me, just for now, just while we're here. That's enough, that's all I am asking."

There was no guarantee that tomorrow would come for either of them, not like today. Their time together was running out. And that was exactly why Yuuto wanted to share these feelings at this very moment.

"I don't want justifications or excuses. Hesitation and doubt only get in the way. If you even like me a little, then take me, Dick."

Dick was speechless at Yuuto's straightforward invitation.

"You made me say all this even though I'm not gay. You're not going to say no now, are you?"

"I give up. You're more of a man than I am."

Throwing away his doubts, Dick kissed him fiercely. Yuuto responded with just as much passion. Dick's skillful, burning kiss left Yuuto breathless, like he was drowning.

As their tongues entwined, Yuuto tugged out the hair tie holding Dick's hair, letting his dazzling blond locks fall loose. It made the already beautiful man look even sexier. Yuuto buried his fingers in Dick's hair, combing through it, stroking it, relishing the feel to his heart's content.

After the long kiss, Dick took off Yuuto's shirt.

"Your skin is really beautiful. It feels amazing, like velvet," Dick murmured in a dreamy voice as he touched Yuuto's skin.

Yuuto's lips curved up involuntarily.

"What?"

"You teased me before," he said against Dick's lips, "saying I was as smooth as ivory."

Dick laughed too and pulled him into a hug. "I give up. Your memory is unbeatable. But I wasn't teasing. I was just pretending to, while saying how I really felt."

"And here I thought you saw me as nothing but an annoying FBI punk?"

"Maybe in my head, but my feelings were different. You always got under my skin, and I hated how much you shook me up."

While talking, Dick began to shower kisses from Yuuto's neck down to his shoulder, then to his chest. Straddling Dick's thighs, Yuuto arched his back in response to the sweet sensations.

Wherever Dick's lips touched, Yuuto's body lit up with pleasure. When Dick sucked on his nipple, a heat bloomed deep in his lower body, and even his groin began to burn. It was the first time his chest had ever felt that good, and though surprised, he adored how honestly his body responded to Dick's caresses.

Yuuto lay back as Dick tugged down his pants and underwear. Without hesitation, Dick lowered his head between Yuuto's legs, as if it were the most natural thing in the world.

"Don't," Yuuto said, pushing his head away. "Oral sex is dangerous. We can't say for sure that there's no chance of HIV infection yet."

"You're fine. You're definitely not infected. I guarantee it."

Overwhelmed by Dick's insistence, Yuuto gave in. Still, he made one thing clear: no finishing in the mouth, just in case.

Once Yuuto relaxed, Dick took his arousal into his mouth. The sensation of warm, wet heat enveloping him was almost too much. A soft tongue followed, slick and slow, coiling around him in a rhythm that sent waves of unbearable pleasure through his core.

Yuuto's breath hitched. Dick's tongue worked him with focused skill, drawing him to the edge in no time.

"Dick, let go," Yuuto cried, shaking his head. Words tumbled out in between broken moans, ones he wasn't even sure were right. "Y-you can't!"

Yuuto gripped his hair, and Dick reluctantly pulled away, finishing him off with his hand. Yuuto arched back as a thick release spilled from him, his body twitching in the aftermath. As he caught his breath, Dick wiped the mess off with his own shirt. Still lying down, Yuuto reached out for him.

"Let me do you, too."

Dick chuckled softly. "Don't push yourself."

But Yuuto ignored him, tugging open the front of his pants. Dick's cock was already fully hard beneath his underwear.

"Don't say I shouldn't do anything. You're like this, and you expect me to just leave it?"

"Yuuto. It's really okay. I'm fine—"

"Shut up."

He pulled down Dick's underwear in one swift motion. The size and thickness made him hesitate, but he leaned forward and took him in as deeply as possible. He couldn't fit all of it, but that didn't stop him, and just like Dick had done for him, Yuuto devoted himself to pleasuring him, moving his lips and tongue around it. The soft skin felt good on his tongue, and the apprehension he expected never came.

As his lips moved with growing fervor, Dick's hand slid from Yuuto's back down to his ass. His fingers gently stroked the space between his cheeks and balls, and the jolt of forbidden pleasure that followed made Yuuto's spine shiver.

Dick licked his fingers, then traced around Yuuto's entrance, coaxing the tight hole open.

"Wait," Yuuto moaned, releasing Dick's cock. Still, the slick finger slipped inside. His muscles clenched around it on instinct, gripping tightly, hungry, and asking for more. Dick let out a quiet breath, admiring the man before him and Yuuto flushed hot with shame. "Not there."

"I'll just touch it a little," Dick whispered, entranced. "It won't hurt. Lift your hips."

Mortified, but desperate to give Dick what he wanted, Yuuto raised his hips. Dick's finger went deeper, gently parting the wet inner walls. The slick, wet sounds filled the space. The finger curled and moved inside, and heat bloomed in Yuuto's lower belly again. He'd just come minutes ago, yet the pressure was already building again, his body betraying him.

As Dick worked him open, the fear and hesitation melted away. Yuuto trusted him. Sitting up, he climbed back over Dick's lap and took hold of his still-wet cock, guiding it to himself.

"Hey, what are you doing?" Dick asked, wide-eyed. "That's not why I touched you."

"Isn't this the natural thing to do?" Yuuto said. "I'll go slow. It's fine."

Dick looked up at him, helpless. "And once it's in, then what? If I lose control and start thrusting hard, I'll hurt you. You know I can't hold back when I'm turned on."

"You won't hurt me."

Even as he said it, Yuuto wondered if he was being cruel—asking to be entered but demanding Dick stay still. It felt unfair.

"Sorry. If you really don't want to, we can stop." He tried to pull away, guilt creeping in. "I just thought… this might make you happy. But it's fine, forget it."

"You're seriously going to turn me on like this and stop?" Dick pulled him back, gripping his waist. "Fine. I'll try not to move. Just come here already. I want you so bad it's driving me insane."

A sweet kiss sealed it.

Relieved by Dick's consent, Yuuto slowly sank back down. But saliva wasn't enough; it didn't go in smoothly, and his body would tense up every time Dick was about to penetrate him. He paused, took a deep breath, and tried to relax. Dick helped, running gentle hands over his skin, murmuring softly.

Eventually, Yuuto loosened, and the thick head slipped in with a wet pop. The rest followed more easily, until he had all of it inside him. The pressure and ache were intense. Yuuto winced, his brows knitting together. He took several shallow breaths.

"That's too much, isn't it? Don't force yourself."

As Yuuto struggled to breathe through it, Dick kissed him softly, trying to soothe. Even though he was inside and unable to move, even though he was likely aching too, Dick held back.

And Yuuto knew—he really meant it when he said he wouldn't hurt him

Moved by his kindness, Yuuto couldn't stay still. Enduring the discomfort, he began to move his hips. As long as he didn't thrust in and out, the degree of pain didn't change much. When he twisted his hips with Dick buried to the base, Dick let out a low grunt.

"It's like a dream. You, riding me like this," Dick said, "shaking your hips like that."

"Did you ever fantasize about having sex with me? Confess."

Yuuto tightened his inner muscles, and Dick groaned again. It made Yuuto feel like he was some wicked woman toying with a man in the palm of her hand.

"I did. I imagined you taking me all the way to the base, begging sweetly for more, to give it to you harder, while you moved your hips. Just picturing you, always so aloof, losing yourself in my arms… my dick would get hard in an instant. I can't count how many times I jerked off in the top bunk after you fell asleep."

He knew Dick was exaggerating, but there was something pitiful and hopelessly male about his words that made it strangely funny.

"Hey, don't laugh," Dick admonished, giving a slight upward thrust. "Get turned on with me."

"I already am—"

Dick's large hand started to stroke his penis in rhythm, reigniting the flame in Yuuto's body. Worried he'd be the only one to climax again, Yuuto responded by rocking his body with deep thrusts, matching Dick's pace.

Dick's hand moved in sync with Yuuto's rhythm. So lost in it, the pain vanished before he realized. Instead, his insides pulsed with a deep ache, and being joined with Dick felt good.

"Dick," Yuuto let out a long moan. "I'm about to come again."

"You've been leaking nonstop. You're soaked." His teasing made Yuuto's cheeks flush. The clear, sticky fluid dripped down Dick's fingers—it was the first time it had ever happened like this.

"Your ass is starting to feel good too?"

He nodded honestly.

"Can I move now?" Dick asked desperately and Yuuto could only nod, shaking his head frantically.

Dick started thrusting upward in small, quick motions. There was no pain—only sharp pleasure that made Yuuto's hips buzz and go numb.

Soon, Yuuto was moaning nonstop. "Dick, I can't. I'm gonna come."

"Me too, me too," Dick muttered, almost incoherently. "You feel too good inside, I can't hold it back anymore."

As both his front and back were stimulated in rhythm, the pleasure surged all at once and then plummeted, overwhelming him with a climax so intense it blurred his senses. It was a level of ecstasy he'd never felt during sex before.

Just as Yuuto arched and came, Dick released deep inside him. In the narrow room, only their ragged breathing could be heard. When the waves of excitement subsided, Yuuto clung to Dick's shoulder. Dick held him tightly in return.

"Are you okay? Does it still hurt?"

"I'm fine. Can we stay like this for a while?"

When he nuzzled against Dick's cheek, Dick ran his fingers gently through Yuuto's hair. "For as long as you want."

Wrapped in Dick's warmth, Yuuto's body and heart began to loosen. He had finally caught the real Dick. He had finally touched the heart that had always felt so far away. Yuuto was filled with a deep sense of satisfaction.

Because they were still connected, Dick's penis began to harden again inside Yuuto. Dick, concerned, tried to pull out, but Yuuto stopped him.

"You're still a beginner. Don't push yourself. It's going to hurt later."

"I don't care if it does. I want to feel more of you. Once isn't enough."

Usually, Yuuto wouldn't have been able to say something so bold. But they didn't have much time left. He threw away his shame and honestly expressed what he felt.

"Make love to me over and over so I'll never forget you. Please, Dick."

Dick sighed and combed his hands through Yuuto's hair. "Don't talk so much," he whispered. "Every time you say something, I fall a little more under your spell."

"Must be an honor to be the one who can break Dick Burnford," Yuuto said with a small smile. Dick smiled too, and their lips met naturally. They kissed gently, playfully nipping at each other, slowly intertwining their tongues as if savoring the moment. Having already climaxed once, there was no urgency left between them.

"Can you turn around?" Dick whispered, and Yuuto nodded. He lifted his hips to break the connection and straddled Dick's thighs with his back to him. As he guided Dick's length back inside, the remnants of their previous round spilled from within him. It acted as a natural lubricant, letting him take Dick in more easily than the first time.

"Is this good?"

"Yeah. Don't do anything. Just lean back on me."

Dick's lips moved passionately across Yuuto's nape and shoulders. His right hand stroked Yuuto's cock, while his left teased the hard peak of his chest.

"Dick, I don't want it to be just me. I want you to feel it too," Yuuto said, writhing on Dick's lap.

"I do. Even if I stay still, your insides squeeze me so perfectly. It's unbearable."

Still, Yuuto knew—as a man, Dick must have the urge to thrust hard. He was probably restraining himself so he wouldn't hurt Yuuto's body, still weak from being sick.

Yuuto wanted to make Dick feel good too. That thought came naturally. He began moving his hips up and down, gently stimulating the hardness inside him.

Dick gave a low groan and held onto Yuuto's waist.

"Does it feel good?"

"Yeah. But don't push yourself."

"How many times do I have to tell you? I want this—" The more Yuuto moved, the more their earlier release leaked out, adding to the wet, obscene sounds that echoed with each motion. The noise only excited him more, and he continued rocking without thinking, moving his hips fervently.

In return, Dick stroked Yuuto's slick cock with his right hand and cupped the sack beneath with his left. His large hands rubbed the two firm orbs together.

"Dick, n-no," he stuttered. "Not there, I don't want this."

"What don't you want? You're feeling it so much."

He couldn't say it felt too good. The pleasure was overwhelming, and he could feel the part of him wrapped around Dick's cock twitching and pulsing. It embarrassed him, but even that embarrassment soon dissolved into something sweet.

"Don't touch me so much, it's too much…" Shaking his head in protest, Yuuto gasped as Dick bit down gently on the lobe of his ear from behind.

"Let it be too much," Dick groaned. "I want to ruin you completely."

Dick's ragged breath tickled his eardrum. Yuuto tilted his head, seeking his lips. Their tongues tangled slowly, descending together into soft, heady pleasure. It wasn't frantic or greedy sex driven by lust. It was slow, tender, like they were making love in the warm haze of an afternoon nap. It melted Yuuto's body and heart in the gentlest way.

It wasn't about the climax anymore. They took their time, drawing it out with long, quiet intervals. They looked into each other's eyes, kissed, and held hands. This achingly sweet happiness felt unreal, like their harsh lives until now had been a lie.

"It really would've been better if we'd had a nice, clean bed."

Yuuto, resting his head on Dick's lap, heard the odd comment fall from above.

Dick sat against the wall, wearing only his pants. Outside, chaos still reigned, but here, it was quiet. It was like the world had left them behind—or maybe this was the center of it.

"What do you mean?" Yuuto asked.

"The place I first made love to you," Dick replied, as if it were the most obvious thing in the world. "Never thought it'd be on some filthy cardboard in a room like this."

"You're more of a romantic than I thought," Yuuto laughed.

"All men are," Dick said, tugging lightly at Yuuto's ear.

Silence set in for a few minutes; they both knew their time together was limited now, and words seemed to fail them. "Dick," Yuuto said at last. "Once you're out of here, you should rest. Just take a day off. Go somewhere peaceful, maybe the beach."

Yuuto was worried. He had a feeling that once they were out, Dick would throw himself right into the chase for Corvus again.

"The beach, huh?" Dick said. "It's been a long time since I've seen it."

"What about that beach house you bought with your friends? Did you sell it?"

"No. It's still there. It's in a town called Wilmington, at a place called Kure Beach. The sand was white, and the view was beautiful… but I won't go back. Not alone. There's no point."

Yuuto gently took his hand. Returning alone to a place filled with memories of friends and lovers, it was too painful. Only the good times would resurface, and the loneliness would hit even harder.

"Dick. If it's okay…" he sat up and faced him. "Could you tell me your real name?"

Dick quietly shook his head. "I can't. I'm sorry."

Part of it was likely because of his work as a CIA contractor, but

Yuuto felt that wasn't the only reason. Dick didn't want to reveal his true identity because he didn't see this as the beginning of something between them. To him, it was the end.

"If I somehow make it out of here and want to see you again, what should I do?"

"You shouldn't. I don't know what lies ahead for me. I can't even make the smallest promise to you," Dick looked away. "Forget about me. That's what's best for you."

Yuuto couldn't blame him for being cold. Before they had even touched, he had already accepted that. He had reached out to Dick knowing full well what he might lose.

"I don't want anything. I won't ask for promises. Just think about me, just for now, just while we're here. That's enough, that's all I am asking."

Dick had said he lived only for revenge against Corvus. But if he ever achieved that goal, then what would he do?

Yuuto hoped he could live a second life, even if it wasn't with him. He hoped Dick would love someone again, like he had loved Noel, and find peace.

Yuuto leaned against his shoulder. He had so much he wanted to say, but no matter what he said, it felt like it would only make things harder. So he stayed quiet.

He felt a gentle kiss against his temple. When he looked up, their eyes met.

"Get some sleep. You must be tired." Dick wrapped his arms around Yuuto's back, and he closed his eyes.

He wished, deep in his heart, that this night would never end.

CHAPTER 24

"Wake up, Yuuto."

Yuuto's eyes flew open as someone shook his shoulder. Startled, he found a man peering down at him—and for a moment, he panicked, thinking he was back in his regular cell.

"It's me, Dick," the man said, taking off his black sunglasses with a smirk at the groggy Yuuto.

"Don't scare me like that."

Yuuto's reaction was understandable—Dick was dressed head to toe in a guard's black uniform, complete with matching shoes and a cap. Where had he gotten all that?

"Where did you get that outfit?"

"It was in the backpack from the start. I had Guthrie stash it for me in advance, for the escape. The National Guard's about to storm the place."

Yuuto jumped to his feet, stunned by the news. "Already? What time is it?"

"Seven in the morning. Seems they moved up the operation because of the high number of guards still trapped inside and the fact that the rioting isn't letting up. They've even started live coverage on the radio."

Sure enough, the radio was reporting on the Schelger Prison riot:

"*—Schelger Prison remains surrounded by over a thousand National Guard troops, and the situation is extremely tense. The inmates are refusing to comply with the police's orders to surrender, and there's no indication that they intend to release the five guards* *they've taken hostage. Smoke can be seen rising from multiple housing units, but the full extent of the situation inside remains unclear—Ah! The troops that had been standing by are now on the move! They're approaching the entrances of each block. It appears a full-on assault is about to begin! I repeat, the operation to suppress the riot by force is now underway—*"

Dick turned off the radio. Slinging the backpack stuffed with his prison uniform over one shoulder, he looked back at Yuuto.

"Time to go."

The moment had come—Yuuto's final goodbye to Dick.

"Dick—" He wanted to say something, but his chest was so tight he couldn't speak.

"I'm glad I met you," Dick said fervently, pulling Yuuto into a hug so tight it felt like his spine might snap. "No matter where you are, I'll be wishing you luck."

Yuuto let out a shaky breath. "Me too."

When Dick finally let go, he kissed Yuuto. The kiss was fierce and aching, a painful reminder of their parting.

"I want to take you with me," Dick lamented between kisses. "I don't want to let you go."

The anguish in his voice brought tears to Yuuto's eyes. He wasn't the only one hurting, Dick felt it too. The pain in his chest wasn't his alone.

"I want to go with you, too. But I can't. I just can't."

"I know, I'm just being selfish."

Even if he left with Dick now, they'd be separated again soon. Once Dick helped him escape, he'd disappear in pursuit of Corvus.

Dick abruptly ended the kiss, as if cutting off his own feelings, and put his sunglasses back on.

"Stay here for a while. Don't go outside until the chaos dies down," Dick instructed. "And one last thing: negotiate with the FBI from a position of strength. You know more about Corvus than you realize. He slipped up a few times in front of you because he got too into playing Nathan."

"What do you mean?"

"The way he boasted about the inner workings of the prison, about the darkness festering in this place, that's where you'll find Corvus."

As Dick opened the door, Yuuto shouted without thinking—

"Wait, Dick!"

Dick turned around. But the sunglasses covered his eyes, hiding the blue that always gave away his feelings. Now, Yuuto couldn't read him at all.

Will we ever meet again? Will fate allow our paths to cross once more? He wanted to ask many things, but held back, forcing a smile instead.

"No matter where you are, I'll pray for your peace of mind. For your happiness."

Dick nodded, then opened the door. After ensuring no one was outside, he took off running without looking back. Yuuto stepped up to the shut door, bracing both hands against it and hanging his head.

The aching hollowness in his chest felt like someone had gouged out a piece of him. All he could do now was pray—pray with everything he had—that Dick would escape safely.

That was all Yuuto could do now.

The Schelger Prison riot was completely suppressed three hours later by the deployment of the National Guard.

With eight dead and over 300 injured, the incident ranked as the second most violent prison riot in United States history, following the 1971 Attica Prison uprising in New York. Including related disturbances that broke out at other prisons, the total number of casualties was expected to climb even higher.

The tragedy reignited national debates about racially segregated housing in prisons and the urgent need for modern security systems, such as remotely operated tear gas dispersal units. These topics dominated headlines and news broadcasts. For the prison administration, however, the most immediate problem was what to do with the inmates from the West Block, which had suffered devastating damage and was now unusable.

As an emergency measure, it was decided that until repairs could be completed, roughly 200 inmates would be housed in the East Block, while the remaining 1,000 would be relocated to nearby state, county, and federal prisons.

Starting the very next day, busloads of prisoners began to be transferred out of Schelger.

During this chaotic process, Yuuto received a visit from FBI agent Mark Heiden. Normally, inmate visits require a guard to be present, but whatever strings Heiden had pulled resulted in the meeting room being occupied only by him and his subordinates.

Heiden, dressed in a perfectly pressed designer suit, greeted Yuuto with a smug, theatrical smile. “What a commotion! I was really shocked when I heard the news,” he said, straight-faced. “But I’m glad you’re safe. Seeing you in good health is a relief.”

The feigned concern irritated Yuuto. It was obvious Heiden didn’t care about his well-being, only whether the riot had interfered with the investigation.

When Heiden asked about any developments in the search for Corvus, Yuuto delivered the lines he had carefully prepared in advance. His message, in essence, was this:

I’ve figured out who Corvus is.

But since he was impersonating someone else, I don’t know his real name or background. There was also a CIA agent in the prison, embedded just like I was, who was tracking Corvus. That agent had a lot of intel on him. During the chaos of the riot, Corvus escaped. The CIA agent broke out too, in pursuit.

Both of them have vanished.

Heiden's face went pale, and he grilled Yuuto, "Why didn't you report this sooner?"

"I was only certain when the riot broke out," Yuuto replied. "I had no time to contact anyone."

When Heiden demanded more detailed information, Yuuto firmly shook his head.

"No. Mr. Heiden, let's make a deal. I'll give you everything I know… in exchange for my release. Let me out of here, and I'll tell you everything."

"Lennix, that's not something we can just do. There are procedures to follow—"

"If you change your mind, come back."

With that, Yuuto cut the conversation short and left the visiting room. Whether the FBI would bite or brush it off as nonsense, Yuuto couldn't tell. It was all up to fate now.

"Yuuto!"

As he exited the Central Block and walked down the hallway of the West Block, Mickey came running up to him. He had a large bruise on his face but otherwise seemed uninjured and in good spirits. Apparently, when the riot began, Mickey had run all over the West Block looking for Yuuto.

"I got my transfer orders. I'm headed to San Quentin. I leave on today's bus."

"San Quentin, huh. That's the closest prison to here."

"Yeah. Can't even get a proper breath of fresh air before being shipped out. Take care, alright?" Mickey stuck out his hand, and Yuuto gave him a firm shake.

Since Yuuto was set to be transferred to the East Block, he was now in the position of seeing others off.

"Mickey, thanks for everything," Yuuto said sincerely. "Your energy always gave me a lift. Do your best over there."

"Yeah. Gotta start the hustle from scratch, but I'll find my way," he said, wholly unconcerned. "Anyway, Nathan and that bastard Dick really pulled it off, didn't they?"

Amid the chaos of the National Guard's storming of the prison, many inmates had attempted to escape, but nearly all were captured and returned with the exception of two: Dick Burnford and Nathan Clark.

Word among the inmates was that the two had coordinated the escape and slipped away together. Some even praised them, saying if anyone could pull it off, it'd be those two.

"Hope they don't get caught," Mickey murmured with a hint of sadness. "I wonder where they are now."

Yuuto clapped him on the shoulder. "They're fine. If it's those two, there's no need to worry."

"Yeah."

Mickey nodded firmly, and seeing that, Yuuto felt a pang of mixed emotion. To Mickey, Nathan would probably always remain a respectable, admirable man. Yuuto thought of Nathan's gentle smile, and deep down, he wished he had never learned the truth about who Nathan really was.

After parting with Mickey, Yuuto headed toward Block C. The air inside the building still reeked faintly of smoke, and fire extinguisher residue clung white to surfaces everywhere.

He peeked into Neto's cell and found him sitting alone on his bed, reading a book.

"Neto," Yuuto called out. "Got a minute?"

Neto looked up and gestured for him to sit.

"How's your injury?" Yuuto asked, looking at his plastered foot.

"I am fine," he said. "This much is nothing."

Neto had injured his leg during the fight with BB and the others. The bone had a hairline fracture, but he was getting around just fine with crutches. With the Black Soldiers mostly transferred out to other facilities, tensions between inmates had noticeably eased, and the prison was slowly returning to a sense of normalcy.

"How about Tonia?"

"She's in the rec room. The Sisters are throwing her a farewell party. You should stop by later, she'd be happy to see you."

Tonia was scheduled to be transferred to a federal prison on tomorrow's bus.

"Got it," Yuuto agreed. "You worried about being separated from her?"

"Nah. Compared to state prisons, federal ones are paradise. Plus, she's got people there too. She'll be fine."

He said it lightly, but his expression looked lonely. Clearly, Tonia still weighed heavily on his mind.

"Yuuto, wanna go out to the yard? I feel like breathing some fresh air."

Neto stood with the help of his crutches, and the two of them walked out of Block C together.

Despite all the chaos that had happened, the yard was full of inmates playing soccer or lounging under the sun like nothing had changed. As long as one didn't think about the wreckage in the West Block, it looked just like any other day.

They sat down together on a bench near the basketball court.

"Nice weather. Feels good," Neto said, narrowing his eyes against the bright blue sky.

Yuuto tilted his head back and looked up, too. The sky was so clear it almost hurt to look at—so vivid it brought Dick's eyes to mind.

"Must be tough, with Dick gone," Neto said, eyeing him.

It was like he'd read Yuuto's thoughts, and he flinched slightly.

"People say he escaped with Nathan, but I don't buy it," Neto said. "Dick's not the kind of guy who'd team up with someone like him."

"You didn't like Nathan?" Yuuto was genuinely surprised. "Most people thought he was great."

"It's not that I didn't like him," Neto said, shaking his head in distaste. "There was just something… off about him. Can't explain it, but he creeped me out."

Yuuto was impressed by Neto's sharp instincts. It was like the man had some kind of sixth sense.

"If there were anyone Dick would've invited to escape with him, it'd be you," Neto said.

"Wow," Yuuto laughed. "Are you psychic or something?"

Neto turned toward him, eyes wide. "So he did ask you? Why didn't you go?"

"I wanted to. But I said no. I want to walk out the front door of this place with my head held high. I don't want to live my life on the run from the law. Still, I might have a shot at release."

Neto's face lit up. "You found the guy you were looking for?"

"Yeah," he nodded. "But I still don't know how it'll go. It's fifty-fifty at best."

"You'll be fine," Neto said before sharply looking up. "Look, Yuuto! A swallow."

Neto pointed, and Yuuto followed his gaze to see a swallow cutting gracefully through the sky.

"Looks like it's enjoying the wind," Yuuto murmured, filled with longing and awe.

Neto reached out and ruffled Yuuto's hair with a rough hand. "You're just like that swallow. You'll be free soon too. You'll soar wherever you want. Believe it. Fortune favors those who believe. Give up, and luck will leave you."

"Yeah..." Yuuto murmured. "You're right."

He realized that Neto *was* right. That belief, having faith, was a kind of strength. The future isn't something you wait for. It's something you take for yourself.

As if burning it into his memory, Yuuto fixed his eyes on the swallow spreading its wings wide against the blue sky.

CHAPTER 25

Two weeks later, Yuuto Lennix was released from Schelger Prison. Just as he had hoped, he walked out through the front gates. But it wasn't because a deal with the FBI had been finalized—instead, the real killer in the Paul McClane murder case had been arrested, proving Yuuto's innocence.

Although the FBI took credit for reopening the investigation and tracking down the true culprit, Mark Heiden's patronizing attitude rubbed Yuuto the wrong way. He couldn't help but suspect that the FBI had already identified the real killer long ago and had simply been holding that card in reserve, ready to play it when it best suited their interests.

Still, a promise is a promise. Yuuto kept his word and promptly provided the FBI with everything he knew: not only Corvus's physical features and the fact that he had once led the cult group White Heaven, but also the suspicion that Schelger Prison's warden, Richard Corning, had helped Corvus escape. Yuuto withheld only the information that would personally endanger Dick—everything else, he laid bare.

What happened next took him completely by surprise: the FBI offered to recruit him as a special agent. With his strong track record as a DEA agent and, more importantly, his rare experience of direct contact with the elusive Corvus, Yuuto was considered a valuable asset to their ongoing efforts.

Yuuto knew the offer was partly driven by the FBI's rivalry with the CIA, but that didn't matter to him. He chose not to return to the DEA but to accept the offer to join the FBI.

He stayed in Arizona for only three days after his release, spending precious time with his family. His stepbrother, Paco, even took time off to come from L.A. to be with them. Along with Leti, Paco, and Leti's sister's family, everyone wholeheartedly celebrated Yuuto's freedom.

On the morning of the third day, Yuuto calmed his tearful younger sister Lupita, who didn't want him to leave, and headed to the airport with Paco behind the wheel.

Yuuto was set to begin training at the FBI Academy in Quantico, Virginia. Although the training was mostly a formality, it was still necessary for him to receive his official credentials as a federal agent.

At the airport, he shared a firm embrace with Paco before parting with a smile and boarding his flight. Somewhere during the flight, Yuuto had a strange dream.

Dick was standing on a beautiful beach, dressed in a white shirt and jeans. Holding his sneakers in one hand, he walked slowly along the shoreline, letting the waves soak the cuffs of his jeans without a care.

Noticing Yuuto, Dick beckoned to him. "Come on in, Yuuto. The water's cold, but it feels good."

Yuuto nodded and started running toward him, but then—

"*Excuse me, sir.* Sorry to disturb your rest, but we'll be landing shortly. Please fasten your seatbelt."

The flight attendant's voice pulled him from his dream.

There was a flicker of disappointment as Yuuto opened his eyes. Yet, he couldn't shake the quiet happiness that lingered—because in that dream, Dick had looked at peace. That alone was comforting. Through the window, the sky stretched wide, blue and full of clouds. As Yuuto gazed out, a renewed sense of freedom settled over him.

If I keep chasing Corvus... maybe I'll see Dick again someday.

The thread that had once seemed severed between them wasn't completely broken. Yuuto had been given a rare second chance.

He felt as though their futures, once thought to run in opposite directions, might again trace the same arc, stretching far into the distance. And he was ready to bet on that possibility.

Hope and anxiety churned in his chest, but there was no fear. His belief in himself would shape the road ahead.

It was hope that would carve open the path of fate.

Yuuto's new life was about to begin.

Afterword

Hello—or perhaps, nice to meet you. I'm Aida Saki. Thank you very much for picking up my humble work.

Deadlock marks my fifteenth book overall, but it's my first publication with Chara Bunko. Despite this being my debut with the publisher, I've gone and set the story in a gritty prison. I was also given a generous number of pages for the afterword... I imagine the editor's thoughtfulness was behind that, probably hoping I'd explain (justify?) *why a prison story*. So, I'll do my best to explain it all here.

Prison stories—I've loved them for some reason since long ago, especially in film. I think the first prison movie I really got hooked on was *Midnight Express*, directed by Alan Parker. It's based on a true story about a young American man who gets arrested while trying to smuggle marijuana out of Turkey and is thrown into a Turkish prison. The overwhelming bleakness and utter lack of salvation in that film left a powerful impression on me.

On the other hand, I also love prison break films with uplifting endings, like *Escape to Victory* starring Stallone (although that's technically more of a prisoner-of-war camp story). Whether the protagonist joins forces with others or meticulously plans their escape alone, the catharsis when they finally overcome hardship and win their freedom is just unparalleled.

This isn't a movie, but I also adored the *Ryōzanpaku* arc in Shinji Wada's classic manga Delinquent Girl Detective *(Sukeban Deka)*. In this arc, the heroine, Saki Asamiya, infiltrates a mysterious juvenile detention center. The nostalgic "worm bath" scene is unforgettable. So, I've watched quite a lot of prison-themed films over the years, and honestly, I believe there's no such thing as a bad prison movie. I think what makes prison stories so compelling is that they come preloaded with all kinds of dramatic tension: justice and evil, crime and punishment, trust and betrayal, despair and hope. It's precisely because the setting is such a closed-off, claustrophobic world that all these elements get densely packed together, resulting in rich, intense human drama almost by default.

It's a world of men only, thick with testosterone. And on top of that, it's a lawless jungle where it's eat or be eaten (laughs). In a place with no escape, these men are forced to confront others and themselves head-on. Enemies are made, but so are allies. At times, hatred blooms; at other times, friendship takes root. And every once in a while, by some mistake or sheer accident, the flower of love might even bloom.

There's something deeply captivating about watching these men desperately try to preserve their pride, even while drenched in humiliation. Or seeing them stubbornly cling to their sense of self through failure after failure. I'm just really drawn to that kind of portrayal. I love watching men who fight, and there's something strangely sexy about strong men when they're completely broken and wounded.

Back around last fall, I had the chance to write an essay about my prison moe for the magazine Shousetsu Chara. I ended up rambling passionately about it then, too. And yet, I still have so much more to say. Once you fall into a moe pit, there's no climbing out—it's a bottomless swamp (laughs).

And so, after passionately expressing my love for prison stories to my editor, I was given the opportunity to write this book. I had always dreamed of one day writing a prison story, so I'm truly happy that dream finally came true.

That said, no matter how happy I was, actually writing it turned out to be quite the challenge (of course). I started drafting around Spring of this year. Before I began, I was so excited, but once I actually started writing, I realized how incredibly difficult it was. It ended up taking me longer to finish than any previous work.

This was also the first time I wrote a story from the beginning with a sequel in mind, and the first time I've ever set a story outside Japan, so there was a lot of trial and error. To top it off, I accidentally went over the page limit (usually I run short and have to add more later), and this turned out to be the longest book I've written. And yet, I still didn't feel like I'd written enough. I honestly wanted to ask myself, *"Just how much do you love prison stories?!"*

To my editor, M-san—*thank you so much.* Even though this was our first time working together, I caused so much trouble. I'm truly sorry and can only bow in apology. Up until I turned in the manuscript, I was so anxious I thought I'd get an ulcer. But thanks to your constant kind encouragement, I was able to hang in there and keep going. I also deeply appreciate your thorough reviews and spot-on advice. Please don't let this experience scare you off. I hope we can work together again in the future. I'd be honored.

To Takashina Yuu-sensei, who drew the illustrations, your beautiful artwork made me squirm in delight. The beauty and sensuality of the characters and the realistic backgrounds are truly stunning. Thanks to your illustrations, I'm sure many readers who might not usually be interested in prison stories will pick up this book. Thank you very much, and I hope we can collaborate again on the next book as well.

And finally, to all the readers: how did you enjoy *Deadlock*, packed full of all the classic prison story tropes? If you enjoyed it even a little, I'd be thrilled. I'd also love to hear your thoughts, so please don't hesitate to share them.

The word deadlock literally means a "stalemate" or "standstill," but in IT terminology, it refers to a situation in which multiple processes are waiting for each other's resources to be released, causing all processes to come to a halt.

Yuuto and Dick were chasing the same man, yet got in each other's way and couldn't achieve their goal. Though they developed strong feelings for each other, the story ends with them parting ways. But in the next book, they are set to reunite. As their story continues outside the prison walls, I'll explore how their relationship changes while they continue searching for Corvus. Please look forward to their reunion story. After all, the more distance there is, the deeper love can grow. I'm personally very excited to write what will surely be a passionate reunion scene.

Next time, may they finally be able to confirm their love…

on a proper bed this time (laughs).

September 2006

Saki Aida

The story continues in

DEADHEAT

A Deadlock Novel

APPENDIX

Disclaimer:

This appendix is basically a prison of spoilers. Handcuff-worthy secrets, twists, and major plot bombs are scattered all over the place. If you choose to keep reading, just know: you're walking into it with your eyes open. We take no responsibility for broken hearts, gasps of betrayal, or the desperate urge to throw the book across the room (or us into prison).

Proceed at your own risk. You've been warned.

NAME Yuuto Lennix

CRIME First Degree Murder (~~disputed~~)

SENTENCE 15 years

ETHNICITY Japanese American

FROM New York, NY

STATUS Released

INMATE PHOTO:

DESCRIPTION:

AGE 27 **BIRTHDATE** April 2

HEIGHT 5"8' **WEIGHT** 143

HAIR Dark Brown **EYES** BROWN

ABOUT:

Former DEA special agent convicted of murdering his partner under contested circumstances. Maintains claim of wrongful imprisonment. Assigned by the FBI to infiltrate and report on a suspected terrorist, named Corvus, operating within the facility.

Officially released.

NAME Dick Burnford (Real Name Unknown)

CRIME First Degree Murder

SENTENCE 30 years

ETHNICITY White American

FROM Norwalk, Connecticut

STATUS Unknown (Escaped Fugitive)

INMATE PHOTO:

DESCRIPTION:

AGE 28 **BIRTHDATE** October 23

HEIGHT 6"2' **WEIGHT** 172

HAIR BLOND **EYES** BLUE

ABOUT:

Identified as a former CIA operative. Incarcerated for the killing of a police officer. Displays a reserved and calculating demeanor; known for his imposing physical presence and emotional detachment. Assigned as cellmate to Yuuto Lennix. Subject exhibits signs of psychological trauma and a complex personal history. Shares an unusually close rapport with Lennix.

OFFICIALLY A FUGITIVE OF THE LAW. DANGEROUS. CURRENT LOCATION UNKNOWN.

NAME Corvus (Nathan Clark : assumed)

CRIME First Degree Murder

SENTENCE Life Imprisonment

ETHNICITY White American

FROM Unknown

STATUS Unknown (Escaped Fugitive)

INMATE PHOTO:

DESCRIPTION:

AGE Early 30's BIRTHDATE Unknown

HEIGHT 5"11' WEIGHT Unknown

HAIR Brown EYES Hazel

ABOUT:

Convicted murderer with military training. Operating under the alias Nathan Clark, Corvus entered Schelger State Prison to avoid external threats. Believed to be orchestrating terrorist activity from within the facility. Leader of the extremist group known as White Heaven. Suspected in the deaths of CIA personnel, including Dick Burnford's unit and partner.

True identity remains unverified.

OFFICIALLY A FUGITIVE OF THE LAW. DANGEROUS. CURRENT LOCATION UNKNOWN.

NAME Matthew Kane

CRIME Burglary/ B&E / 2nd Degree Assault

SENTENCE 2 Years

ETHNICITY White American

FROM California

STATUS Hospital Inpatient

INMATE PHOTO:

DESCRIPTION:

AGE 20 BIRTHDATE Unknown

HEIGHT 5"5' WEIGHT Unknown

HAIR Blond EYES Brown

ABOUT:

Young, non-violent offender incarcerated for being an accomplice in an unintentional stabbing of an elderly civilian during a robbery.

Vulnerable due to age and stature.

Subject was sexually assaulted early into his sentence and required hospitalization and surgical intervention. Expected to be returned to general population once cleared.

NAME Michele "Mickey" Ronini

CRIME Bank Robbery

SENTENCE 8 Years

ETHNICITY Italian American

FROM California

STATUS Transferred to San Quentin

INMATE PHOTO:

DESCRIPTION:

AGE 30's BIRTHDATE Unknown

HEIGHT 5"10' WEIGHT Unknown

HAIR Dark Brown EYES Brown

ABOUT:

Served 5 years of his 8 year sentence before being transferred to San Quentin.

Personable and well-liked inmate known for his easygoing demeanor. Serves as an informal supply broker within Schelger State Prison, managing the internal black-market trade of goods and contraband. Acts as a neutral intermediary among inmate factions.

NAME Bob "BB" Trenkler

CRIME Four Counts First Degree Murder

SENTENCE 150 Years (Four Life Sentences)

ETHNICITY Black

FROM California

STATUS Under strict security

INMATE PHOTO:

DESCRIPTION:

AGE 30's BIRTHDATE Unknown

HEIGHT 6"1' WEIGHT Unknown

HAIR Black EYES Brown

ABOUT:

Known as Bab Bob, he is a high-ranking, volatile member of the Black Soldiers gang.

Known for extreme violence and erratic behavior.

Involved in the sexual assault of inmate Yuuto Lennix.

Pending disciplinary and criminal review for involvment in a recent riot.

NAME Ernesto "Neto" Rivera

CRIME Third Degree Assault

SENTENCE 3 Years

ETHNICITY Mexican American

FROM Los Angeles, California

STATUS Active in General Population

INMATE PHOTO:

DESCRIPTION:

AGE 30's **BIRTHDATE** Unknown

HEIGHT 6"3' **WEIGHT** 186

HAIR Black **EYES** Brown

ABOUT:

Leader of the Locos Hermanos, the largest Chicano-affiliated street gang with significant power both in and outside of prison. Attacked by Bob "BB" Trenkler and subsequently held in solitary.

Trusted ally of Inmate Yuuto Lennix, often providing key intelligence and assistance. Allegedly romantically linked to Tonia.

NAME Tonia [Unlisted]

CRIME [Unlisted]

SENTENCE 3 Years

ETHNICITY Mexican American

FROM Los Angeles, California

STATUS Active in General Population

INMATE PHOTO:

DESCRIPTION:

AGE [Unlisted] **BIRTHDATE** Unknown

HEIGHT 5"9' **WEIGHT** 152

HAIR Black **EYES** Brown

ABOUT:

Assigned male at birth with the name Antonio; identifies and presents as female. Younger sibling of Ernesto "Neto" Rivera.

Acts as a maternal presence for vulnerable and younger inmates. Core member of The *Sisters*, an informal community of gay and transgender inmates who provide mutual protection and solidarity.

OTHER INMATES

Name: Choker [Full Name Unlisted]
Race: Black
Age: Under 40

Status: Deceased – Homicide under review.

Notes:
Former leader of the Black Soldiers. Terminal cancer patient housed in the infirmary, cared for by Dick Burnford. Known for his calm demeanor and love of reading. Killed by Nathan Clark in an apparent act of mercy.

Name: Henry Galen
Race: White
Sentence: Life without parole

Status: Active in general population. High-risk designation due to extremist affiliations. Under ongoing investigation for inmate death.

Notes:
Leader of the ABL. Formerly affiliated with a right-wing extremist group. Known white supremacist and neo-Nazi ideologue. Previously involved with Tonia. Suspected in the death of fellow inmate Lindsay, with whom he reportedly had a relationship.

Name: Hawes [Unlisted]
Race: Black
Age: Elderly
Sentence: 20 years

Status: Released

Notes:
Long-term inmate nearing release. Cellmate to Matthew Kane. Despite his calm demeanor, he played a role in luring Yuuto Lennix into a staged assault by Bob "BB" Trenkler.

Name: Bernal [Full Name Unlisted]

Race: Chicano

Sentence: 120 years

Conviction: Sexual Assault, Aggravated Battery

Notes:

Violent offender with a history of predatory behavior. Convicted pedophile and known sadist. Raped and severely assaulted inmate Matthew Kane. Considered highly dangerous and volatile.

Name: Lindsay Scott
Race: Black

Gender Identity: Female

Status: Deceased – Homicide suspected. Case under internal investigation.

Notes:

Inmate involved with Henry Galen. Known for engaging in transactional sex despite warnings from Tonia. Believed to have been killed by Galen following escalating tensions in their relationship.

SCHELGER STAFF

Warden Richard Corning: Warden of Schelger Prison. Secretly collaborates with Corvus (Nathan Clark), facilitating his movement in and out of the facility.

Officer Guthrie: Senior correctional officer at Schelger Prison. Acts as the de facto head of the guard staff. Maintains covert ties with the CIA and collaborates directly with Dick Burnford on classified operations within the facility.

Dr. Spencer: Infirmary doctor at Schelger Prison, with five years of service. Operates as a covert CIA asset within the facility and collaborates closely with Dick Burnford.

Cowen: Prison guard at Schelger. Took bribes from gangs and participated in their betting activities.

OTHERS

Paul McClane: Yuuto's DEA partner. Four years his senior. Murdered prior to Yuuto's imprisonment.

Mark Heiden: Investigator with the FBI's Counterterrorism Division, Domestic Terror Unit. Known for his polished appearance and high-end suits.

Leticia "Leti" Lennix: Yuuto's stepmother. Chicana.

Lupita Lennix: Yuuto's 12-year-old half-sister. Japanese and Chicana.

Paco: Yuuto's older stepbrother. Officer with the LAPD.

Frank: Dick's former teammate. Killed in an explosion orchestrated by Corvus. He lived at Kure Beach in Wilmington, North Carolina, along with three other Delta Force members.

Jonathan: One of Dick's former Delta Force teammates. Killed in an explosion orchestrated by Corvus. Spent downtime with the unit at Kure Beach in Wilmington, North Carolina.

Noel: Dick's teammate and lover. Two years older than Dick. Killed in the same explosion caused by Corvus. Lived with the Delta Force team at Kure Beach in Wilmington, North Carolina.

GROUPS

CIA: The Central Intelligence Agency is a civilian foreign intelligence service of the federal government of the United States tasked with advancing national security through collecting and analyzing intelligence from around the world and conducting covert operations.

DEA: The Drug Enforcement Administration is a United States federal law enforcement agency under the Department of Justice. Its primary mission is to combat illicit drug trafficking and distribution within the United States. The DEA also coordinates and pursues U.S. drug investigations both domestically and internationally.

FBI: The Federal Bureau of Investigation is an agency of the United States Department of Justice, and reports to both the attorney general and the director of national intelligence. A leading American counterterrorism, counterintelligence, and criminal investigative organization, the FBI has jurisdiction over violations of more than 200 categories of federal crimes.

Black Soldiers: A predominantly African American gang known for their strict hierarchy and discipline. They play a significant role in the prison's power structure.

Locos Hermanos: "Crazy Brothers" A Chicano gang involved in the prison's internal conflicts. Their rivalry with the Black Soldiers leads to violent clashes.

ABL: White supremacist gang.

TRANSLATIONS

Orale, amigo: Okay, friend

Golondrina: Swallow.

Muchas gracias: Thank you very much.

De nada: You're welcome.

Excerpt From Dear Benjamin, Volume 1

Originally published under the title 디어 벤자민
Copyright © 이드 (ID), 2018

First published in Korea by BookCube Networks Co. Ltd.
This English edition is published by BLoved Publishing LLC in 2025 by arrangement with BookCube Networks Co. Ltd. through Rightol Media (copyright@rightol.com).

Prologue

Huff! Huff! Huff!

Ragged breaths formed into wisps of white in the cold night air. A man tore through the darkness, sweat dripping down his jaw as his soaked shirt clung tightly to his heaving chest. He didn't stop running. He *could not*.

Bang! Ba-bang!

Explosions echoed in the distance, booming one after another like earth-shattering thunder. It was hell on earth, but his ears barely registered the noise. What mattered now was the state of his body.

Fuck! Of all days!

Profanities spilled haphazardly from his chapped lips, his breath hitching with desperation. His body was feverish, hotter than he'd ever felt in his twenty-seven years of life, but he kept running. Darkness threatened to swallow him as he veered toward a solitary building in the distance.

An old, rundown warehouse.

It was situated some distance away from the noise. He knew it wasn't safe but it was his only option.

Crack!

He kicked open the door, relieved that it held together despite its dilapidated state. He slipped inside and quickly shut the door behind him, his eyes darting around, scanning his surroundings.

Thankfully, the warehouse was empty. Considering the chaos outside, it seemed unlikely anyone else would hide here.

Another explosion echoed in the distance, yet the man felt an unsettling detachment from everything. Remaining on high alert, he moved cautiously through the shadowy warehouse, eyes scanning every corner with unwavering vigilance.

The space was cluttered with piles of hay, old farm equipment, and a jumble of forgotten junk. It was far from ideal, but it seemed safe for now. He quickly crouched among the haystacks, positioning himself beneath a cracked window through which a thin beam of moonlight spilled.

Much like the door, the window was old and battered; its glass, clouded with grime and scarred by a jagged crack, seemed ready to shatter at the faintest tremor. Still, it was an escape route if things went south, and he relied on the dim light to inspect the pills he'd pulled from his pocket.

In his trembling hand lay a mix of pills—suppressants. The dim light blurred the pills into indistinct shapes, making it impossible to tell their color or form—they were nothing more than smudged shadows resting in his palm. But it didn't matter; he didn't have time to sort them out. Desperation clawed at him as he tossed all the pills into his mouth, swallowing them in one go. The uncontrollable heat surging through his body distorted his vision and clouded his judgment. Breathless, he waited, praying for relief.

But it didn't come.

If anything, his fever was worsening, like an unrelenting fire consuming his veins.

"Shit!" he cursed under his breath.

The suppressants weren't working—none of them. He'd brought a variety as a precaution, but all proved utterly ineffective. Panic ignited as his breaths quickened, each inhale fueling the fire within him, like a furnace roaring with every desperate gasp.

He had spent his entire life believing he was a beta. But when he came of age at nineteen, everything changed. He unexpectedly presented as a recessive omega—a revelation that shattered his world. It was unthinkable, a secret he couldn't let anyone discover. Thankfully, his recessive status gave him a fragile sense of security.

Though he presented as an omega, his pheromones were faint, barely more potent than when he was a beta. A single pill taken once a month had been enough to keep his omega status hidden. He had lived among alphas without their pheromones ever affecting him, and he had never experienced a heat cycle—until now.

If only it had stayed that way.

His first heat cycle was hitting him with full force, and it couldn't have come at a worse time. In a final, desperate attempt, he swallowed the last of his pills before curling into himself as the searing heat raged through him.

He couldn't believe this was happening. It was the worst-case scenario—a nightmare beyond anything he had ever imagined. It couldn't get any shittier than this. Grinding his teeth in frustration, he struggled against the relentless heat waves, but his body refused to obey.

The heat grew more unbearable with each passing moment. Sweat poured off him like rain, soaking his clothes. His vision blurred until everything around him became a hazy, indistinguishable fog. The pressure between his legs was unbearable—his cock was so hard it strained painfully against the front of his pants, the pressure so intense that the seams looked ready to give way. His underwear was already sopping wet with precum.

The man trembled, his breath ragged as he fought the overwhelming tide of heat consuming him. Panic clawed at his chest—if the alphas outside caught even a trace of his scent, it would be over. Desperation overtook him as he yanked down his pants, his mind clouded by primal need. His hand gripped himself tightly, the cold touch against his fevered flesh sending a shudder through his body. Broken gasps and curses escaped his lips, raw and unrestrained.

His moans echoed through the warehouse; his strokes became frantic, his breath escaping in hot, ragged gasps. The rhythmic slap of flesh against flesh filled the air, blending with the moans that escaped his throat, growing louder and more desperate with each passing moment. The two sounds seemed to merge in perfect sync.

Time slipped away as his mind dissolved into a murky haze, swirling with the intensity of a hurricane. He clamped his other hand over his mouth, stifling a loud moan as he climaxed, hot semen spilling over his palm and fingers. But the relief was momentary; the hunger within him surged with renewed ferocity, a relentless, insatiable tide that only grew more excruciating and unbearable.

This wasn't enough.

This feeling, this overwhelming need—it wasn't something he could satisfy with his hand.

The inside of his ass was slick, overflowing with watery fluid, becoming unbearably needy. He had never been with a man; he never even *thought* about being with another man before and had spent his entire life pretending to be a beta. But an omega was an omega, and his heat-ridden body craved more. The realization hit him like a ton of bricks, sinking in as his brow unfurled, forcing him to acknowledge it for the first time. It devastated him, but what was more devastating was how helpless he felt as his body heated up, turned on against his will.

Is this what a heat cycle feels like? Now he understood why omegas would throw themselves at alphas when they forgot to take their suppressants. The realization made him curse, but deep down, he couldn't escape the truth. Some part of him secretly longed for one of the alphas outside to catch his scent, track him down, and end this unbearable torment.

His body felt like a cruel joke, betraying him at every turn. If this went on, he feared he might throw open the door and crawl into the chaos himself. He had to do something—anything—before it got that far. Despite the anger and resentment simmering inside, he reached back, his hand trembling as it moved toward his ass.

Shuddering, his thoughts scattered and unfocused, he spread his cheeks. It was his first time using his body this way to satisfy his desires, and he groaned with effort as he awkwardly eased a finger inside. Tight as it was, the slickness eased the discomfort, making the intrusion bearable. Yet, no matter how deeply he prodded or how many fingers he used, it was never enough.

His frustration boiled over, a hot breath escaping his lips as his flushed face pressed against the rough floor. Quiet, desperate whimpers slipped from him as his trembling fingers worked feverishly. Yet, the searing ache only intensified, an insatiable fire consuming him and dragging him perilously close to the edge of madness.

"Someone…help…" he begged, his voice trembling, his tear-filled eyes pleading for mercy.

As if answering his desperate plea, a flicker of movement caught his eye—a shadow shifting just beyond the edges of his vision. A voice broke through the haze, rich with amusement and mockery, "Wow, this is great. You're really turning me on."

The omega's eyes snapped open in shock.

Was it a ghost? No—it couldn't be.

The omega froze, his skin turning deathly pale as if doused in icy water, his fingers still buried deep inside himself. He hadn't even had the chance to withdraw them before the gravity of his situation came crashing down, rendering him motionless and exposed.

Even though his senses struggled to catch up, he was sure there had been no sign of anyone else when he entered the warehouse.

Unbeknownst to him, the large warehouse had a second story—not a full level, but a shadowy balcony tucked away in the darkness. He hadn't noticed it before, but now someone stood there, leaning casually over the railing, watching him with unsettling calm.

"Go on. I want to see more." The voice was relaxed, laced with a casual amusement that clashed sharply with the gravity of the moment.

Then, a powerful wave of alpha pheromones hit the omega, leaving his body trembling uncontrollably. The sudden presence of the alpha, combined with the suffocating pheromones, shoved him to the brink of panic.

"An alpha?"

BLOVED PUBLISHING